Room for Suspicion

Room for Suspicion

A Cluttered Crime Mystery Novel

Carol Light

TULE
PUBLISHING

Room for Suspicion

Copyright© 2023 Carol Light

Tule Publishing First Printing, June 2023

The Tule Publishing, Inc.

ALL RIGHTS RESERVED

First Publication by Tule Publishing 2023

Cover design by Croco Designs

No part of this book may be used or reproduced in any manner whatsoever without written permission except in the case of brief quotations embodied in critical articles and reviews.

This is a work of fiction. Names, characters, places, and incidents are products of the author's imagination or are used fictitiously. Any resemblance to actual events, locales, organizations, or persons, living or dead, is entirely coincidental.

ISBN: 978-1-959988-61-8

Dedication

For Marta Justak, whose steadfast support and wise advice is priceless. We have always encouraged each other to reach for our dreams, and I couldn't have achieved this one without you. I value our friendship more than words can express.

Make new friends,
but keep the old.
One is silver,
the other is gold.

—Girl Scout song based on Joseph Parry's poem "New Friends and Old Friends"

Chapter One

As Crystal Ward turned into her client's driveway, she noticed the signs were missing. Last week there had been two identical political ads proclaiming Scott Danforth for U.S. House of Representatives planted in the grass. The double dose of smiling headshots of Danforth against backgrounds of the red, white, and blue of the American flag would have been hard to miss, even with her mind still focused on the argument she'd had with her husband this morning.

Who had removed the signs? The original one had been stolen, and her client, Farrah Compton, had doubled down, replacing it with two signs. Now the question was whether Farrah would respond with three or increase the signage exponentially to four.

The mental picture of Scott Danforth's smiling face multiplying across the yard made Crys grin as she parked in the driveway. Sometimes having an eye for detail was a curse, but today she welcomed the distraction from what she could have said—should have said?—to Rick to convince him that her work as a professional organizer was important to her and potentially life-changing for their family. Not that anything she said would have done any good. Rick just wasn't ready to listen. She wasn't giving up, though.

She steered her thoughts to the task at hand: helping Farrah Compton reorganize her home office. Farrah's suburban American Dream residence with its unfenced expanse of manicured green lawn (currently uncluttered with signs) represented everything Crys dreamed about in a house. Not that she didn't appreciate her own Craftsman bungalow in a much less affluent Chicago suburb, but imagine having more green space than concrete and mature oak trees already changing into their fall colors. Even better, imagine not having to worry about money or the mowing and fertilizing, pruning and raking of this little slice of paradise. And then there was the spacious interior...

Enough house envy. The grass is always greener on the other side of the fence, as her mother would say. Literally, in this case.

Crys unclipped her seat belt. By some miracle, she had arrived a few minutes early for their ten o'clock appointment. Traffic in Chicago, even in the northern suburbs, was as unpredictable as the autumn weather. Today the road gods had smiled and the weather had cooperated, although a cold front was expected to blow through around midday. That was why at the last minute before leaving the house, she had decided to add a linen blazer to her outfit. Locating and pressing it to look more professional for this meeting had cost her an extra fifteen minutes, but she was willing to take the risk to make a good impression. Farrah, a stylish professor at the University of Illinois-Chicago, favored suits, silk blouses, and scarves tied in an endless variety of styles. Crys glanced down, hoping the blazer hadn't wrinkled too badly during the drive.

She shouldn't have looked. In the sunlight, the black fabric appeared faded to a dark gray. The wrinkles, like the sign thief, had returned. *It's my linen look*, she decided. She would wear the wrinkles and crinkles, natural to this fabric, with dignity and hold her head high. She could remove the jacket as soon as she was inside.

She grabbed her handbag and binder and stepped out. As she locked her van, a travel-worn black Jeep Cherokee pulled up next to her and shuddered to a stop.

The man in the black leather jacket who emerged gave her a wide smile and a "hiya."

"Are you one of my sister's students?" he asked, his focus shifting to the notebook she carried. "I'm Randy, Farrah's brother." His friendly smile broadened, and he stuck out a hand.

She took it and gave him a firm squeeze. Other than his coloring and the shape of his eyes, he didn't resemble his sister. Instead, he looked like a hipster slipping into middle age, with a double chin under his unshaven jaw and a slight paunch lounging on top of his jeans. A scar by his left eye made his lid droop into a skeptical slant, but his smile challenged that impression.

"Crystal Ward. I'm helping Farrah organize her office."

"Geez, really? She's the neatest person I know. No offense. You wouldn't want to see my place."

He was trying hard to be charming, so Crys smiled. "I'm helping her to improve it." She glanced at her watch and saw it was ten. "As a matter of fact, she's expecting me now."

He walked a step behind her toward the front door. "I just have to ask her something quick. She's a busy lady these days. Guess that's why she wants to clean things up."

"Organize. It's not the same as cleaning."

"Got it. Straighten things up. Does that work?"

"Close enough." She often had to educate people about her profession. Ten years ago, she'd had no clue that people actually earned money helping others arrange their spaces, using techniques she had learned by necessity as a wife and mother. Not that Rick appreciated that she had marketable skills.

She stepped onto the small concrete porch. Black electrician's tape covered half of the doorbell, a model with a video camera above the ring button.

"Huh." Randy stopped behind her, close enough to be breathing down her neck. He smelled like the inside of a fast-food hamburger joint, a mixture of grease and ground beef. "Look at that—someone's taped over the camera. I hope she hasn't been burgled."

He knocked on the teal front door, a rare concession to color for Farrah, who preferred whites and shades of cream and beige. They glanced at each other and then away as they listened for footsteps. Randy tried the doorknob, but it was locked. Crys pulled out her phone and scrolled to Farrah's number.

"You calling her?"

"Yes."

"She's gotta be here. Maybe she's in the john."

The phone began to ring in Crys's ear. From inside, she

heard the faint musical notes of a common ringtone. It sounded about five times and then switched to voicemail.

Crys hung up without leaving a message. Odd—Farrah hadn't seemed like someone who would forget an appointment. Maybe Randy's guess was correct: she was in another part of the house, away from her cell.

"I know the code," Randy said, reaching around her to punch in four digits: 9-8-2-1. With a beep, the door unlocked. Crys stepped back as he pushed it open.

"Hey, Farrah," he called as he led the way in. "You here, sis? It's me."

His announcement was greeted with a deep silence.

"Maybe she's out back," Randy suggested. "I'll check."

That worked for her. She would wait while he had his chat with Farrah, which he'd promised would be quick.

The wide entry faced the staircase to the second floor. Her client's office was to her left, and Crys couldn't resist the invitation of the open door to see what had changed since her last visit. The room was vacant—no Farrah and not much of anything else. They had cleared the built-in cabinets and bookcases on her last visit. The middle of the room held half a dozen boxes containing the items from the shelves. There was a vacant space where Farrah's desk had been. She must have found a charity to take it. Soon the new one would arrive, and then—

"Jesus, Mary, and Joseph!"

She found Randy in the living room. The shock on his pale face alarmed her even more than his exclamation. She followed his gaze to the fireplace. A man lay on the floor in front of the white marble hearth. The blood coating the side of his face had formed a red pool on the white carpet.

Crys's hand flew to her mouth. She turned her gaze away, and another splash of color on the carpet caught her eye. The teal-and-navy geometric pattern on a silky fabric looked like a scarf. She stepped closer, her heart rate accelerating.

Farrah lay sprawled on her side in front of the white sofa. Ignoring Randy, who was still calling for divine help, Crys rushed to her client.

"Farrah?" She noticed blood droplets in a spray pattern on her white shirt. Splatter, not an injury. One end of the scarf puddled like its own stain beside her neck. Her eyes were open but fixed in an unblinking stare. Her skin tone was pale, but a tiny twitch of her fingers indicated that she was alive.

"Farrah? It's me, Crys. Are you hurt?"

There was no response. Crys hesitated to touch her, knowing that this was most likely a crime scene. She extended a shaky hand under Farrah's nose and thought she felt a wisp of breath.

"Uhh—" Randy moaned behind her. She jerked around. As a mother she recognized that sound. Sure enough, he raised his hand over his mouth and began to gag.

"Not in here you don't." Crys seized his arm and spun him around. There was probably a half bath on the ground floor, but she didn't know where it was. She hustled him into the kitchen and shoved him into one of the chairs at the island. "Put your head down and take some deep breaths."

He obeyed her and gulped in air like a trout in the bottom of a rowboat.

"That's it. Breathe in—breathe out."

She opened cupboards and searched until she found a mixing bowl to place beside him in case deep breathing didn't work. Keeping an eye on Randy, she pulled out her phone and dialed 911.

"I never thought she'd kill him," Randy moaned, rolling his forehead on his folded arms. "Geez. What am I gonna do now?"

"Who?" she asked as the 911 operator answered the phone, but Randy only moaned.

Crys provided Farrah's address and asked for ambulance and police. She hesitated when the operator asked again for the nature of the emergency. She pictured the man's bloodied face. Head injuries could bleed profusely, as she knew from seeing her brothers' and son's sports injuries. What she'd seen in that one quick glance had been more than blood. She'd seen bone and gray matter. She had also seen a bloodied sculpture of a woman on the carpet near Farrah's outstretched hand.

"There's been a murder," she said, bile rising in her throat. "A man's been killed."

RANDY HAD STOPPED moaning but still looked pale with a faint hint of green around his lips. Crys suspected her own color was a close match. She tried not to think of the dead man in the next room as she filled a glass of water with one hand while pressing the phone to her ear with the other. They should have left the house immediately and not disturbed the crime scene, but it was too late now. Randy's hand shook as he drank the water. If his legs were that unsteady, he'd never make it outside.

The 911 operator had insisted on remaining on the line with her. Crys had already explained how she and Randy had discovered the victims and described the scene in the living room. Crys knew she could hang up, but the woman's voice was as reassuring as a hug.

"Is there anyone else in the house with you?"

Crys drew in a sharp breath. She glanced over her shoulder and listened. There was a hum from the refrigerator, the sound of Randy's ragged breathing, and the pounding of her heart, but she heard no other noises. They seemed to be alone with Farrah and the dead man.

"I don't think so, but we haven't checked it out." She realized she'd lowered her voice. No point in broadcasting their presence if they did have company.

"You just stay where you are, Crystal," the operator advised. "The police are almost there. They'll make sure no one else is around."

After that, she had no desire to leave the kitchen. Randy had been accurate in describing his sister as neat. The room was spotlessly clean with no signs of disturbance or recent occupancy. Farrah didn't leave dishes in the sink or even a washed cup in a drainer. For that matter, she didn't leave a dish drainer in the sink or on the countertop. Even the tea towel looked as if it were displayed more for show than use. Crys touched it. White pressed linen with tan lines in a modern, large checkered pattern. There wasn't a wrinkle to be seen. Had Farrah starched it? She glanced down at her black jacket again and shook her head. *Linen look.* Not that it mattered now.

Still holding the phone to her ear, she slid into the chair at the island next to Randy. The operator told her the police were three minutes away. Randy's breathing was quieter, although he moaned again that he didn't know what he was going to do.

He didn't seem concerned about his sister. She wanted to check on Farrah, but from what she'd seen, there didn't appear to be any need for first aid. As she'd told the operator, the patient wasn't bleeding, her breathing was unobstructed, she didn't appear to have any fractures, and she wasn't in immediate danger. Unless the killer was still in the house.

Crys glanced over her shoulder again. It was a big house. Plenty of places to hide. She wanted to phone Rick, to hear his voice reassure her, but she would have to disconnect the 911 call to do that.

Come on—hurry!

"You should be hearing the sirens soon," the operator assured her.

Crys rubbed her palm across the cool surface of the white quartzite countertop. She wasn't a fan of all-white kitchens, but she became calmer as her gaze rested on the white cabinetry and walls. So many negative spaces, like the white expanses in this kitchen or the green lawn minus the campaign signs. Beautiful in their own right, they were restful places for the eyes. Maybe this feeling of clean tranquility was why Farrah liked white.

A knock at the front door startled her. Randy raised his head and glanced around.

"They should be there now," the 911 operator said. Crys thanked the woman and hung up.

The four uniformed officers at the door told her to remain in the kitchen with Randy after she led them into the living room. From her seat at the end of the island, she watched as paramedics and firemen entered with a stretcher. The knot of their bodies blocked her view, but they seemed to be talking to Farrah. She thought she heard a moan, but she couldn't be sure. Randy held his head in his hands with his elbows propped on the island. He had stopped muttering fears of his impending doom.

Everyone dealt with shock and grief differently.

Crys had to do something, so she refilled his glass. When she returned to her seat and peered into the living room, she noticed that two more officers—a man and a woman in plain clothes—had joined the gathering. The man glanced in her direction, and their eyes met. He said something to his partner, who turned to look at her.

The knot in Crys's stomach tightened. Growing up with three brothers, she had learned a choice collection of words never to be uttered in their mother's presence. All of them came to mind as she watched Mitch Burdine approach.

Chapter Two

"I HEARD YOU called it in. I was hoping it was another Crystal Ward."

What Mitch meant was that he was hoping it wasn't Lieutenant Rick Ward's wife. She should have realized who the homicide detective to catch the call would be. Fate was being fickle again.

"I'm working with Ms. Compton. I had an appointment at ten."

His eyes drooped at the outer edges as if he were chronically burdened with sad news and sympathetic. It was a look that promised more than it delivered, at least in her experience.

"Are you okay?"

She nodded, afraid that she was going to be sick as the seriousness of what she'd stumbled upon struck her. As a homicide detective, Mitch had no doubt seen his share of murder scenes, but this was her first.

She wasn't going to be sick. Not here. Not in front of him.

Randy pulled himself away from his pity party. "Is Farrah all right?"

Crys found her voice. "This is her brother, Randy. We

arrived at the same time."

Mitch glanced back toward the living room. "The paramedics are examining her. She seems to be in shock, but—"

Before they could stop him, Randy jumped off the stool and rushed toward his sister.

"Hey!" Mitch tried and failed to grab him. He hurried after Randy, and Crys followed.

Farrah was still on the floor, but she was now lying on her back. Her brown wavy hair was tousled, making her appear younger than her almost forty years, or maybe it was the blank expression on her face softening it. Her eyes were open but still unfocused, and her jaw was slack. Her scarf hung limply from her neck.

"Are you okay, sis?" Randy asked. He waved his hand in front of Farrah's unseeing eyes. "Sis?"

The paramedics, who were unbuckling the straps on the gurney, had turned to watch him. One of them stepped toward him when he grabbed Farrah's arm and began to shake her. Mitch's partner and a uniformed sergeant near the body also looked up. Both reached hands to gun butts.

Farrah gave no indication that she'd heard Randy. He shook her harder, shouting her name.

"That's enough." Mitch jerked him back, causing him to release his grip on his sister. Farrah's head lolled to the side.

The paramedic who had also reached out to stop Randy glanced at Mitch. "Is this family?" he asked.

"I'm her brother." Randy shrugged out of Mitch's grasp. "What's wrong with her?"

"Mostly shock. There doesn't seem to be any injury, unless she hit her head," the paramedic told him. "She hasn't said anything or reacted to pain, but there could be internal injuries. She needs to be checked out by a doctor."

"Step back and give them room," Mitch said, grabbing Randy's arm, but more gently this time. "They'll take her to the hospital. Do you recognize the man over here?"

His gaze flickered to her. Crys shook her head.

Randy swallowed hard and quickly averted his eyes. "It's her husband, Wes. Are those his brains? Geez, I think I'm gonna be sick."

"Take him outside," Mitch said to a uniform. "I'll talk to him later."

Crys had seen enough, too. "I'll wait with him."

"I GOTTA GET outta here," Randy said, pacing along the concrete path that connected the driveway to the front door.

His color seemed better. He rubbed his unshaven chin. On some men, facial hair looked rugged and masculine, but Randy's jowls and patchy beard didn't quite make the *GQ* cut. His broad smile might compensate for what wasn't a handsome face, but at this moment he was far from happy.

"They'll be out soon to talk to us," she said.

Crys wrapped her arms around herself, grateful that she'd worn the blazer, wrinkles and all. Another gust of wind scattered leaves from oak trees in the neighboring yard. The homeowners must spend hours raking each fall. She couldn't imagine her immaculate client doing that. Had Wes maintained the yard, or did they have a lawn service?

Before she could reach a conclusion, the front door opened, and the paramedics emerged with Farrah on a stretcher. Her eyes stared up at the sky, unseeing, as if her soul had left her body and was floating above it. Crys found herself shivering, despite her jacket.

"Where are you taking her?" Randy asked.

"Rush Oak Park," the EMT answered.

Randy didn't object. He took a step to follow them and then stopped. Maybe he did have feelings for his sister after all.

They were watching the paramedics place Farrah into the ambulance when another man joined them.

"What's going on here?" he asked sharply.

Crys turned. The new arrival was about fifty and shorter than her by a couple of inches. His dark eyes, close together under bushy brows, focused on her since Randy's attention was still on the ambulance.

"I live over there." He jerked his thumb backward toward a split-level house diagonally across the street. A new-looking white Chrysler sedan was parked in the driveway. It seemed a surprising choice of vehicle for the short man in baggy jeans and a gray sweatshirt. But she shouldn't judge a book by its cover.

She resisted the urge to smooth her linen blazer.

"I saw all the cop cars, so I knew it was more than a medical call. What was it—a robbery? I figure she's a woman who would fight. Is she gonna be okay?"

"She'll have to be checked out. Have you had a lot of robberies here in the neighborhood?" she asked.

He looked insulted. "Here? This is a safe neighborhood. I should know. I'm president of our neighborhood guard."

She was about to ask him what that was when Mitch and his female partner appeared.

"Can I help you, sir?" Mitch asked, all business.

"Just checking on things. What happened here? If a crime was committed, I may have some information. Been keeping an eye on this place."

Mitch pulled a small notebook from an inside pocket and clicked his pen open. "I'll be happy to talk to you, mister—"

"Zygman. Gary Zygman. I live over there—2473."

"Someone will be over shortly," Mitch said after he'd taken Zygman's contact information. "Now I'll have to ask you to wait off this property."

"Yeah, yeah. Sure," Farrah's neighbor said, backing away.

Mitch waited until Gary Zygman had crossed the street before introducing his partner as Detective Alvarez. He told her to interview Randy. She nodded, her face impassive. She probably knew who her partner would want to interview and why.

"Your color looks better," Mitch said after Alvarez had steered Randy toward the driveway. "I almost couldn't spot you in that white kitchen."

She expected him to laugh or at least grin at his joke,

but he remained serious. Dead serious. He looked a little pale himself. She wasn't going to offer any commiseration.

"I'm okay. Don't you have some questions you have to ask? I'd like to leave."

"Right." His brown eyes softened. "My first question is, do you want me to call Rick?"

Anger welled up inside her. "No. I'm perfectly capable of calling him myself. I told you I'm okay."

Was that relief she saw when he nodded and said, "Got it"? Maybe he didn't want to upset her husband, either. The one thing they agreed on was Rick's welfare.

He returned to professional detective mode and had her repeat how she had found the body. She described her arrival and how she and Randy had entered the house together.

"You're sure the door was locked?" He raised his head from his notes to look at her.

She bit back a sarcastic comment, and instead said, "I didn't try to open it, if that's what you mean. Randy tried the handle and it was locked. That's when he said he knew the code."

"So neither of you pressed the doorbell."

"Correct." She realized they could have—the button encircled in red wasn't covered by tape.

"Was the doorbell camera taped like that when you arrived?"

"Yes." She might as well help him wind up this interview as soon as possible, so she added, "It wasn't like that on Friday when I came."

"But you noticed it this morning." He kept his gaze on

her. "You could have been walking into a crime in progress."

He didn't want or need an answer. If Randy hadn't been with her and known the door code, she never would have gone into the house. But if Randy hadn't arrived, how long would Farrah have lain on the carpet in shock? Hours? Days? It didn't bear thinking about.

Mitch's gaze fell to her hands rubbing her arms.

"Are you cold? We can go back inside."

"No. I'm fine." She just wanted him to finish.

He picked up the pace, questioning her on how she'd met Farrah—*a referral from another client who teaches with her at the university*, how long she had been working with her—*about two weeks*, and the scope of her project—*just her office, mostly her desk and filing system*.

A cool breeze chilled her synthetic trousers, and she tugged the blazer closer to her chest, crossing her arms to hold it in place. At least she didn't have to explain her profession to Mitch. He'd known about it from the beginning. He'd also known about her husband's concerns about her safety and frustration over their need for a second income. Although Mitch had never expressed an opinion about her decision to start her own business, she suspected he shared Rick's reservations. Maybe he'd sensed that his opinion wouldn't be welcome. He was right about that.

She glanced over at the sound of Randy's raised voice. He was gesturing with his hands and shaking his head. He looked over his shoulder toward his Jeep, probably wishing he could escape. She knew how he felt. Detective Alvarez said something else to him, and he turned back toward her, his head lowered. She was a small woman, about five four, who had perfected a no-nonsense look known to most parents, teachers, and apparently cops. She appeared to be in her early thirties, not much younger than her partner.

"What about the victim?" Mitch asked, regaining her attention. "What do you know about him?"

"Her husband? I've never met him. He wasn't home when I visited." Now that she thought about it, Farrah hadn't said much about him, but why would she? It was her office, not his, and organizing the space to suit her needs was mainly what they'd talked about in their three meetings. Farrah didn't waste time in idle talk.

Mitch's sandy eyebrows had risen. "She must have said something to you about him." He flipped a few pages back. "Wes Compton. Maybe short for Weston?"

She tried to think of anything that had been mentioned. "Farrah said he owned his own business, and they were a case of opposites attracting. She's a college professor in political science. I have the impression that he…"

Mitch waited, watching her.

"I'd just be speculating," she said. Ah, but she was talking to him as she would with Rick about the case. He needed to move on, interview someone else. She'd told him all she knew.

"You're a good judge of character. Go ahead."

She flushed, not sure how to take that remark. Before, when he'd first become Rick's partner and protégé and a frequent visitor to their home, it might have been a compliment. Now, she sensed sarcasm, but she couldn't tell if it was directed at her or at him. Was he referring to her choice of client, a woman now involved in a homicide, or her low opinion of him since that day they had stopped being friends? Even after five years, the words they'd exchanged after Rick had been shot and left bleeding alone in a filthy alley still stretched like a minefield between them.

Before she could answer, his cell phone buzzed. He glanced at the screen and then excused himself, turning his back and stepping away with the phone to his ear.

"Hi, honey. What's going on?" he asked in a fake slow drawl that made him sound more like a Texan than a native of Illinois. No doubt the women he dated loved it. Did he see himself as some sort of cowboy? Her son had outgrown that fantasy, and he was only fourteen.

Crys turned toward the other interview in progress. She stepped closer, pretending to give Mitch space.

"They had their fights," Randy was saying. "What couple doesn't?"

"Physical fights?" Detective Alvarez asked. Her blond hair was short with dark roots. She had an attractive face, with small, neat features that probably softened when she smiled. She glanced sideways at Crys, who recognized the cop instinct to always be aware of her surroundings. Crys gave her a nod and moved back toward Mitch, pretending that she hadn't been listening. She gazed across the street. Gary Zygman stood in his open garage and watched them, his hands on his hips.

"Sorry about that," Mitch said, pocketing his phone. He glanced down at his notes. "Where were we?"

She raised her eyebrows but didn't comment on his obviously personal call with a woman. "You were asking me about Wes Compton."

He met her gaze then. She had to give him credit. He appeared to be genuinely interested in what she had to say. It must be a helpful technique when interviewing witnesses. Probably something Rick had taught him and just as fake as his drawl.

"I was just going to say that I didn't think they were spending a lot of time together. My impression is that he was busy with his business and she had her career. They each did their own thing."

He nodded. If he was disappointed in her less-than-earthshaking observation, he didn't show it. The truth was, she didn't know Farrah well enough to form any helpful opinions. However, Crys trusted her instincts, and they told her that Farrah and her husband weren't close. Whether that was a new problem in their marriage or a slow slide down from the peak of wedding day bliss, she couldn't tell.

"Any children?"

"No." That was one thing she knew. She had asked that question the first time she had visited Farrah in her home. The white carpet and sofas in the living room and the lack of kid clutter had suggested that only adults lived there.

"You said you'd only met with her three times. During the daytime, right?"

"Yes. The first was a phone call, and the other two meetings were in the late afternoon, after she finished work. Today she scheduled it for the morning."

Mitch continued to be all business, treating her as he

would any other witness, she assumed. Or maybe he had a date for lunch with Honey, whoever she was. After a few more questions, he had her retrace her steps into the house to see what she or Randy may have touched. She had to wait in the kitchen with Randy for a tech to fingerprint her and then Mitch told her she could go.

"If I have any more questions, I know where you live," he said with a grin.

She didn't return it. Here, away from Rick and the kids, she didn't have to pretend that all was well between her and Mitch. Besides, a murder had occurred. Death deserved more respect.

As she walked to her van, she felt a headache coming on. She would have to tell Rick and then he would have more ammunition to argue that she needed to find a safer job. He didn't understand how much she loved helping people better organize their spaces and their lives. With Farrah Compton as a client, she had hoped for future referrals to other university staff to earn enough money to make their own home more accessible for Rick. Instead, she was now a material witness to a homicide, a homicide that her own client may have committed. She could forget about referrals and new business. If Farrah Compton was a murderer, the last thing she would be needing was an organized office.

Crys settled inside the van and resisted the urge to rest her head on the steering wheel. Mitch was bound to have more questions for her. She would have to cooperate with him, like it or not. She was a cop's wife and knew her duty, however much she detested Mitch. Besides, she wanted to know what had happened inside that teal door this morning.

She shoved her key in the ignition. *Damn it all!* Life could turn on a dime, and once again it had.

Chapter Three

CRYS'S HANDS HAD stopped shaking by the time she arrived home and changed into jeans and a sweatshirt. Taking a ham and cheese sandwich on a plate downstairs, she listened to phone messages at her desk in the basement as she nibbled. One call was from her friend Maggie, who couldn't wait to share more ideas about promoting Organizing Chicago, her idea of a name for Crys's business. Another was from a potential client planning a move. Crys played the message again. Maybe she had a future as an organizer despite what had happened this morning. As Maggie had predicted, word of mouth about her services was spreading.

The thought of growing her business was both exhilarating and scary. Maggie had built her own PR firm from scratch, and Crys was grateful to have her as a friend and mentor by her side to help birth this baby enterprise. But what would people think if they knew about the murder she had discovered today in her client's home?

"Mom!" Kurt yelled, slamming the front door behind him.

"Down here."

She heard the thud of his backpack hitting the floor

followed by footsteps clomping down the stairs. "You'll never guess what happened in school today!"

The front door closed again, firmly enough to be heard in the basement, but not quite a slam. "I get to tell this time," Dana yelled. She ran downstairs to join her brother. "You told first last time."

They both started talking at once, their voices escalating in volume.

"Whoa!" She raised her fingers to her mouth and whistled. Their hands came off their hips, fingers jammed into ears, and mouths shut. It was one useful trick her older brothers had taught her growing up in Wisconsin.

"Now," she said when they unplugged their fingers from their ears, "as I seem to remember, Kurt, it is Dana's turn today. What's the big news?"

Dana's long, serious face widened in a smile. "Humph!" she said to her brother with a superior look. "Today we had a really cool convocation about smoking, and the doctor cut open a real lung. He let two kids touch it."

"They were wearing gloves," Kurt said.

Dana ignored him. "They showed it on the big screen and it was gross, like a dirty sponge full of black tar!"

"It wasn't that gross," her brother said, flipping open one of the boxes stacked near her desk. "What's this?" he asked, pulling out a plastic tray with a dozen spindles.

"It's for sewing—thread spools go on those posts. So have you both sworn off smoking and putting tar in your lungs?"

Kurt shrugged. "Basketball players don't smoke. I'd rather spend my money on cool tattoos."

"Eew," Dana said. She came over to give her mother a hug. "I'll never smoke or get a stupid tattoo."

"Good." Crys returned her tight squeeze, drawing comfort in their closeness for the few seconds Dana tolerated it. Her day's story would top theirs, but she wasn't about to burden them with it. Instead, she clicked her mouse to put her computer to sleep.

"I'm starving," Kurt said, eyeing her half-eaten sandwich. He dropped the thread organizer and headed toward the stairs.

"There's peanut butter and apples," she called to his disappearing back.

In the kitchen, Kurt was already slicing and coring his apple. She fetched the smooth peanut butter he preferred from the cupboard. She set out two plates and washed an apple for her daughter, who usually didn't eat much after school.

Dana took time to neatly arrange her backpack in her cubby compartment below the stairs. She didn't seem to have much in it, but Crys wasn't surprised. Her efficient daughter used her spare time during the school day to complete most of her homework. Her son was the opposite, hence the Cs that seemed to be enough to satisfy him. By the time Dana returned to the kitchen, Kurt was halfway through his snack. As soon as he stuffed the last bite in his mouth, he placed his plate in the sink and headed up to his room.

The doorbell rang as Crys slid a plate of apple slices in front of her chattering daughter. Dana ran to answer it.

"Uncle Squeak!" she yelled.

"Hello," Crys said as her older brother Gregg, known to her children as *Squeak*, appeared behind his niece in the kitchen.

He nodded to her over Dana's golden head and then set down his toolbox by the stairs, a tricky maneuver with her daughter's arms around his waist. "Easy, girl. You're squeezing the life outta me." He patted her with one arm and held a narrow rectangular box out at his side with the other.

"Goodness, Dana, let him go. He'll be Uncle Squeal if you keep hugging him so tightly."

Dana released him. "You haven't been here in at least a week!"

Gregg's lips twitched. He smiled too infrequently, but he had a fond spot for Dana. "Missed me, squirt?"

She grinned and her nose tilted up again. "No, I've been too busy."

He laughed. "Uh-huh. Tough life being twelve. Too bad you don't have time to come out to the farm and help me with my new colt this weekend."

"A colt?" Crys said over Dana's squeal of glee.

His blue eyes twinkled. "Yep."

"Well, don't just stand there," Crys said. "Sit down and tell us about it."

"Not much to tell. It was a rescue from a farm. The owner had dementia, and his animals were in bad shape." Judging from the glance he gave Dana, there was more to the story not appropriate for young ears. "I'm fostering it for now."

Which meant food, shelter, and money he probably

needed for the mortgage on his small farm. Crys had given up trying to counsel Gregg about his finances. He was an impulsive spender and seemed content to work two or three jobs at a time to have enough to pay his bills, rather than plan ahead. *Uncle Squeak By* would have been an even more appropriate nickname for him.

Gregg declined an apple, but she slid the plate of slices within reach in case he changed his mind.

"Kurt doing okay?"

She glanced at the ceiling and nodded. The sound of a heavy musical beat thumped above them. "They just came home from school."

"And guess what happened, Uncle Squeak? We saw a doctor cut up a smoker's lung. It was gross!"

"Is that so? Guess you learned something today."

"I always learn something. That's because I listen." She shot a sly glance at her mother.

Uh-huh. Little eavesdropper or budding detective, she didn't know which. Either way, she and Rick had learned to be aware that young ears could be listening.

Her uncle sat back with a grin. "Smart girl. Chip off the old block." He turned to Crys. "How was your day?"

"Complicated," she said, unwilling to talk about it in front of her daughter.

The music upstairs abruptly ended in mid-song, and a door banged. Dressed in baggy nylon shorts and a T-shirt, Kurt bounded down the stairs and slammed the front door.

"Mr. Basketball," Crys said. "He's hoping to make the team this year."

Gregg nodded. He had played basketball through junior and senior high school, as had her other three brothers. He accepted an apple slice neatly slathered in peanut butter from Dana.

"You aren't parked in the driveway, are you?"

"No, I'm in the street. I didn't want to block Rick if I'm still here." He pointed to the box he had placed on the kitchen table. "I brought that new showerhead to install—the one you picked out."

The picture on the package was exactly the simple and inexpensive replacement she'd selected online. "Perfect. Thanks for picking it up. Did you keep the receipt?"

He pulled it out of his flannel shirt pocket and handed it to her.

"Thanks for fixing it, Gregg."

He nodded and accepted another apple slice from Dana. They weren't a family that talked much about feelings, but hopefully, he knew how much his help meant to her. Rick could no longer go upstairs, much less replace a showerhead. She blinked away the sudden tears that burned her eyes. The shock of the murder, no doubt.

She sensed Gregg watching her, but Dana was oblivious. Her daughter finished spreading peanut butter on the last slice and announced she was going upstairs.

"You okay?" he asked when Dana had left the room.

"Can't tell you about it now." She didn't want to provide food for her daughter's hungry ears. "Went to see a client this morning, but she—was ill. Anyhow, you'll stay for dinner?"

"We'll see," he said, rising. He would stay if Rick was going to be late. Although Rick had never said anything to

Gregg, he knew her husband's pride hurt to have to rely on his brother-in-law for help.

Dressed in play clothes, Dana bounded back into the kitchen and hugged Gregg's neck. "What color is the colt? Can I feed him?"

He described the latest addition to his farm and promised her that she could feed him on her next visit. "He's too small to ride, but you can give Sophie a workout. As soon as you feed the chickens, that is," he added. Dana detested the dirty creatures.

She wrinkled her nose. "If I have to," she surprised Crys by answering. Her daughter was growing up.

Finishing his soda, Gregg rose from the table and ruffled Dana's hair, drawing another squeal from her. "Time to go to work," he said.

After her uncle headed upstairs with his tools, Dana hung around the kitchen a few more minutes, telling Crys about her classes before retreating to the den. Sounds of television voices and laughter soon emerged.

Crys drew a deep breath and closed her eyes. How was Farrah doing? What had happened this morning to cause her to kill her husband? She couldn't imagine the well-educated, professional woman she'd worked with reacting in such a violent way. Then again, some marriages were a series of battles, fights to the death or, more often, to a victor emerging and the other spouse being vanquished. But Farrah? The woman in deep shock in that white living room hadn't seemed like someone who would wield a murder weapon in anger, smashing her husband's brains out.

Crys shuddered and rubbed her arms. She pictured the bloody images curling up like photographs in a fire and floating away into a night sky. Breathe in, breathe out, breathe in—

A burst of laughter from the comedy Dana was watching intruded, and then Crys's cell phone began to ring. Rick's picture was on the screen when she pulled it out of her handbag. Oh, no—she had forgotten to call him. She drew another deep breath to steady herself before answering.

"Kids home?" he asked after they exchanged hellos.

Rick wasn't a husband who called during the workday to chat. He must have heard, probably from Mitch. "Yes. Dana's watching TV, and your son's outside shooting baskets."

He chuckled, but the sound wasn't lighthearted. "No surprise there. I remember practicing until after dark to try to make the high school team. And I did—mainly warming the bench that first year. Guess it was good practice for the game I play now."

It was no game, but she kept quiet. He didn't want sympathy.

"I heard what happened this morning." His voice was low. "You should have called."

She sighed. "I meant to. I'm still processing it."

"It can hit you that way." There was a long pause, and she let his empathy embrace her. Rick had seen death many times when he worked homicide. "I was thinking of going to the gym after work, but I'll come home."

"No, I'm fine. Go to the gym. I'll feed the kids, and

we'll eat later."

There was another pause, another deciphering of what wasn't being said. Usually Rick was quick to put their arguments behind him. She was the one who rehashed them endlessly and needed time to move on. Last night's had been the same subject—her work—but more intense than usual. They both had gone to bed angry, something they had once vowed never to do.

She could hear the basketball hit the backboard above the garage door. "If you're sure," he said at last. "I could use a workout, even a short one."

"Please—go to the gym. Sweat your socks off."

"I love you," he said, surprising her. The phone clicked, ending the connection before she could say anything in reply.

She closed her eyes and breathed deeply. She hadn't heard those words in a long time.

GREGG LEFT AFTER a noisy early dinner with the kids. Kurt claimed the computer upstairs to work on a report for science class, and Dana snuggled with a library book in Rick's recliner in front of the television. A multitasker, she liked to read and watch television at the same time.

Crys heard the garage door go up a few minutes before seven. She opened the door and watched Rick maneuver into his wheelchair and then roll up the ramp and into the kitchen. His dark hair, graying at the temples, was mussed and glistening from exercising, and shadows darkened his eyes. His black gym bag rested on his lap.

She kissed him. "Must have been a good workout. You're soaked." He looked exhausted, too, but she didn't say that.

"You told me to sweat my socks off. Besides, I had some frustrations to work out."

She didn't bite. Whatever was on his mind could wait, especially if it was about the murder she'd walked into.

She squeezed his shoulder. "I'll warm up dinner."

He raised his hand to cover hers. After a moment, he reached for the hand rims on his wheels. "I'll go wash up."

Later, after Dana and Kurt had spent some time with their father and gone to bed, they sat in the den that had served double duty as the main living room since Rick's injury. They had converted the front parlor into a new master bedroom due to his inability to use the stairs. Installing an elevator remained a distant dream.

At ten, Rick clicked on the local news. The murder was the third story behind reports of the sentencing of a former councilman who'd run for mayor and a carjacking on the northside.

The reporter clutched her microphone with the exterior of Farrah's house in the background. It looked just as Crys had left it. The camera crew must have arrived not long afterward, as the segment had been filmed in full daylight. The camera shot then moved to the front porch as crime scene technicians left with their equipment. According to the brief story, *family members* had found a man dead and a woman with *undisclosed injuries* this morning. The woman had been taken to a local hospital, and her condition was unknown. Mitch, caught on camera exiting the house, paused as the female reporter extended her microphone toward his face before telling her he had no comment.

The reporter then interviewed Gary Zygman, still dressed in his jeans and gray sweatshirt. His hair appeared wet with deep grooves where his comb had plowed through. He told the reporter that it was a quiet neighborhood, and the people who lived in the house mostly minded their own business. His tone indicated that he preferred it that way. The report ended with the statement that the police wouldn't release the names of the victims until the next of kin had been notified.

Rick muted the sound when the report concluded. "So, what happened?"

"Didn't Mitch tell you?"

"I haven't seen him today. Seems he was busy with a new case."

She ignored his sarcasm and told him what she'd reported to his former partner. Sometimes it was annoying to be married to a cop, a former homicide detective at that. He frowned as he listened. How frustrated was he having someone else in charge of this investigation?

"Sounds like the wife has some explaining to do," he said when she finished.

"She must have witnessed it. That could explain her shock."

He gave her a skeptical look. "You don't think she's innocent, do you? Most homicides are committed by family members or friends, and spouses are usually at the top of the suspect list. This looks like a clear-cut case of domestic violence."

"I can't see Farrah murdering anyone. She's a professional woman, very calm and cool."

"Yeah, but how well do you know her?" His words had sharpened. "I've arrested more professionals than I can count, and I'm not talking about hookers. They may be well dressed, but they're just as crooked."

He leaned closer to her, shifting his weight to his right elbow on the arm of his wheelchair, and lowered his voice. "You don't know these people, Crys. You're walking into their houses without a clue of what might be waiting inside for you. I thought we agreed that you were only helping friends or family."

"Norah Kelley referred her. They both teach at U of I Chicago." She lowered her voice. "Norah is a friend of a friend, and Farrah is her friend. You make it sound like it's my fault that her husband was killed."

"It's dangerous. You could have walked into an active crime scene and been hurt."

He frowned at her and kept his voice low, too, typical of their arguments after the children were in bed. Sometimes they hissed at each other like cats circling, ready to scratch and bite but unwilling to risk being hurt or inflicting pain on the other.

"I'm not going to carry a gun," she whispered back. "I'm selective about who I work for, and I won't walk into a situation that looks dangerous." Although she had walked into Farrah's house after she'd noticed the tape on the doorbell camera. Mitch had pointed that out. "Why can't you trust me?"

"Because you're still assuming you can judge people by how they dress or what kind of house they live in. You think there aren't crooks living in nice quiet suburban homes or those mansions on Michigan Avenue?" He jabbed his hand at the television, now showing the weather. "What did that neighbor say—things like that don't happen here? How often have you heard that after a violent crime?"

"It's usually true, though. I bet if you looked at the crime statistics for that street—"

He threw his head back. "You always want to argue! Haven't we been through enough as a family?" He straightened in his chair, pulling away from her, and scowled at the muted screen.

That was a low blow. She glared at him but then noticed again the dark shadows beneath his eyes, the hollowness in his cheeks. Her anger burned out, leaving her just wanting to turn back the clock. Or the years.

She reached for his hand, but he flicked her away. His chest rose and fell with his breath.

Later, in bed, she apologized to make peace.

"I'm just tired of this," he said in the darkness.

That makes two of us. He didn't reach for her, so she turned out the light before rolling onto her side with her back toward him.

Chapter Four

HOSPITALS RAISED HER blood pressure. She'd spent too many weeks here after Rick had been shot and then more hours with him in a rehab center, which hadn't been much of an improvement. Waiting at the reception desk, she sniffed a yellow rose in the floral bouquet she'd brought for Farrah. The natural scent reminded her of her mother's garden and calmed her.

She found the room number on the fourth floor not far from the elevators, but she could have guessed which one it was. A policewoman sat in a chair outside the door. She rose when Crys told her she was there to visit.

"She's not allowed any unauthorized visitors," the young officer whose name badge identified her as Rosa Puente said. "Are you family?"

"No, I'm a friend. I'm the one who found her."

"That must have been a shock. I'm sorry, but you'll have to obtain clearance from the detectives in charge. I can—"

"I'll talk to Mrs. Ward, Officer," Mitch said, emerging from the elevator. His partner followed him, her face expressionless.

Mitch lightly touched Crys's arm and led her farther

down the hall. Detective Alvarez met Crys's backward glance but didn't follow them. She began talking quietly to Officer Puente.

"Didn't expect to see you here." He was unshaven, and his sand-colored hair looked, as usual, like a casualty of the freaky gusts of the windy city. Before the shooting, she might have teased him about his shaggy look or nagged at him like a big sister to get a haircut. Now, she couldn't imagine making a personal suggestion like that.

"If you're checking on her," he continued, "she's the same as yesterday, from what I've been told. We're not allowing visitors, except for family. She's still out of it, anyway."

She glanced back at the two policewomen. They were peering in the glass panel of Farrah's door.

"What did the doctor say? Is it a head injury?"

"Well, I'm probably not supposed to tell you, but she's in what they call a catatonic state. They didn't find any other injury, although she does appear to have a small bump on her head. They don't think she's concussed, though."

She'd heard of the condition but didn't know much about it. "Isn't a catatonic state basically a psychological condition? When will she come out of it?"

He frowned. "She'd better come out of it soon. At the moment she's our chief suspect."

Crys had been afraid he would say that. She must have shaken her head. He took it as disagreement.

"Her brother said they weren't getting along." His eyes were dark but not unfriendly. "If I had a dollar for every domestic violence killing by a spouse I've investigated, I could retire."

She looked away. He sounded like Rick. Also, Randy's first thought had been that Farrah had killed her husband, but that didn't prove that she had.

"Just because they weren't getting along doesn't mean she'd bash his head in. Besides, how do you know it wasn't self-defense?"

"Because she didn't have any injuries, and he didn't have any weapon."

He didn't need a weapon. He was bigger and stronger than his wife. He could grab her and kill her with his bare hands.

"She didn't have any bruises?"

He shook his head. "Nada."

A nurse walked by, so she lowered her voice. "What about the blood on her shirt? It looked like spatter."

"CSI is working on it. They have her clothes."

"I just don't see her as a killer." Her voice sounded like a low hiss and reminded her of the argument she'd had last night with Rick.

Mitch straightened. He looked weary even though the day wasn't half over. Then his lips curled in a crooked smile. "Wanna bet on it?"

"No!" She felt her face flushing. This was just another crime to him, but the woman lying comatose inside the room down the hall didn't deserve cops making light of the trauma she'd experienced or peering in through the window on her door as if she were a lunatic in a padded cell. "I just want to know what happened, and I don't need a cynical homicide dick telling me the case is already solved when you don't even know her side of the story!"

"*Dick*, huh?" He held his palms up. "I'm not gonna touch that one."

She clenched her jaw. Why had she let him push her buttons again?

"We're just starting to investigate," he said in his infuriatingly low-key way. "The husband's office said he was in Milwaukee and not due back until today. Looks like he returned early, they fought, and she hit him hard enough to end their marriage."

"Or they fought and—"

Mitch glanced past her shoulder and unfolded his arms. "Hey, Dr. Park."

The woman in the white coat approaching them stopped. She smiled at Mitch as she recognized him.

"Detective. How can I help you?"

"Excuse me, Crys," Mitch said, dismissing her. He steered the doctor farther down the hall, leaving her abandoned in the corridor as he'd left his partner earlier. Typical.

She was still holding the vase of flowers. The two policewomen were still talking in low tones by Farrah's door. She doubted they would let her leave the flowers inside the room. She saw a nurses' station in the direction Mitch had taken the doctor and headed there. There was no point in hanging around, especially if Farrah was still—what had Mitch said?—*catatonic*.

No one was at the nurses' station. As she rested the vase on the counter, she was just close enough to hear Dr. Park updating Mitch on Farrah's condition.

"With the medication, we expect she'll come out of it in a day or two, but this condition can be unpredictable, depending on the patient and the nature of the events that brought it on."

Mitch's back was toward her, and she didn't hear what he said next, but the doctor replied that she would be making rounds again that afternoon, around four. Mitch nodded and the two parted. He headed back toward Farrah's room, where his partner was now alone, waiting in the chair by the door and talking into her phone. Detective Alvarez rose as he approached, her cell still held to her ear, and they headed toward the elevators.

The harried nurse who returned to the desk a few minutes later agreed to deliver the flowers to Farrah. Crys thanked her and turned to find a man waiting behind her. He was just over six feet and stocky, but his jeans, pale blue shirt, and sports jacket fit him well. Something about him looked familiar.

"Excuse me," he said to her. His brown eyes looked troubled. "Are you a friend of Farrah's? I heard you mention her name."

"Yes, I was hoping to see her, but they're not allowing visitors."

"Oh god." He rubbed his face. "I went by the house, but there was police tape. A neighbor told me there'd been a murder, and Farrah had been brought here. How bad is she hurt?"

He didn't look like Farrah or Randy. She glanced behind her. The nurse had left, and there were no hospital staff in sight to provide answers for him. "Are you family?" she asked.

"I'm her husband."

Chapter Five

"You... Wes?" That's why he looked familiar. She'd packed a framed picture on Farrah's desk of the couple in happier times taken on a vacation to what looked like the Caribbean.

"Yeah, Wes O'Malley. I gotta see her. They told me downstairs that she's in 417."

"That's right. She's resting." She shifted to peer around him. Mitch and Detective Alvarez were gone, and Officer Rosa Puente had not returned to her post. "I imagine they'll let you see her, but you'll have to wait until the police officer comes back."

"Police? Is she in danger here?"

"I don't think so, but they're not taking any chances." She didn't want to tell him that his wife was a suspect in the murder. "I'm Crystal Ward, by the way."

"I don't understand," he said, rubbing the back of his neck. "What happened?"

She told him about finding Farrah unconscious in the living room. "She's not injured, not physically, from what I understand. It's more like she's suffering from severe shock."

"I still don't get it. Who hurt her? And who was the

dead guy?"

Apparently, the helpful neighbor hadn't known that detail. "The police thought it was you, Wes."

"What? I wasn't even home. I just came back today from Milwaukee."

"Business trip?" she asked, remembering what Mitch had told her.

He glanced up as a staff member in scrubs emerged from a room. "Yeah. Business."

Rick had asked last night how well she knew Farrah. Not well at all, apparently. Here was a husband who had only been mentioned in passing once or twice, and there was another man, now in the morgue, whose identity and relationship with Farrah were unknown.

"Do you know if she was expecting someone?" Seeing Wes's tired face and sad eyes, she hoped the dead man wasn't a lover.

He shook his head. "We're separated. I stopped by last Friday to see if she needed anything. We kinda argued then, but she said there wasn't anyone else."

A separation explained why she hadn't met Wes or heard much about him from Farrah.

"It was her idea, not mine," he continued. "She called it a *trial separation*. She didn't want to give up the house, at least not yet."

"It sounds as if she wasn't ready to give up on your marriage either."

"You think so?" When Crys nodded, he frowned again. "Then who was this guy? Did he break in? Is that what happened?"

She wasn't sure how much she should say, but she felt sorry for him. "The police didn't find any evidence of a break-in, although someone had taped over your doorbell camera."

"Yeah, I saw that."

He rubbed his face again and then his jaw tightened. "Wait a minute. You said the police thought I was the dead guy?"

"Yes."

"Do the cops think she did it? Is that why there's a police officer guarding her—they think she's a killer?"

"They—" She found herself quoting Mitch. "They're just starting to investigate." And place bets that Farrah was guilty.

He stared at her, and she could see his thoughts had moved out of shocked confusion. "They've gotta know who the guy was. Didn't he have a driver's license?"

"I don't know." She hadn't seen them check the dead man, but she hadn't been able to see much from the kitchen. Wouldn't they have checked for a wallet or ID or other clues in his pockets and asked her and Randy about what they'd found? Or did they wait for the crime scene investigators to do that? She wasn't sure.

Wes rose and jammed his hands in his pants pockets. "So, they figured I was the poor schmuck?"

"Well, your brother-in-law Randy—"

He glared at her. "Randy? He butted in? What the hell was he doing there?"

She drew back from him, her spine pressing into the edge of the reception desk. "He arrived just after I did. He said he needed to talk to Farrah, and it wouldn't take long." Wes's eyes were mere slits now, a good reason not to mention that Randy knew the door code.

"Yeah, like two seconds for her to say *no*. So he said it was me?"

"We couldn't really see the man's face clearly. Randy must have assumed it was you." Now that she thought about it, Farrah's brother hadn't looked closely at the corpse. The sight of blood had made him nauseous. She could see a resemblance between Wes's hair and what they'd seen of the victim's, but Wes appeared to outweigh the dead man by thirty pounds. No, Randy hadn't looked closely at all.

"And he figured that Farrah had killed me? Geez. I can't believe he'd think his own sister could do something like that. That's low even for him."

She couldn't say much in Randy's defense. He had all but pointed his finger at his sister and named her as the killer.

"The dead guy must have been a burglar." Wes had started to pace. "Farrah didn't always check the camera before answering the door."

"She couldn't check the camera. It was taped."

He stopped. "You're right. He must have rung the bell and forced his way in when she answered."

She didn't comment. Wes's scenario didn't jive with what had looked like a visit by a guest who'd been invited into the living room. And wouldn't a burglar have a weapon or some sort of tool? He didn't seem to have a bag, either, for loot, but he could stuff money or jewels into his clothes, if his intention was to rob her. And where was his getaway vehicle? Had he arrived on foot?

Wes peered down the corridor. Presumably, Officer Puente hadn't returned, because he strolled back to the nurses' station where she was standing.

"Did you say your last name is O'Malley?"

"Yeah. Farrah kept her maiden name when we married. She'd already made a name for herself writing articles and doing lectures. Did she tell you she's up for promotion? Her boss is retiring. She'll be head of her department."

"Yes, she did. She said that's why she wanted to hire me to organize her home office."

He stifled a yawn. "I think she told me about that. Couldn't see that she needed someone to help her do that, no offense."

"None taken. Sometimes a fresh eye and new ideas can help, and that's what I do for clients."

She didn't think he was listening. He was gazing past her at the blank wall of the empty corridor, apparently lost in thought.

Crys glanced at the clock. She should go. She would have already been on her way if she hadn't run into Wes, but meeting him had changed everything. The murder wasn't a "clear-cut case of domestic violence," as Rick and Mitch assumed. Who was the dead man, and what had happened in that room that had left Farrah catatonic?

Maybe the man was a home invader who had talked or pushed his way in, as Wes had suggested, and hadn't known Farrah at all. Rick would have to admit that it had just been bad luck that her client had been a victim of crime. Yes, she had discovered the crime, but that, too, was just a matter of luck. She knew in her gut that Farrah wasn't a killer. The shock of killing a man, even in self-defense, would be traumatizing to anyone and possibly explain her catatonic state.

But why was the camera taped and who had done that? Why had Wes hesitated when she asked if he was in Milwaukee on business? Had he really been out of town when the murder occurred?

Questions cluttered her brain, begging to be answered. There was only one way to tackle them—one at a time.

"Wes, you said you returned this morning from Milwaukee? Does your office know you're back?"

A nurse approached the desk. Wes watched as she dropped off a chart. She didn't seem to notice them and disappeared around the corner of the hallway.

His attention swung back to her. "The office? No, I was supposed to come back this afternoon."

"But you came back early. Was it because you wanted to talk to Farrah?"

He frowned at her. Was he becoming frustrated with her questions? It wasn't her business. He had every right to tell her that, but until he did, she was going to ask her questions and try to sort through this mess so that all of their lives could return to normal. Besides, separated or not, Wes was close to Farrah. He probably knew her better than anyone.

"I thought something was wrong." He patted his suit pocket and pulled out his cell. Even though it was one of the larger models, it seemed like a business card in his large hands. "My phone tells me whenever someone rings the doorbell. I had it turned off during my meetings, but then I saw there had been several alerts yesterday. When I checked, all of the camera recordings were black. I tried to call Farrah, but she didn't answer, so I thought I'd better see for myself."

He stared at the face of his cell as if he expected it to announce that his life hadn't been turned upside down. There were new messages, but he didn't seem interested in checking them.

"Do you still have the camera pictures on your phone? You might be able to help the police if you can tell when the lens was taped. Whoever did that might have something to do with the murder."

He shrugged. "Yeah, it's all here. I checked before I went to bed the night before last. Guess I just thought it was dark. It was late. I was tired from leaving early to drive and—" He seemed to rethink what he was going to say. "And spending the day in meetings."

"And before that night? Was everything normal?"

He nodded. He probably checked the camera at bedtime, if not more often. Who could resist being a secret watcher, a spy? Not a separated spouse. It sounded as if the tape might have been placed over the camera lens the night or early morning before the murder.

"Wes, you said there were multiple alerts yesterday morning about the doorbell."

He swiped on his phone and tapped on an app. "Three: eight thirty, nine ten, nine nineteen."

She and Randy had arrived at ten, but they hadn't rung

the bell. One of the earlier alerts was probably the victim, whoever he was. But who were the other two visitors? Farrah had been busy that morning.

"Tell me about Randy," she said, hoping to keep him talking.

"Huh?" Wes had tapped into his text messages and was reading a lengthy one.

"Randy. Are he and Farrah close?"

He stuffed his phone back into his jacket pocket. "Only when he wants money. No, that's not fair. I guess you could say they're close enough, for a brother and sister. They grew up without much, and Farrah looked after him."

"So he comes to her when he needs help?"

"Something like that. He's always got a new idea for a business, usually a restaurant. He had one a few years back—a pizza bar, he called it. We helped him with that one, which was our mistake. Turned out he hadn't checked into what it took to get a liquor license. It failed in six months. Farrah has tried to give him advice, but even she's run out of patience with him."

Randy had moaned about what he was going to do. "He seemed to be desperate to talk to his sister, like she was his last resort."

A flash of anger sparked in Wes's eyes. "That sounds like him. I bailed him out once after the restaurant fiasco when he claimed he owed money to some guys who would break his legs, but I told him that was the last time. He's all big ideas and no sense. I've tried to tell him he has to work on a business plan, hammer out the details before he starts spending money. You gotta lay a foundation before you build. For a guy who went to college, he doesn't seem to know much." His tone became less sharp. "I started O'Malley Construction from scratch, but I asked questions and learned what I had to do to borrow money when I needed it. You can't just borrow from anybody. If the bank won't loan it, you probably haven't done your homework."

She smiled at him. "You're a self-made man."

"Yeah, I guess you could say so. Hey, do you think that police guard is back? I really want to see Farrah."

"Let's go see."

CRYS'S PHONE RANG as she reached her car. She wasn't surprised to see it was Mitch. She'd asked Officer Puente to call him and let him know that Farrah's husband had shown up at the hospital. She'd left Wes with the policewoman, who was allowing him to only look at Farrah through the glass in the door until the doctor and Mitch signed off on closer contact. She wasn't sure Wes would comply for much longer.

"I'm on my way back," Mitch said. "Are you sure it's her husband?"

She clicked her van door open as she approached it. A Kia with a SCOTT DANFORTH sticker on the rear bumper pulled into the space next to her.

"I didn't check his ID, but that's who he said he was, and he looked exactly like the man in a picture I saw in Farrah's office last week."

He swore. "I thought you identified him as the vic."

"If you recall, that wasn't me. I just met the man today, and I had no idea who the victim was." She nodded at the woman who stepped out of the Kia. There was no passenger emerging from the side she was parked on, so she opened her door and slid into her seat.

She heard a sigh before Mitch said, "You didn't mention seeing a picture of the husband. Couldn't you tell if the victim was him or not?"

She held her phone away from her ear and counted to ten before answering. "The man's face was covered with blood and his head bashed in. I couldn't have recognized you in that condition."

"Okay, okay," he said over a low chatter of a police radio and some honking. She heard his partner swear. "You might as well fill me in. We've just hit traffic."

She looked at her watch. She had an appointment in thirty minutes, which meant she might arrive on time if the roads weren't congested, but she would be pressing her luck to expect that kind of a break two days in a row. She didn't regret taking time to talk to Wes, but she couldn't afford to risk losing a client by being late. It wasn't her fault that Mitch had to return to the hospital and find a new identity for his victim. As she'd reminded him, she wasn't the one who had identified Wes as the dead man.

She started the engine to turn on some heat as she gave him a quick summary of how the doorbell camera blackout had caused Wes to go to Farrah's house and how he'd learned of the murder and his wife's hospitalization from a neighbor. Then she dropped the other bombshell.

"By the way, his last name isn't Compton—it's O'Malley. And before you ask, I didn't know he had a different last name than his wife until he introduced himself to me."

Mitch swore again. "Weston O'Malley. That explains why there were no hits on DMV."

She heard Detective Alvarez say, "I'll run it."

"Crys, stay put. We'll be there in—"

His partner muttered something that sounded like "a couple of hours at this rate."

"Twenty to thirty minutes," he finished.

"Sorry, but I'm on my way to an appointment. You know where to find me." She disconnected before he could argue.

Chapter Six

CRYS EXAMINED HER business calendar on her computer. Next week, the first of October, had several dates with appointments. There were also two possible new clients she was confident would sign up for her services. She was on the right track. Local advertising and word of mouth were working. At least for now.

The prospect she had visited this morning after leaving the hospital promised to be profitable, judging from the multiple rooms in the woman's Albury Park house full of accumulations from thirty-five years of marriage and three grown children. She'd liked Judy Woodbine, who had laughed at herself for being too busy in the past to deal with what she called *the junk*. She would email Judy her standard contract today.

Despite Rick's doubts, she trusted her instincts about people and her safety. She really hadn't been in any danger at Farrah's house. The woman was not a killer, unless she'd been fighting for her life. She wasn't so sure about Wes, though. Had he returned earlier and killed the man visiting with his wife? He checked her visitors on his camera access, which could be perceived as a form of stalking. How jealous was he of other men in Farrah's life? His concern for his wife didn't seem like an act, but domestic abusers proclaimed their love even after beating their significant others nearly to death.

Now she wanted to know why Farrah and Wes had separated. Hopefully, it wasn't because of violence. Farrah had never mentioned much about her husband and had never said anything about them living apart. Domestic violence occurred even to partners who were well educated and affluent. It crossed all social and economic boundaries in society. Farrah was a proud, independent woman who would never admit to having that sort of problem. She would try to handle it herself and keep quiet. No, Wes was still a suspect and so, unfortunately, was her client. But who was the dead man and why had he been there?

Behind her, the furnace hissed and huffed as it came on, reminding her that she was sitting in the basement. Her gaze traveled up to the concrete block walls painted white years before they had moved in. Unlike Farrah's kitchen, this room seemed dingy and cold. At least the walls weren't the original unpainted gray. *Baby steps.* Many successful companies had started in a basement or garage. There was no shame to it.

She slipped into a favorite daydream of renovating this space. If she had the money—no, *when* she had the money, she would add a walkout with a ramp for Rick to the backyard and windows next to the new exterior door. Her office would also have a high window at ground level and be framed in as a proper room, with a dropped or plaster ceiling hiding pipes and beams.

What color would she paint the walls? Perhaps a calming blue. She could hang artwork that inspired her, like the picture of a skier balancing at the top of a long downhill slope. Crys ran her hand over the surface of her secondhand wooden desk, envisioning a sleeker, modern teak table with metal legs. Her old but not antique goose-neck lamp would be replaced by a hinged Anglepoise model with a techy vibe. There would be an ergonomic chair and a colorful rug under her feet on the concrete floor.

The furnace rattled as it shut off. She shook her head, dispelling the fantasy, and gazed at her workspace as it was. Lighting currently consisted of an exposed lightbulb over the stairs and florescent fixtures dangling on chains over the dusty workbench and the laundry area. She hated florescent lights, which she also had to live with in the kitchen. One of these days she would have canned ceiling fixtures installed that could be brightened or dimmed at will via voice control. Imagining *intelligent* lights and appliances in their eighty-year-old bungalow made her smile. Perhaps that was a dream too far.

She sighed, saved the calendar, and logged off her computer. Her chair squeaked as she rolled it backward. Cardboard boxes were stacked around her, the product of too much of her guilty pleasure—online shopping. She spied the spool holder Kurt had pulled out of a box yesterday and tucked it back inside. She would find a place to use it instead of waiting for a future client to need it for sewing. The same was true with her other purchases. Use them or lose them—wasn't that what she told her clients?

Beyond the stack of boxes, her washer and dryer stood silent. She noticed the basket of laundry she'd forgotten to start when she came downstairs and rose to take care of it. From her new perspective by the washer, her battered desk looked like an island surrounded by a sea of boxes. Everything in the basement seemed to be waiting for her to do something.

With a sigh, she began to check pants pockets and load the machine. At least Rick couldn't see this mess. Her office would confirm his skepticism about her ability to run a business.

Then the guilt set in.

Rick couldn't see it because he couldn't walk down the stairs. They had built ramps for him in the garage and at the front entrance, but his paralysis prevented him from independently navigating beyond the main floor. An elevator would make a huge difference, but they couldn't afford it. Not yet. Since the shooting, Rick's limited use of the house had changed his life—their lives, too. He couldn't help with the laundry, as he used to do on weekends when the kids were little. The workbench that had been his domain downstairs had been collecting dust for the last five years. She'd encouraged her brother to use it, but he'd said he'd feel too much like a trespasser. She understood. She hadn't touched Rick's tools, either, other than a hammer and screwdriver that she'd taken upstairs. Everything had changed because of a single bullet fired in a dark alley.

Now you're going to blame him for this? And then a familiar rebuttal: *It's just not fair.*

She waited for the wave of sadness and regret to wash over her but instead only felt anger. The grief counselor she'd met with, courtesy of the police union's medical plan, had taught her to allow herself to feel her emotions rather than try to stifle them. That advice worked—usually. But damn it, after another sleepless night, she wanted to do more than *feel*.

Her hands gripped the side of the washer. She filled her lungs with all of the air they could hold. Before she could unleash a blood-curdling scream of frustration, someone knocked at the front door.

She released the breath she was holding and pushed the button to start the wash cycle. She was already heading up the stairs when she heard her friend Maggie's cheerful "yoo-hoo!"

"I CAN'T BELIEVE it!" Maggie said after Crys told her about walking into the murder scene. "And you don't know who he was?"

"No. I believed Randy when he said the man was Farrah's husband. You'd think he'd recognize his own brother-in-law." Crys set her glass of wine down on the table. She always invited Maggie into the living room, but her friend claimed she preferred the coziness of the kitchen. The first time she'd seen it, she had commented that it reminded her of her grandmother's kitchen. "In a good way," she'd added.

"Wow." Maggie topped off her glass from the bottle of pinot noir she'd brought *to start the weekend*, as she put it. She had changed from her business attire into skinny dark blue jeans and a cowl-neck sweater in peach that warmed her light golden-brown skin. Her hair, which changed more often in a month than Crys's had in a lifetime, was straightened and gathered into a casual ponytail.

"Maybe she had a lover, and the husband walked in, surprising them. The he shows up the next day, pretending he just returned from his trip."

"Maybe, but he seemed to be in shock and really worried about Farrah."

"Or he's a good actor."

She laughed, thinking of Wes. "He seems like a *what you see is what you get* kind of guy. I'm sure Mitch and his partner will be checking his alibi."

"Wait a minute, did you say *Mitch*? He's the detective on this case?"

She nodded. "Yep."

"That must have been awkward. He doesn't think you're a suspect, does he?"

Crys looked at her in surprise. "Me? No."

"I would hope not, but you two are like alley cats fighting over the same scrap of food, ever since—"

"I know, I know. But Mitch knows me better than that. He's not out to get me, Mags." At least she hoped not. She had refused to wait for him at the hospital this morning. He might want to cuff her and haul her in for hindering his investigation (not that she had), but he'd never do that. Mitch wouldn't do anything to upset Rick. Besides, he hated writing reports. Rick had threatened more than once to chain him to his desk to finish case notes when he'd supervised Mitch.

"You can't have everything," Rick had told her. "I'll take a good detective in the field over a desk jockey any day."

Maggie must have come to the same conclusion. "Maybe you're right about that. Anyhow, let's talk about Organizing Chicago. Have you thought any more about creating a website?"

"I've been putting my business cards up in shops and handing them out."

Maggie shook her head. "Not good enough. In today's world, you need more than handing out cards or relying on word of mouth. You need to be on social media—Facebook, Twitter, Instagram, for starters."

"I don't know if I'm ready for that yet."

"What's stopping you? Is it Rick?"

"Mostly. He's against advertising, at least on the scale you're talking about. He's worried about my safety. Walking into a murder at a client's house didn't help."

Maggie winced. "No, I guess not."

"Anyhow, he hasn't told me to stop. He just thinks I should vet my clients by only working for people known to our friends and family."

"That might net you two jobs a month. I thought you wanted to earn real money. How about starting with a simple website? I know a good webpage designer, and I could arrange a discount for you. That's not advertising, not really. It's just a place where people who hear about you can find out what services you provide and how to contact you."

"I don't want to stress Rick out. He has enough to deal

with. Maybe when this murder is solved…"

"If it's solved. No offense, but with our current crime rate in the city, that could take a while." Maggie tapped a polished nail on the base of her wineglass. "You could really be a huge success, Crys. I'm sure of that. You love this work, the same as I love my PR business. And you're good at it. Besides, you told me the extra money is helping. Picture a website—and that's all I'm talking about here—showing prospective clients some of your before-and-after shots." She held up both hands, fingers L-shaped as if framing a picture. "How impressive would that be? Everyone loves seeing possibilities and real examples of people improving their homes."

"I know, but—"

"Meanwhile, you can keep convincing Rick that you know what you're doing and how great the income will be for the entire family. Rick's a reasonable guy. He'll come around."

No wonder Maggie was so successful in her public relations business. She was very persuasive. And she was right. Bills never stopped coming, and there was so much Crys wanted to do to make the house more accessible for Rick. They'd been fortunate that he had great insurance and his medical costs had been paid, thanks in part to a fundraiser more successful than anyone had imagined. Even so, months of hospitalization and rehab, followed by remodeling the house to accommodate his wheelchair, had drained those funds. Now they were facing two children going to college in a few years. Wasn't the extra income and boosting their depleted savings the reason she had started this venture?

"Hello?" Maggie waved a hand at her. "Earth to Crystal."

"Okay," she said, glad for her friend's faith in her. "How much are we talking about to design a webpage and who is this guy you know?"

Maggie texted her the contact's information. Taking this next step would be good for all of them. She just hoped Maggie was right about Rick changing his mind.

Chapter Seven

KURT CAME HOME with a new friend. She intercepted the boys before they headed upstairs, forcing her son to give a mumbled introduction. Rafe was a few inches shorter than Kurt and had smooth brown skin and hair with a rich shine like a black limo. The boy was polite, which showed he'd been taught manners, although his evasive eye contact made him seem secretive. The kid was probably just anxious to see Kurt's room and play basketball. She remembered how parents had faded into the background of her own teen years as peer relationships moved to the forefront. Introductions to friends' parents and adults were both boring and awkward. As Kurt's mother, though, she wanted to know who his friends were.

Dana followed the boys inside, taking her time to report on her day before going to change. All three kids soon reappeared for a snack of cheese sticks and crackers. She risked Kurt's ire by questioning Rafe to learn that he was new to the neighborhood and lived a few blocks away. Before she could ask about his parents, Kurt said, "Let's go."

The boys were outside shooting hoops when Rick came home. They stood in the grass to let him access the garage.

Glancing out the kitchen window, Crys frowned as she recognized the car that pulled up to the curb in front of the house.

"I invited Mitch over for a beer," Rick told her when he rolled into the kitchen.

"So I see." She bent down to give him a quick kiss.

It wasn't much of a warning, considering Mitch was the last person she wanted to see again today. Another glance outside revealed that he had stopped to talk to the boys on the driveway. Kurt passed him the basketball, and he aimed for the backboard. The shot was good. Rafe chased the ball and Kurt gave Mitch a high five.

Resentment formed a knot in her stomach. It should have been Rick out there.

"Not a problem, is it?" her husband said, seeing her expression. "He said he saw you at the hospital today, visiting that woman."

She felt her face flushing. Mitch was still reporting to Rick, even though they were now in different units. Or had he been annoyed enough to vent to his former partner about how his wife was interfering with his work? Not that she had interfered. It had just been luck that Wes had approached her at the hospital and she'd discovered who he was. She had let Mitch know as soon as the policewoman returned.

"I went to see my client, Farrah. They wouldn't let me see her, though."

"You must have missed the excitement. Her husband showed up."

Her look of surprise was genuine. Mitch hadn't told

Rick everything.

"Alive and well. Crys, about visiting this woman." Rick reached for her hand, but the sound of the front door opening stopped him from saying more. He released her before Mitch appeared in the kitchen.

"Hey, Crys," he said, his face impassive.

"Hello, Mitch." She managed a tepid smile for Rick's sake. It was all he deserved for blabbing to her husband, even if he hadn't shared everything.

With that social duty done, he turned to Rick. "Kurt sure has those three pointers nailed. I can tell he's been working on them."

"He's putting in a lot of time out there," Rick agreed. "Who's the new kid?"

"Rafe," they both answered at the same time.

Mitch grinned at her. "Jinx."

He sounded like her brothers in teasing mode, but she wasn't amused. Ignoring him, she told her husband, "Rafe is a new friend. I don't know if he likes basketball or just wants to hang around Kurt."

"Oh, he's as big a basketball nut as Kurt. He seems nice enough," Mitch said. "A little shy, but he's new here. Said they just moved in a couple of weeks ago."

"Sounds like you're pals now," she said, resenting his befriending Kurt's buddy. "I'd like to meet his parents."

"So would I," Rick said, "but it's probably time we started trusting Kurt's judgment. He's almost in high school." He looked up at his former partner. "I'll go change. Make yourself at home. There's beer in the fridge."

She turned back to the stove. Rick was willing to trust

Kurt's ability to assess people and not hers? The heat of her anger alone could have kept the chili simmering.

"Something sure smells good," Mitch said, leaning on the counter next to her.

"Chili." Crys turned away to pull out two beers from the fridge. She handed them to him. "Here. The remote is on the table or in the recliner."

He straightened and accepted the beers. She resumed stirring, even though the ingredients were mixed well enough.

"Look, about this morning, I don't mind that you didn't wait around at the hospital. O'Malley was still there when we arrived."

"Terrific." She didn't turn around.

"All righty, then. Was that *chili* you said or *chill,* 'cause I have the feeling I upset you."

She was too angry to have this conversation. "Chili and chilled beer. Take it or leave it." She could feel him staring at her.

He straightened after a moment. "Thanks. I'll take the beer and leave you to your, er, simmering."

TEN MINUTES LATER, the men were both settled in the living room. Crys heard Rick laugh. At least Mitch was good company for him, but she had no desire to join them. She squeezed out the sponge she'd used to wipe the countertop. The chili was bubbling on the stove, Dana had gone upstairs to read her new library book, and the boys were still shooting baskets outside. She turned the stove burner down further and escaped downstairs to begin laying out the memory book she was creating as a gift for a client whose kitchen she had recently finished organizing.

Thirty minutes later, she had the before-and-after pictures in order and laid out on colored pages. She had found quotations from lyrics of her client's favorite singer to commemorate her achievement in organizing her home. Sandi was a fellow shopaholic, although television shopping networks were her vice. She'd been surprised to find how many duplicate items were crammed into her bulging kitchen cupboards. Three large bags full of virtually new graters, spiralizers, colanders, spatulas, pans, and dishes had been donated to a women's shelter, enabling her to reclaim her space. In the process, she had rediscovered a love for cooking and lost five pounds by eating healthier at home. Her new goal was to lose the twenty-five pounds she'd been carrying since her children were born. Crys felt confident she would do it.

Footsteps on the wooden stairs brought her back into the present.

"I'm guessing someone's hungry," she said as she carefully stacked the pages and photos in order. "I'm coming."

"I can't stay, but thanks for the in-vite," Mitch said in his fake Texas drawl. She turned to find him standing behind her and looking over her shoulder.

"Making a scrapbook?"

"It's a gift for a client." She reached for the desk lamp to turn it off.

"A gift, huh? That must make the customers happy.

Your business must be growing."

She spun her chair around, but she couldn't see sarcasm in his face. It didn't help that his back was to the lightbulb dangling over the stairs and casting his face in shadow. He tilted his head, waiting for her response.

"It is. Little by little."

"Word's getting around?"

"Somewhat. I have a few new potential clients," she added and then regretted it. It was none of his business.

"That's good." He looked around the cluttered basement, probably wondering how she could possibly sell her services as a professional organizer.

Enough. This was her space, and he had no right to judge her. Why had he come downstairs anyway?

She rose. "Look, if you have more questions for me, you might as well ask them. Otherwise, I'd better go see about dinner."

He turned to her, his expression serious. "Yeah, I do have a question. Can you set aside your anger at me until I make an arrest in this case?"

"What?"

"Crys, I'm sorry that you walked in on a crime scene and became part of this case, but I have a job to do here. The thing is, you know these people—"

"Not really."

"You know these people better than I do. Apparently, you talked to Weston O'Malley for a while. He said you told him to show us the doorbell video. *That nice friend of Farrah's*, he called you and said he told you everything already."

"Look, Mitch—"

He held up a hand. "Let me finish." He drew a breath. "I know you didn't know he was alive or would show up there at the hospital. I'm not mad about it. My point is, you're part of this investigation, and I have to be able to talk to you without feeling like you'd rather stick me on a spit and slow roast me over a fire."

She folded her arms. "I can't forget what happened in that alley, Mitch. I live with it every day."

Even in the dim light of the basement, she could see him flinch.

"Fair enough." He jammed his hands in his pockets. "Can we at least call a truce for now?"

She stared at him. Had he listened at all to what she'd just said?

"A truce?"

"With this case. It would help to set aside—you know, the past. I don't mean forget it—oh, hell. I just need to be able to talk to you without upsetting you, or vice versa."

She was sure the range of expressions crossing her face would probably encompass twenty emojis, ranging from shock to anger to what? Curiosity? No, he couldn't be serious. He wanted her to *set aside* his inexcusable failure to provide backup to Rick in the alley that night? Impossible. And hadn't they been operating under a truce of sorts ever since? She had tolerated him coming to their house and pretended to be friendly when they were around Rick. Wasn't that enough?

"Okay, right," he said, looking away from her. "Not yet, I guess." The polite, neutral expression she was used to seeing settled on his face. "I may need to ask you some more questions as we learn more. Let me know if Rick—or you—need anything."

He headed toward the stairs. "Mitch," she called. He hesitated and then looked around at her.

"I can do a truce." *For Rick and only until this murder was solved.*

"Cool," he said like a teenager from a past era, giving her one of his slow, lazy grins.

"As long as you keep me informed about the investigation."

His grin faded. "As much as I can."

She nodded. CPD had its own regulations. She understood that. "Have you identified the dead man?"

"Not yet. Turns out he didn't have an ID on him."

"No wallet?"

"Nothing, unless you count some coins in his pocket and a card for Midtown Taxi. We're running his prints through AFIS. The husband didn't seem to have any idea of who he might be." He looked questioningly at her.

She shook her head. "No, he didn't. He seemed to think it was a burglary."

"It doesn't look like it. We confirmed the victim arrived by taxi, but he paid with cash."

She thought of Maggie's theory. "Do you think Wes is involved?"

"We're checking out his story. Looks like he did go to Milwaukee when he said and checked into a hotel there two nights before the murder. He left his access card in his room, so we don't know exactly when he left. We're waiting to hear back from the customers he claimed he met with yesterday to see if they can account for his time."

Milwaukee was about a two-hour drive from Chicago. Wes could have driven home and then returned for his meetings, which would give him an apparent alibi. Maybe she was wrong and he was a better actor than she suspected.

Mitch's phone buzzed. He reached for it, glanced at the screen, and pocketed it again. "I'd better head out."

Business or pleasure? Probably pleasure. It was Friday night, and he was a single guy. He used to tell her about his dates, back when they were friends and he was like a kid brother. Before.

She looked up at the sound of a toilet flushing upstairs. Her family was probably ready to eat. Rick would expect her to invite Mitch.

"There's plenty of chili—and chilled beer. Sure you don't want some dinner?"

"Yeah. Rick offered, but I can't stay tonight. Maybe next time." With another grin and a wave, he disappeared up the stairs, bounding like Kurt and just as noisy.

She added installing carpet on the staircase to her dream basement makeover.

Chapter Eight

"WHO'S THAT BOY Kurt's been playing with? Seems like he's over at your place every day. I don't like the looks of him."

Connie Byrne, Crys's neighbor, didn't miss much that happened on the street. As the widow of a cop, she had long practiced keeping an eye on things, as she liked to say. From her seat at her neighbor's sturdy oak kitchen table, Crys had a clear view of her own driveway and the road, both deserted after the earlier Monday morning school and work departures.

"That's Rafe, a new friend of his."

"Rafe?" Connie's gray eyebrows shot up. "What kind of name is that? Must be Rafael or one of those other Spanish names. Kids should use their given names when they talk to adults, even if they're stuck with these new ones, like Mason or Sunshine. Don't even get me started on those made-up names with hyphens or apostrophes. Stick with family or Bible names, I say."

"I hear Smith is a popular boy's name these days," Crys said, feigning innocence.

Connie frowned at her and then gave a bark of laughter. "Sheesh! Well, Rafe or whatever his real name is, knocked the ball into my rosebush, or what's left of it. He didn't even apologize."

The rosebush in question was well past the last bloom of youth and only produced one or two flowers a year, but her neighbor was sentimental about it. "I'm sorry, Connie. I'll talk to Kurt about it."

"Not your boy's fault," Connie grumbled. She had a soft spot for both Kurt and Dana.

"To tell you the truth, I don't know much about Rafe myself, other than he likes playing basketball. I asked Kurt about him, but all he told me was that Rafe had moved here a few months ago from Florida."

Connie shook her head. "Who moves here from Florida this time of year? Don't they know winter's coming? Have another piece of banana bread."

"No, thanks. It's delicious, but I had breakfast before I came over."

"I'll wrap some up for Rick and the kids before you have to leave."

Crys sneaked a look at her watch. She didn't want to rush Connie, but she had an appointment at nine this morning. Her new client was a soon-to-be newlywed neighbor two blocks over. She needed to reorganize her garage to accommodate her new husband's tools and his need for space to park his car. Rick wouldn't have any reason to disapprove of this job.

Connie must have seen her check the time. "Remember I told you I have a friend from church who said she needed help cleaning out her husband's stuff?" She reached for a scrap of paper under the saltshaker. "She said I could give you her information so you can give her a call. Name's Betty Angelis."

"Thank you. Did her husband leave her?"

Connie's smile was grim. "You could say that. Died of the cancer a couple of months ago. He was a retired fireman. I keep telling Joey he'll end up with the cancer if he isn't careful around all that smoke and chemical stuff."

Joey was Connie's son who worked for the fire department, the youngest of her three boys. The oldest, Pete Jr., had followed in his father's footsteps and joined the police, and the middle son, Eddy, better known now as Father Byrne, was a priest. All three were fiercely protective of their widowed mother and often came over to check on her.

"That will be a big step forward for her, I imagine," Crys said. "Parting with her husband's clothes and belongings."

"I told her, 'Betty, there's no hurry.' Took me eight months before I had a yard sale for Pete Sr.'s clothes, the ones the boys didn't want, which was most of them. Took a year before I decided to call the trash collectors to come get his recliner and haul it away." She shook her head. "I never thought I'd hang on to that old chair a second longer than I had to. I kept threatening to pitch it when Pete was still alive."

"It reminded you of him." Looking around the kitchen with its mismatched appliances and 1970s orange-and-brown floral wallpaper that was faded and peeling at the seams, Crys didn't think much else had changed in Connie's home since Pete Sr. had died four years ago. Connie was hanging onto memories of her own, like the almost dead rosebush her husband had planted.

The lines of her neighbor's face had softened. "That's the truth, but he would have laughed at me for being sentimental over that worn-out hunk of junk. It only reclined for him, you know. He said I was too small to push it back, but I think the chair was just being ornery."

Crys smiled with her. Rick's recliner still sat in her living room, although he didn't use it anymore. It had been purchased new only a year before the shooting, which was why she kept it. That and the fact that the kids liked to curl up in it. She thought of it as theirs, while Rick's was now his wheelchair. She couldn't imagine feeling the least bit sentimental about that.

"Call Betty soon," Connie said. "She's expecting to hear from you."

Crys looked at the scrap of paper. Rick would approve of this client, too. Connie's late husband had been a mentor to him when he joined the force. They owed their house purchase to Pete Sr. He had told them about the house next to his before it came on the market, allowing them to make an offer before anyone else could swoop in.

"Thanks, Connie. I'll call her today."

CRYS SPENT THE rest of the morning helping Marci Newton, soon to be Mrs. John Freitag, sort through her garage. She was relieved that the woman wasn't sentimental or someone who had to be coaxed to part with her belongings, however out-of-date, broken, or unlikely to be used the item was. Too bad all of her clients weren't as practical as Marci.

During a break when she was alone, Crys called the hospital to check on Farrah. Her condition remained *satisfactory*, a vague description but not the worst status. Without any details, she assumed Farrah was much the same or she would have been discharged over the weekend. Still waiting for Marci to reappear from inside the house, she checked her email. Crys drew in a sharp breath—several items she'd ordered for Farrah's office had been delivered. An attached photograph showed three cardboard boxes stacked to the side of the teal front door.

WES O'MALLEY WAS in the yard gathering up crime scene tape when Crys drove by shortly after noon. She hadn't expected him to be there. Her plan had been to put the packages in her van and keep them until she could complete the job with Farrah. As her van drew closer to the driveway, she could see that the packages were no longer on the front porch. They were probably safely inside, so there was no need to stop to talk to Wes, who was still technically considered a murder suspect. She was here, though, and anxious for an update on Farrah. She pulled into the driveway.

Wes approached with an angry scowl on his face as she stepped out of her van. She was again struck by his size as he drew nearer and had a moment of doubt about being with him.

"Hi, Wes. I would have called, but I don't have your number. How are you doing?"

"Okay."

He looked a little puzzled, as if he couldn't remember where he'd seen her before, so she introduced herself. "We talked at the hospital, remember? I've been organizing Farrah's office."

"Yeah, right." His scowl relaxed. He had dark smudges under his eyes, but he was shaved and his hair was combed. Wearing a pressed blue shirt, dark trousers, and a sports jacket, he was dressed more for an office than for yardwork.

"Farrah's still out of it—no change."

"I'm sorry to hear that. What does her doctor say?"

"She's not sure what's going on inside Farrah's brain. They gave her medication, but the doctor said it may take a few days to kick in, if it does. They let me see her anyway."

"That's good. I'm praying for her recovery."

"Thanks." He waited, crumpling the tape into a ball in his huge hands.

"I was notified that three packages for her office were delivered. I didn't want them sitting out on the porch, especially with thieves in the neighborhood." She wasn't sure he knew about the political signs being stolen, but living in a city, he wouldn't be surprised that she wanted to safeguard her order.

"Yeah, I put them inside."

"Thank you. Would it be okay for me to have a quick look to make sure they sent what they were supposed to?"

He looked vaguely around toward the front porch.

"Sure, I guess." He seemed to become aware of the yellow tape he still held. "I'll go put this in the trash."

When Crys reached the front porch, she noticed the black tape on the doorbell had been removed. The sticky residue and evidence of fingerprint powder that remained would have to be cleaned. That was the least of Wes's worries today.

She tried the door handle on the teal door, but it was locked. She looked for Wes, but he must have gone into the garage or wherever their trash bin was located. He had given her permission to go inside but had forgotten to tell her the code. Maybe he assumed Farrah had given it to her. She remembered the digits Randy had punched in.

The lock buzzed and she swung the door open.

So how many people knew the code? The dead man could have been another regular visitor, perhaps a lover, as Maggie had suggested. Or someone could have obtained the code and decided to use it for criminal purposes. It would be easy to observe Farrah, Wes, Randy, or now even her using it. The skin on the back of her neck tingled. A neighbor with a good pair of binoculars might have been able to read the keys as they were punched in. She glanced across the street. Gary Zygman's broad front window was dark and his garage door was closed. It didn't appear anyone was at home, unless someone was standing in one of the darkened rooms. She wouldn't be surprised to learn that he also knew the code.

She stepped inside and closed the door. If only it could tell her what had happened and explain why there had been no breaking and entering. All they knew was that Wes had received three doorbell notifications that morning before she and Randy had arrived. If the killer was one of them, who were the other two? There was a peephole in the door for Farrah to check. But was she in the habit of using it and would she have opened it to someone she didn't recognize or expect? There was also the possibility that the killer had knocked, as Randy had, and not used the doorbell at all. In any case, if Farrah had opened the door, with or without checking the peephole, her visitor could have forced his way inside. That matched Wes's theory.

Too bad there wasn't a camera in the entryway where Crys now stood.

The air in the foyer seemed stale, as if the house had been unoccupied for weeks, not days. The energy level felt low to her, like a depressed mourner. She listened but heard nothing in the unnatural quiet. It was as if the house were waiting and listening for a human presence to give it life. Or maybe it was the miasma of death lingering. Thankfully, she couldn't see the living room from where she stood.

The garage door rumbled. She would soon be alone at the scene of a murder with a man being investigated as the perpetrator of the crime. And there was Rick's question—how well do you know these people? She thought she knew Farrah well enough, but this was only her second encounter with Wes. Mitch had indicated that they had only partially verified his alibi.

She hesitated. She could skip checking the contents of the boxes and leave, or she could act as if she didn't consider Wes to be a threat. Although his size was intimidating, she had no instinctual tingling or other signal that he was dangerous. Her internal radar about people had never let her down.

At least not so far.

Digging in her shoulder bag, she found her Swiss Army knife and popped open the larger blade. She would stay, for now.

Chapter Nine

WES HAD STACKED the three packages inside the office. Crys checked each label for the sender's name and slit them open with her knife. She had examined all of the contents before she heard him approaching.

"Looks like everything arrived in one piece," she told Wes as she straightened.

He didn't seem to hear her as he gazed around the office with its bare shelves and missing desk. To Crys's surprise, he raised his hand to his mouth and his eyes teared up.

"Wes—she'll be okay." She folded her knife and stowed it in her handbag.

He wiped his eyes. "It just looks like... she left."

"But she hasn't! I know it looks empty, but that's temporary. We ordered a new desk, and all of her books and photos will be put back. I promise." She remembered then that they had been living apart. "She'll be showing it off to you before you know it."

He was quiet for a moment. She hadn't meant to make him sadder, but she didn't want to offer false hope of a reconciliation. For all she knew, they had parted angrily and Wes hadn't been back in the house since they'd separated.

"The separation was her idea," he said, his thoughts paralleling hers. "I always saw us with a couple of kids, growing old together in this place."

"It's a beautiful house. How long have you lived here?"

"Five years." A faint smile touched his lips. "It was her choice—her dream house. Kinda big for just the two of us, I thought, but we'd hoped for children. At least I had. I figured we'd grow into the space."

"That's what a lot of couples do—plan ahead for growing families. It makes sense."

"Yeah, she wanted kids, but then it didn't happen. I thought she was working too hard. She's a professor, you know. Political science. She's written some articles and is making a real name for herself. I told her she could do both, be a mom and have her job. Then she started working for Danforth."

"Scott Danforth? She's working for him? Do you mean volunteering for his campaign?"

"No, they hired her. She runs statistics for them, analyzes trends. Projections, she calls it."

No wonder she had a ready supply of Danforth signs. "Oh. I thought she was still teaching at the university."

His face darkened. "That's the problem. The university said she could cut back on her class load, but not enough. It was too much, even though she didn't think so. We argued about it. She thought I was mad because of the guy's politics, but it wasn't that. We found out early on when we were dating that we had different ideas about that stuff."

A mixed marriage between a Republican and a Democrat. It sounded as if the campaign had been at least a catalyst to their separation.

"You don't like Scott Danforth?"

His scowl returned. "He's a politician, so he makes sure you like him. She had him and his crew over here a couple of times. She said she wanted some practical experience with a campaign, but it's like a shot of adrenaline for her, you know? All the rah-rah stuff. Vote for Scott. I told her she was like a different person around that bunch."

"Not the Farrah you knew."

He shook his head. "She'd been like that when we met, all excited about teaching. She'd just been hired by the university then. I was surprised she even noticed me."

Crys didn't know why men like Wes believed well-educated, professional women wouldn't be attracted to blue-collar guys. Good character and the ability to provide financially went a long way, especially if the woman wanted children. Higher education, as her mother said, was gravy, but meat and potatoes could stand on their own.

"Then when she didn't get pregnant… I wanted to adopt, to raise a kid before we were too old. She said maybe she wasn't meant to have kids." He sniffed. "Kids or no kids, I can live with whatever. I don't care if she works for the damned campaign if that makes her happy. I just want her to be okay."

Going through pregnancy or adoption followed by years of childcare was a big commitment and hard to juggle with a professional career. Crys couldn't imagine life without Kurt and Dana, but maybe Farrah was one of those women who didn't need children to feel fulfilled.

"Wes, do you know who the dead man was?"

He looked at her for the first time. "No. The police showed me a picture of him, but he didn't look familiar. Not that I could tell much."

Probably not, even if the man's face had been cleaned up to help identify him. "Did Farrah have any enemies? Anyone who was mad at her or might be trying to cause trouble for her?"

"No one. She's popular, you know. Her students love her."

His mouth twitched. He looked like he might start crying again but fought it. A lump formed in her throat. Rick had looked that vulnerable in the hospital after the doctor had told them that he would probably never walk again. The only time she had ever seen him cry had been after the doctor had left them, closing the door softly behind him.

She cleared her throat. "I'm so sorry you're going through this. Do you have any family in the area?"

"They're in Indiana." He hesitated and then added, "Most of them."

"What about Farrah's folks? Besides Randy, I mean."

"I called them."

Judging from his lack of enthusiasm, he didn't seem inclined to rely on them for support.

"They must be worried about her," she probed.

He shrugged and then his fists clenched at his side. "Whoever he is, I'm glad the bastard's dead." His face twitched again. "I should've been here."

Crys reached for his arm and squeezed it. "That's not

realistic, Wes. You can't guard someone 24/7. For what it's worth, I don't think Farrah killed him."

He looked up. "You think someone else was here?"

"I do. Remember your alerts about three people ringing the doorbell that morning? One of them could have killed him. Farrah saw whatever happened and… it was too much for her. We'll just have to wait until she can tell us." Or until Mitch and his team identified those other visitors.

He released a sigh big enough to expel hours of tension. "I should get back to her."

Crys patted his arm. "Yes, she needs you. Is there anything I can do to help?" She doubted that he'd considered what needed to be done while Farrah was ill. "Have you notified the university?"

He looked stricken. "Ah, hell. I should've called her boss. Maybe he heard about it on TV?"

"They didn't give her name in the story I saw. Do you have her boss's number? I can call."

He scrolled on his phone to find it, and she noted Farrah's department head's name and number on her own phone.

"What about the campaign? Is there someone there I should notify for you?"

He gave her a blank look. "I don't have a number for them."

"They should be easy enough to locate. I'll take care of it," she promised. She handed him one of her cards. "Here's my number. Maybe I'd better have yours. The new desk should be delivered here soon. I'll let you know when they email me with the date."

She needed to check when the other items she'd ordered were due, she realized as she entered Wes's name and number into her phone's contacts list. She would have to make at least one more visit to finish this project, after Farrah returned home.

If Mitch didn't arrest her.

Wes walked her to the door, a silent companion. He thanked her for coming and seemed reluctant for her to leave.

"If Farrah is awake, say hello for me," she said brightly, trying to give him some hope. He managed a nod before closing the door behind her.

As she reached the driveway, a Kia Forte pulled up. The dark-haired woman who emerged was about her age and wore jeans, a sweatshirt, and athletic shoes. She opened her trunk and pulled out a plastic red pail with cleaning solution bottles on one side. A pair of blue rubber gloves was on top of a sponge and whatever else filled the other half.

"Hi," Crys said. "Are you here to clean?"

Her brow furrowed. "Clean, yes." She raised the pail as if to confirm what she'd said.

Crys smiled. English didn't seem to be the woman's first language, so she decided not to mention cleaning the doorbell. "That's good. Have a nice day."

The woman smiled back. "Good. Clean," she said before reaching back into her car to grab a mop.

Chapter Ten

THAT AFTERNOON AS Crys sat in her basement office, cinnamon and ripe apple scent filled her senses from the autumn candle she'd lit. Maybe there was a little too much apple pie smell. It was making her hungry, despite having enjoyed a toasted cheese sandwich as soon as she had arrived home.

She dialed Professor Raskin, Farrah's boss, and reached a secretary, who took her message that Ms. Compton was in the hospital and unable to call. Crys told her that the earliest she would be back was two weeks at a guess. The secretary expressed concern and promised to deliver the message as soon as the professor returned to his office after class.

She found a number for Danforth Campaign Headquarters on the internet. A woman with a sales rep's enthusiasm promised to deliver her message to Evan Kruper, the campaign manager and Farrah's presumed boss. "Be sure to vote for Scott," the woman said after Crys thanked her, instead of the usual *Have a nice day*. Maybe she should end her own calls to clients with a cheery *Stay organized!* Somehow, that seemed over the top. Maggie probably wouldn't think so.

Later, Kurt came home from school, boisterous over the prospect of going to a Bulls game with his dad and Mitch, who had organized the outing a few weeks earlier.

"Remember the deal," she told him. "Homework after school today since you won't be home until late."

He jammed half of a peanut butter and jelly sandwich into his mouth. "I know," he mumbled with his mouth full, or so she translated. He bounced toward the stairs, nearly knocking his sister over as she entered the house.

"Watch it, you idiot!" Dana said.

By the time Rick came home, Kurt could barely contain his excitement. He filled his dad in on the stats for the visiting Pistons while Dana told Crys in great detail about her science teacher's promise of a field trip next month to the Museum of Science and Industry downtown. It was a relief when Mitch rang the doorbell. Kurt jumped up to answer it.

"Thought we might get an early start," Mitch said to him. "No telling about traffic."

More like he wanted to allow extra time for Rick to manage. "Would you like something to eat or drink?" she offered.

"No, thanks. I'll get a dog at the game."

"Me, too!" Kurt said, practically bouncing on his toes. "Or maybe pizza."

Mitch grinned. "How about both?"

Rick shook his head. "You two are bottomless pits. Speaking of which, I think I'll make a pit stop before we leave."

As his father rolled toward the master suite, Kurt asked,

"Mitch, are you going to buy a program? It's a new season, you know."

"Kurt! You have your own money. Mitch is providing the tickets, remember?"

"Ah, Mom. I was only asking if *he* was going to buy one."

"We'll see," Mitch said. "Nice jersey, bud." He pinched it with his left hand and then faked a punch with his right to Kurt's midsection, causing him to laugh and pretend to hit back.

"Get your jacket," Crys reminded her son, "and money, if you want a program." He grinned and flipped the peace sign at Mitch before bounding upstairs.

She was left alone with him for the moment—as good a time as any to test the truce term he had agreed to. "Anything new with the investigation?"

"We had a hit on the prints and identified the victim."

"Really? Who is he?"

He jiggled his keys, looking pleased with himself. "Turns out he's a reporter, name of Jason Norman."

"I don't think I've heard of him."

"That makes two of us. Apparently, he's a big deal with *The New York Times*. One of their prize-winning journalists."

She heard a brief squabble from upstairs but could tell it was nothing serious. "But what was he doing here?"

"That's what I'll be working on tomorrow. I'm waiting until his family is notified. We just obtained the ID late this afternoon." He grimaced. "Not that I'm expecting the *Times* to tell me much. News media tend to be secretive about the stories they're investigating."

She heard a toilet flush from the master bedroom and a door slam upstairs. They wouldn't be alone much longer. "What about Wes O'Malley? Did his alibi check out?"

The key jingling stopped. "We're still working on it."

"What do you mean?"

Rick emerged from the bedroom as Kurt bounded downstairs.

"All set?" Rick looked up at Mitch.

"Yeah, let's go! Bye, Mom," Kurt said.

"Have fun and listen to your dad," she told him. Rick reached for her and she bent down for a kiss. Mitch held the door for him.

He winked at her. "Don't wait up for us, Mom."

She smiled despite herself. "Thanks for taking my guys to the game. It means a lot."

He grinned. "Are you kidding? You think I'm doing it for them? Kurt has nothing on me as a Bulls superfan."

She didn't completely believe him. Maybe if he'd worn a jersey or painted his face red and black. He flashed the peace sign at her and pulled the door closed.

SHE'D PROMISED DANA they would order a pizza as their special treat. Garballi's was their favorite local pizzeria, and they opted for a thin crust cheese and pepperoni pie. Crys sat on the sofa with her daughter curled up next to her watching *Wheel of Fortune* as they waited for the delivery.

After the guys had left and she'd phoned in the pizza

order, she'd searched online for Jason Norman. Mitch had been right about him being a big deal in journalism. He even had a biography on Wikipedia (not yet updated with his death, of course). She clicked on that page. Jason, known as *Jase*, was thirty-nine. He lived in New York City, where he'd been born, and had worked for the *Times* for a decade. He'd won many awards, including two Pulitzers, for his articles as a foreign correspondent. She scrolled down to his personal life. There was no mention of a wife or children. Probably too busy with his career and world travels to settle down. She had found no mention of Chicago or any current assignments.

The doorbell rang, and she motioned to Dana to stay put. She peered through the spy hole in the door and recognized the bulky shape of their usual delivery guy.

"Hi, Austin," she said to young man who took their pizza from the insulated carrier and handed it to her. "How's college going so far this fall? Any good classes?"

He wrinkled his pug nose. "Still high school 2.0."

"Darn. No good computer courses yet?"

He shrugged. "I'm taking advanced game design, but I learned all that stuff when I was ten."

"Well, maybe next semester they'll catch up with you. Hang in there."

The cost of the pizza was just under seventeen dollars. She set down the fragrant cardboard box and pulled two twenties from her pants pocket. She held up the two bills. "If you want a challenge, I could use your help with a little computer research."

His face lit up. No surprise there. Austin worked for a

rideshare company in addition to his pizza deliveries to make money for tuition.

"Thanks, Mrs. Ward." At nineteen, he still didn't have much facial hair, and she doubted that he shaved yet. With his rounded cheeks, he still looked more boy than man, although his voice was surprisingly deep. He reached for the money and then hesitated. "What kind of help do you need?"

"I have two names. I want to see if there's any connection between them. Maybe in the past they were in the same place at the same time. That kind of link. They may not have met before, so don't spend a lot of time on it. And this is just between us."

He nodded and took the money from her. Tucking the empty carrier bag under an arm, he pulled his cell phone from a shirt pocket. In a second he had opened the screen he wanted. "Ready."

"Farrah Compton of Chicago and Jason Norman, a journalist in New York." She spelled the names for him. "And Austin, don't do anything…you know."

"No hacking government websites. Got it." He pocketed his phone and gave her a two-finger salute before heading to his idling old Toyota sedan with the Garballi's sign lit on the roof.

Crys closed the door and carried the pizza to the kitchen. She had more than one reservation about what she'd just asked Austin to do. She was being nosy, but why not take advantage of the best computer researcher in the neighborhood and contribute to his college education fund at the same time? It should be all right, as long as he didn't do something illegal.

Chapter Eleven

CRYS DIDN'T HAVE a chance to catch up with Rick until the next evening after the kids had gone upstairs. Kurt had homework, but he was more likely to be checking in with friends on his phone. Dana didn't yet have a cell phone, and she was probably reading. Crys was determined to not hover over them. If they failed a test or didn't have their work completed, then she would talk to them about better time management and impose sanctions, if needed. They were old enough to learn to take responsibility for their choices.

She was curled up on the sofa as she listened to political commentators on a national network talk about the upcoming election. Rick shifted in his chair and blinked. He'd been dozing for the last twenty minutes and hadn't noticed when she'd switched channels.

"You were up late last night," she said. She had fallen asleep by ten. She hadn't looked at the clock when he'd transferred himself into their bed.

He yawned. "It was a good game, especially since we won. Too late for a work night for an old guy like me, though."

"I'm glad you guys had fun. Kurt loved every minute. It

sounded as if he ate his share of dogs and pizza."

"That's on Mitch. He was egging him on." He turned toward her. "You seem to be getting along better with him."

She knew he was talking about his former partner, not Kurt. "It's this case. We have a common interest besides you." She grinned at him.

"Uh-huh." He didn't smile. Something was on his mind.

"He told me last night that the victim had been identified as Jason Norman."

"A big-league reporter," he said, his face crinkling as if he'd smelled spoiled chicken. "He worked for *The New York Times*."

"The *Times*? Wow—that is big league. Does Mitch know what he was doing in Chicago?"

Rick used his arms to push up and stretch his upper body. He hadn't gone to the gym today. Hopefully, his muscles weren't beginning to cramp.

"He was on assignment here. Something to do with the election."

"In Chicago? Wouldn't a reporter of his caliber be working on at least a national angle?"

Rick glanced at her. "Maybe he was. We have a couple of federal seats up for grabs, the House reps and one senator this year. Anyhow, Mitch is trying to learn more. The *Times* wasn't helpful. If it were my case—" He cut himself off and his expression darkened.

But it wasn't his case. He was no longer in homicide. That didn't mean he couldn't contribute his considerable detective skills to help solve this murder.

"What do you know about Scott Danforth?"

Her question seemed to penetrate the dark thoughts that had shut him down. "Danforth? Isn't he a politician? A Democrat? The name sounds familiar." He jerked his head toward the television. "Is that who you've been watching? What happened to the game?"

"You fell asleep. It couldn't have been that exciting." She handed him the remote, and he switched back to the Nets and the Lakers game. It still had five minutes to go, and the teams were huddled during a timeout. The score was close enough now to be interesting. To her surprise, Rick left it on mute.

"Why were you asking about Danforth?" he asked.

"He's our state senator from this district, but he's running for Congress now. Farrah Compton is working for his campaign."

"No surprise there."

"What do you mean?"

"She's a college professor, isn't she? They're all Democrats."

"Maybe not all."

"Around here? Illinois isn't exactly a hotbed of conservatism."

"True." Wes had told her that his wife was doing statistical reports for Danforth and helping him to strategize. "I wonder if that's why he contacted her," she said aloud.

"Who?"

"Jase Norman. If he was reporting on Danforth's campaign, he might have been referred to Farrah. She could share statistics and projections." She explained what Farrah's work had been, at least as well as she understood it from what Wes had told her.

He yawned again. "Why would she kill him, then? Not that I have any sympathy for reporters."

She elbowed his arm. "She wouldn't. That's the point. As you great detectives say, she has no motive."

"No known motive. My money is still on the husband, if we can prove he was in town that day. Even if he wasn't around, he could have hired a killer."

She hadn't considered that possibility, but it didn't seem to fit her sense of Wes as a hands-on type of guy. "I don't think so," she told him, loving him for challenging her theory. "If he hired a hit man—"

"Or woman," Rick said, giving her a wry look.

"Or woman, to go to their home, wouldn't Farrah be the target? And hitting him over the head? Come on! What kind of hit person would do that?"

He laughed. "I didn't say he hired a pro."

"Okay, but that's a lame theory. And if Jase Norman was the target, how would Wes or the hired amateur killer know he would be there? He didn't live in Chicago."

Rick pursed his lips. "You're right. The method of killing isn't professional, more of a heat-of-the-moment attack."

"Yes, exactly. It was unplanned. The weapon could have been the statue I saw on the floor."

"And since your client wasn't killed and you don't think she's the murderer, the most likely suspect is the husband. He came into the house and caught them together."

She sighed, remembering her own suspicions about a jealous Wes catching Farrah with another man. "It still seems unlikely. They were in the living room, not the bedroom. Wes said she's had people from the campaign over. She probably also invited colleagues from the university to their house, maybe even students. If Norman was doing an interview, she would have just introduced him and explained why he was there. End of story."

Rick tapped the television remote against his thigh and then unmuted the game. The sound was still turned low. A whistle signaled a timeout.

"Crys, you know it's looking bad for Farrah Compton, unless we find evidence that someone else was there."

"I know. Wes thinks it was a burglary, but nothing was stolen." As soon as the words were out, she realized that she was wrong. "Wait a minute. Jase Norman's ID was missing. That has to mean that a third person was in the room and took it."

"You're assuming he had an ID to take. A lot of people in New York City don't drive."

"No, but they have wallets, don't they?"

He had begun to massage one thigh with both hands. "Let it go, Crys. Mitch is on top of it. He'll sort it out."

His words cut off the conversation as effectively as a door slamming in her face. She snatched the remote from his lap and muted the TV again.

Rick looked at her in surprise. "What?"

"You're shutting me out. *Let it go*? And as for Mitch—" She stopped herself just in time. They had argued once before about her anger toward his former partner. Besides, this wasn't about Mitch.

His eyes darkened. "Mitch is doing his job."

"Yes, and he's at least willing to listen to my thoughts on the case."

"Cryssie, I'm just trying to protect you."

"Argh." Jumping up, she tossed the remote toward him. He caught it mid-air.

She left him and retreated to the kitchen. Rejecting the urge for a glass a wine, she slumped at the table. She knew she was making more of it than she should, but they hadn't talked about a case since Rick had been investigating Dominick Ricci last year. Before the shooting, he had shared what he could about cases from time to time, telling her once that he liked how she thought beyond the obvious. She missed those conversations: speculating with him about crimes, analyzing evidence, testing out theories together. Sometimes, the closeness they shared in those conversations was better than sex, even before the shooting.

When she returned to the den, Rick was stretching by raising his torso out of the seat of his chair before bending his elbows to lower back down. "I think I'll head to bed."

"Go on. I'll unplug our offspring. I think we could all use an early night."

Chapter Twelve

MAGGIE RANG THE doorbell the next morning not long after Kurt and Dana left for school.

"I can't stay long," she said, setting a bakery bag, keys, and purse on the kitchen table. "I have a meeting at ten with a potential new client. I need to review my proposal before then, but I couldn't resist picking up some cheese Danishes at Milow's. You know they're the best in Chicago. Is that coffee I smell?"

"I just made a fresh pot." She found cups and plates while Maggie made herself comfortable at the kitchen table. She was dressed to make an impression in a black pantsuit, silky turquoise-and-orange patterned blouse, and black shoes with heels higher than Crys had ever worn. Unlike her, Maggie wasn't six feet tall and had no reservations about adding a few inches to her height. She also had a new French manicure.

"I brought you this morning's paper about the murder. What's the inside scoop?" she asked as Crys set a mug of coffee in front of her.

"Nice," she said, tapping her friend's fingers and taking the paper. "Farrah is still in the hospital, and Mitch is checking her husband's alibi."

Maggie was admiring her nails. "Spoiler alert—the paper says the victim was a famous reporter, Jase Norman." She tapped a fingertip on the picture of an unsmiling man staring into the camera lens. "Or did you already know that?"

"Actually, yes."

"Hmm. Well, according to social media, he wasn't happy being taken off the international beat. What a shame he's gone—so brilliant and cute, too."

In the newspaper photograph, one she had already seen online, Jase Norman appeared handsome and intelligent, as befitted a celebrity journalist. He had a long, ascetic-looking face and a carefully tousled haircut that had probably been expensive. Of course, the man in the photo looked nothing like the bloodied and crumpled body on Farrah's white carpet. She must have made a face, because Maggie snatched the paper from her.

"I'm so sorry! I shouldn't have brought it up. Let's have a Danish and talk about something else, like my fabulous PR plan for Organizing Chicago." She pushed the paper aside and retrieved a manila envelope from her bag.

"I'm still not sure about that name. Isn't it too ambitious sounding? As if I'm going to organize the whole city?"

Maggie's dark eyes sparkled. "It's a *lot* ambitious, but you need to aim high. One of these days, you'll have a team of organizers and more business than you know what to do with. Trust me, this city is full of people desperate for your services, and who better to do it than you? Have you contacted Ty about the website?"

Crys opened the waxy paper bag and placed a pastry on

each plate. They appeared to have a strawberry and cream cheese filling. "No, not yet."

"Crystal!"

"It's just… I've been busy."

Maggie wasn't buying her lame excuse. "Okay, let's take it one step at a time. I want you to feel comfortable about this, but as your friend, it's my duty to give you a nudge."

"A shove is more like it." She grinned to let Maggie know she wasn't upset with her.

"All you have to do is talk to Ty. No commitment, just have a conversation. Have you looked at other organizers' sites?"

"I've seen a few, back when I was checking out how much to charge."

"That's not the same as examining their website design and content."

They both took bites of their pastries.

"Best bakery in Chicago," Maggie said. She reached for a napkin to wipe her hands and then pulled out a pen. On the manila envelope, she wrote:

1) CHECK OUT TEN LOCAL ORGANIZERS' WEBSITES.
2) IDENTIFY WHAT INFORMATION/FEATURES YOU WANT ON YOURS.
3) MAKE A LIST OF QUESTIONS FOR TY.

She turned the envelope around for Crys to see. "How's that for a plan, Ms. Organizer? Better? I was aiming for bite-sized steps this time."

When she didn't receive an immediate answer, she

crossed out the ten and changed it to five websites to check. She spun the envelope back around.

Crys licked sugar from her finger. "It's not that I have a problem making a call. I just need more time."

"You haven't talked to Rick." Maggie's dark eyes studied her.

"Not yet."

Maggie tsked. "I can't believe you're the same woman who told me she would start climbing walls if she didn't get out of the house and do something useful, like earn money to have a closet in her bedroom or redo her kitchen."

"I do want that, but—"

Maggie wagged a finger. "No *buts*. Rick is more reasonable than you think. If he rejects the idea the first time you propose it, keep working on him. Use charm, threats, or whatever it takes to whip him into line."

Crys faked a shocked look. "Whip?"

"It's just an expression, although I bet you have access to a pair of handcuffs." Maggie winked and took another bite, chewed for a moment, and rolled her eyes in delight. She pushed her list back toward Crys. The pen rolled off the page and stopped when it hit Crys's mug. "I know marriage negotiations can be tricky—"

"Especially when a murder has occurred in your client's house."

"Okay, very tricky for now. Keep this and let me know when you're ready. Meanwhile, remember why you started this business in the first place."

"Thanks." A little internet research wouldn't hurt, but she didn't want to make any major moves without Rick.

His concerns about her safety were understandable. Besides, her decisions and their consequences would affect all of them.

"I appreciate your work on Organizing Chicago, Maggie. I know you have paying customers who need your time."

"Hmm. Well, friend or not, I wouldn't be offering you my professional expertise if I didn't think you were worthy of it. I don't share Milow's with just anybody, you know." Maggie dabbed her mouth with her napkin. "Anyhow, as long as Farrah isn't the murderer, I don't see that it was anything more than bad timing or luck that you were there. The suburbs are usually safe. It's not like we live in the city."

"I tried that argument. I think he just needs a little more time, Mags." She reached for the newspaper. "Does this article say anything about Farrah?"

"It mentions that she and her husband are the homeowners. It doesn't say that she was the woman taken to the hospital."

"That's good." She scanned the article. There was another headline about the upcoming election. "What do you know about Scott Danforth?"

Maggie froze with her mug halfway to her lips. "Scott Danforth? The hot politician? Is he involved?"

"Farrah is working for his campaign."

"I thought she taught at the university."

"She does, but she's been involved with his team. Her subject is political science, and her husband said she wanted some practical experience."

"Makes sense. I've considered volunteering to work on his campaign myself, although he already has a PR team, of course."

"What have you heard about him?"

"Nothing bad, actually, which is surprising for a politician in this city. He seems to have done a good job as a state senator." She tilted her head. "Charismatic, charming—people seem to really like him. His wife, Laura, is an attorney at a legal aid center downtown. Or at least she was. They have two or three children and live in Inverness. Both grew up in Chicago."

"No scandals?"

"Not that I've heard. Of course, he is an Illinois politician on the way up. Now if he were running for governor, I'd be really suspicious." She laughed and Crys grinned, even though it was dark humor. For a while, it had seemed that every Illinois governor had ended up in prison.

Maggie's eyes glowed. "How would you like to meet Scott Danforth? He's going to speak at the POW gala Friday night. Our theme this year is *Striking a Blow for Democracy*."

She had mentioned POW, the Professional Organization of Women, before. It was one of many groups she belonged to. Great for networking, she claimed, but large enough so she could avoid being drafted to serve on the board.

Maggie pulled out her phone and began tapping on it. "I wasn't going to go, but what the heck. It's at the Riverview in St. Charles, very classy with fabulous food."

"Are you sure you want to go? That would be great!"

She could find out more about Farrah's role with the campaign. Rick wouldn't have to know why she was going to the meeting. He wouldn't care about her going to a women's organization's event with a friend.

"You can be my guest," Maggie said as she continued to tap on her phone. "I'll tell them that you're a prospective member, which you are. It'll be fun! Oh, no."

"What?"

Maggie made a face. "They're all sold out."

CRYS'S CLIENT LOVED the photo album. "I'm so proud of my kitchen, I'm telling everyone I know about you!" Sandi had gushed, which was exactly what Crys wanted to hear. She did the before-and-after albums as gifts to her clients, but they might prove to be a useful advertising tool if she continued to grow Organizing Chicago by word of mouth. A picture was worth a thousand words, or, as Ludwig Mies Van Der Rohe, the designer of Crown Hall, one of her favorite buildings in Chicago, had said, "Less is more." She often shared his famous quote with her customers. Maybe she would put it on her future website.

She then met with Connie's friend, Betty. The house where Betty and her late husband had lived for fifty years was full of happy memories, and Crys had no intention of removing his presence. Helping Betty to go through his clothing and toiletries might be the extent of that project, although Betty had suggested that she might want to also clean out the organized but overly full basement and garage. She'd left a contract with Betty and her card. She had a feeling she would be hearing back soon, especially with Connie pressuring the poor woman.

Returning home, Crys mixed up a tuna salad sandwich for lunch. She flipped through bedroom and closet pictures on her phone as she ate. Ideas were beginning to form as she imagined the reordered spaces and how she could help Betty to envision the next phase of her life. Her phone rang. She frowned when she saw the name of her caller.

"I have a few questions," Mitch said. "Is now a good time?"

Hello to you, too. "I'm just finishing eating lunch."

"Same here. Guess we're on the same schedule. Great minds and all that." He chuckled.

Hardly. Millions of other Americans were also probably eating now, as it was just past noon. "So, what's up?" she asked to encourage him to quit trying to make small talk.

"Okay, so according to Jason Norman's editor, who wasn't very helpful, Jason, or Jase as he's known, was working on a story about the next crop of Congressional representatives and came to Chicago to look at the Danforth campaign. We checked it out, and he had made contact with the campaign manager and had scheduled an interview with Scott Danforth. They were supposed to meet the day he was killed. I also learned that Ms. Compton was advising Danforth. Did she ever mention anything about working on his campaign?"

"No, but I heard something about that this week. She's still teaching at the university, although they assigned her a lighter class load this semester."

There was a pause. Either he was chewing or she'd surprised him.

"What did you hear about her work with Danforth?" he asked.

She deflected. "Couldn't the campaign tell you what she was doing?"

"Advising, polling—whatever that means. She seemed to be working closely with Danforth and his campaign manager, but she wasn't one of the people Jase Norman talked to when he visited their headquarters on Wednesday. Apparently, that wasn't one of her normal days in the office due to her teaching responsibilities." She heard some paper rustling. "She never mentioned the campaign to you? Or anything about having an appointment with Norman?"

"No. I knew she supported Danforth. She had his signs in her yard."

There was silence again for a moment. "I don't remember seeing any."

"You didn't." She told him what Farrah had said about a sign being stolen and then replacing it with two more. "I noticed they were missing that morning when I arrived. I figured the thief had returned."

"Great—another crime to solve."

Could the sign thief have taped the doorbell camera to avoid being seen? In that neighborhood, probably everyone had cameras or kept an eye out, like Mr. Neighborhood Watch across the street. "That neighbor, Gary Zygman, said he had some information."

She heard the sound of a pop top being opened and the hiss of a soda. "Yeah, Zygman said she'd had some company before you and the brother arrived. Two cars were there earlier."

"That would match up with Wes's three doorbell notifications, including Jase Norman."

"Yeah. Hold on." She heard a page being flipped and took advantage of the pause to take another bite of her sandwich. Mitch didn't seem in a hurry to end the call. She was beginning to feel like his token lunch date, so she might as well eat.

"Now that I think about it," he said, "that guy said something about signs... oh yeah, here it is. He said she'd practically accused him of stealing her sign. That didn't sit well with him. Said he's the captain of their version of Neighborhood Watch but couldn't resist saying that maybe she should rethink who she supports if she doesn't want her liberal, socialist candidate's signs disappearing."

"Charming."

"A real prince. No record, though. He owns three of the All Cars Auto Parts stores around town. Even his record with the Better Business Bureau is clean."

"What about cameras? Do any of the other neighbors have them, or is this Neighborhood Watch commander so good they don't need them?"

"He's not that good if her signs were stolen right under his nose. But no, the house directly across has the same kind of doorbell camera, and it was taped, too. Looks like the same black electrician's tape. We took it to analyze for prints."

"Sounds like the same person." Possibly the sign stealer or even the person who killed Jase Norman. Someone had planned carefully, too, in making sure neither camera would capture whatever crime was planned—theft, murder, or both.

"The good news is Zygman has a camera. Not the ideal sightline for us, but there was a figure the night before the murder who seemed to be headed toward your client's house. Possibly male, wearing a hoody and those fancy tennis shoes with the florescent stripe on the heel."

"I know which ones you mean. Kurt's been wanting a pair. They're expensive, though."

She heard voices in the background.

"I have to go. Catch you later."

The line went dead. "And you have a good day, too," she said to her phone before setting it on the table.

She finished her sandwich and carried her empty plate to the sink. So much for Mitch handling it. He had learned what she knew already about Farrah's second job, and he had forgotten his conversation with Gary Zygman about the disappearance of the political signs in Farrah's yard. The theft of the signs could be relevant to the murder, but how? The hooded figure caught on camera sounded like a teenager. He could be the sign thief or just a kid roaming the neighborhood at night. Why would a teenager kill a famous reporter inside Farrah's house? It made no sense.

She slotted her plate into the dishwasher. It hadn't been too unpleasant talking to Mitch, at least not after they had gotten past the awkward small talk. His calls before this murder had always been about Rick, checking in with her about his recovery or status during subsequent setbacks, asking questions about what the medical professionals were doing, or offering suggestions or help that she hadn't needed from him. Often, he just texted. This time the call hadn't been about Rick at all, and he had been the one to volunteer information. He had answered her questions about the murder investigation—all of them. And he hadn't made her angry once. That had to be a record in recent years.

So, this was what a truce looked like. The question was, how long would it last?

Chapter Thirteen

WITH THE SUN trying to remind Chicagoans of summer warmth while spotlighting the reds and gold of turning leaves, Crys couldn't face working in her windowless basement office. It was a shame not to enjoy autumn weather at its best. This afternoon she would have been working with Farrah in her office, but the poor woman was still in the hospital, according to the limited information she could obtain over the phone. Had the medication brought her back to consciousness? She didn't want to bother Wes. She had several hours before Kurt and Dana returned from school, so she decided to run errands and squeeze in a visit to the hospital.

Today, a policeman wearing a uniform that appeared as new and crisp as his crewcut stood guard in front of Farrah's door, but he wasn't alone. A small group of three men and one woman with a microphone were fanned out in a semicircle surrounding him. One of the men, dressed in jeans with a puffer vest over his flannel shirt, stepped backward as he hefted a camera onto his shoulder. A bright light switched on and the young officer blinked. Crys recognized Farrah's doctor rushing toward the group from the nurses' station.

"Turn that off," Dr. Park told the cameraman. "You all need to leave. Now."

"Are you Farrah Compton's doctor?" the well-dressed woman asked, shoving her mic toward the physician. She didn't seem to realize that the camera had been turned off.

"Yes, but I'm not giving any interviews."

One of the two men in business suits said impatiently, "This is Senator Danforth. Ms. Compton is an employee. He's come to pay his respects."

The candidate put a hand on the other man's shoulder. "Ms. Compton is a colleague, Evan, and she's not dead, at least I sincerely hope not. Please tell me that's not true—is it, Doctor?"

He turned his face toward Farrah's physician, giving Crys a view of his profile. Scott Danforth's pictures on the signs in Farrah's yard had not exaggerated his handsome features. He looked exactly like the healthy thirty-something in his ad, with tousled brown hair and a wide mouth that wasn't at this moment flashing his toothsome smile. Somehow, he was able to simultaneously project sympathy for Farrah and respect for the doctor, addressing her as if she were the most important person he'd ever met.

Dr. Park's anger seemed to melt, and she shook her head. "She's stable, but no visitors except family allowed."

"Thank you, Doctor." Danforth turned to the reporter and cameraman. "Nothing to film here. Let's respect the doctor's wishes. She's taking excellent care of Farrah."

The woman with the mic nodded and jerked her head to tell the cameraman to head toward the elevator. Danforth's companion frowned as he watched them go.

"Told you it would be a waste of time," the cameraman grumbled as they passed Crys.

When she looked back, Scott Danforth was shaking Dr. Park's hand. "I'm glad she's receiving good care. I have a lot of respect for this hospital. All of my children were born here. But tell me, Doctor, what's the prognosis? Do you expect a full recovery, and soon, I hope?"

Dr. Park wasn't won over by the senator's concern or charm. "All I can tell you is that she's stable. Now, if you'll excuse me—"

"Sure." Danforth turned to the policeman as Dr. Park hurried back toward the nurses' station. He offered a handshake to the officer.

"I appreciate your diligence in protecting Ms. Compton. She's a valuable member of my team."

The young officer mumbled what sounded like "just doing my duty, sir."

The unhappy man Danforth had called Evan shifted his feet and glanced at his phone. He was a few inches shorter than the politician and wore glasses. His hair was starting to recede, causing baldness to begin a slow race for domination of his head with the gray appearing at his temples. The cheery woman at campaign headquarters who had taken her message about Farrah's hospitalization had mentioned an Evan Kruper as the campaign manager and Farrah's boss. Apparently, her message had been delivered.

Crys studied a sign about hand washing on the wall; hopefully, the men would assume she was waiting for someone. Evan's gaze seemed to pass over her, and he didn't look her way as they headed toward her and the elevator beyond.

"I still don't think this was a good idea," she heard Evan tell the candidate. "She's a suspect in that reporter's death. That's why the police have a guard posted."

"Come on, Evan. This is Farrah we're talking about. She's a professional woman, not a killer."

Crys jumped when a voice close to her ear asked, "Is that Scott Danforth?"

"Randy! You scared me to death."

"It is him." He ignored her and stepped toward the senator and Evan, who had stopped to wait for the elevator. "I'm Randall Compton, Farrah's brother." He stuck out his hand, which the senator shook. "Thanks for coming to visit her."

Danforth placed his left palm on top of their clasped hands. "I'm sorry that your sister was hurt. How's she doing? We've been very concerned about her."

"She's starting to come around," Randy said. "The doc's optimistic that she'll be okay."

"That's great news, isn't it, Evan?"

"Sure—great," Evan said as he tapped on his cell phone. He didn't sound convincing.

Danforth introduced Evan Kruper as his campaign manager and then looked past Randy's shoulder directly at her. "Hi, are you family, too?"

Crys realized that she had moved closer and now appeared to be with Farrah's brother. She extended her hand. "Crystal Ward. I know Farrah will be anxious to return to help you win this election."

Randy gave her an amused expression. "That's right.

We all want to see you win. As a restaurateur, I'm hoping you'll look after the interests of small businesses, maybe give us a tax break or two."

Scott Danforth had been looking between the two of them, probably noticing there was no physical resemblance. His attention returned to Randy. "Small businesses are the heart of the American economy, and I fully support them."

"That's great." Randy flashed a smile. "I told Farrah that she was backing the right horse in this race."

Crys winced.

Evan pocketed his phone as the elevator door opened and said, "We should be leaving."

Danforth didn't seem offended at being compared to a horse, or maybe he was a consummate politician. "I'm speaking on Friday night at a dinner at the Riverview Conference Center in St. Charles, if you'd like to hear more." He turned to Evan, who was holding the elevator. "Let's give Mr. Compton and Ms. Ward two tickets each." He flashed his camera-ready smile. "Bring some guests. I hear the food is great. It might even make up for having to listen to speeches while you eat."

Evan released the elevator door, which closed behind him. He reached into an inner jacket pocket.

"Gee, thanks," Randy said, accepting the tickets from Evan but directing his comments to the politician. "I'll tell Farrah you were here."

Danforth clasped him on the arm. "You take care. I know this must be hard on your family, but your sister is a tough lady, a real fighter."

His puzzled glance at Crys suggested that he was still

not sure about her relationship to Farrah. She thanked him and shook his hand again. He placed his free palm on top of their joined hands, as if their meeting had a special meaning for him. The man certainly had charm.

Maggie would sure be surprised that she'd scored tickets for the big POW event and had met Scott Danforth. He seemed like a concerned employer to Farrah, even a friend. Had he or Evan arranged for Jase Norman to meet with Farrah? If she could talk privately to Danforth or his campaign manager, even for a few minutes at the POW dinner, maybe she could find out why Jase Norman had been at Farrah's house and who might have had a reason to kill him.

Chapter Fourteen

FRIDAY NIGHT THE Riverview Convention Center was decked out for a glitzy evening. With light shining from almost every window and spotlights showcasing the exterior, the limestone building on the hill sparkled like a crystal chandelier. They crossed the Fox River and turned into the entrance, entering a glamorous world beyond Crys's expectations.

Maggie, more accustomed to these events, ignored the arrows pointing to the parking lot and drove to the front, where red-jacketed valets were helping other guests emerging from the cars ahead of them. She pulled up behind a Lincoln with non-personalized Illinois plates and SCOTT DANFORTH bumper stickers on each side of the rear fender. Crys recognized Evan Kruper when he emerged from the driver's seat. He tossed his keys to a valet, snatched his parking stub, and hurried inside. No one else was in the car. Scott Danforth and his wife were probably arriving separately, unless they had been dropped off at a back entrance to avoid the crowd. Probably not. Danforth would want to be noticed and press the flesh of potential voters.

Maggie moved to the front of the line of cars, and Crys grabbed her small handbag as a valet opened her door. She kept her knees together to make a ladylike exit appropriate to wearing something other than her usual pants. What a relief it had been to learn that cocktail attire was the extent of the formality required. Her little black dress still fit her, despite not being worn for more than a year. The upstairs closet cupboard had been bare of other options. She hoped that her black heels wouldn't pinch her feet beyond endurance before the evening was out. Next to Maggie, who wore a dark green sheath that complemented the golden brown of her skin, she wondered if she wasn't looking more funereal than glamorous. Not that she could ever compete with her friend in any style category.

"Isn't this fun?" Maggie said, squeezing her arm. "I was ready for a girls' night out."

They found the designated banquet room downstairs. Crys presented her tickets, and they followed the hostess's direction to create name tags before entering a huge room filled with round tables, each seating ten people. Maggie stopped to chat with several women wearing pre-printed name tags identifying them as officers of POW. Half listening to their conversation, Crys glanced around at the other guests. Most looked sophisticated and at ease in their dresses and suits, as if they attended events like this on a regular basis. Their closets probably had wardrobes more like Maggie's than hers.

She spotted Randy without any trouble. His pastel-green sports jacket and tieless shirt marked him as an outsider. That color might have worked in Miami or Martha's Vineyard in the summer, but not here. The fabric had to be linen. She recognized the wrinkled look. The wealthy-looking couple he was chatting up wore expressions indicating they were being politely tolerant but weren't interested in what he was selling. The woman, a blond in a form-fitted black-beaded cocktail dress, appeared to be about twenty years younger than the middle-aged man, whose full head of silver hair shone under the soft lights of the chandelier above them. A younger woman wearing a short summer dress in a colorful floral print stood nearby. She also wore a bored expression. Crys decided her own black dress, as simple and boring as it might be, wasn't such a bad choice after all.

Maggie ended her conversation with the POW women and took Crys's arm. "Let's find our table. I bet we're near the front since we have tickets from the guest of honor."

She was right. Their table was in the front row but on the far side. It had a better view of the doors to the kitchen than the stage. Only two chairs of ten appeared to have been appropriated, so they were able to select seats with a view of the podium.

"It looks like Scott and his wife are already here," Maggie said as they placed their jackets on the backs of their chairs to claim them.

Crys followed her gaze to the table in the center front closest to the podium. A small crowd had gathered, but she easily spotted Scott Danforth in the middle.

"Which one is his wife?"

"I think she's the one off to his right. She's wearing the blue dress, brown hair."

Maggie had said that Laura Danforth was a lawyer who worked in a legal aid clinic downtown. The woman looked well groomed, but her dress and hair style were more natural and simple, rather than fashionably chic. She was more girl next door than high-society glamour queen, which made her more approachable. Crys found women who dressed like they were on a first-name basis with top fashion designers intimidating.

"Have you met her?"

"No, but we will. We'll have to thank them for the invitation at some point." Maggie nudged her. "Looks like we have some local press here."

Bright lights from cameras on shoulders came on, and Scott Danforth draped his arm around his wife and smiled. Laura Danforth seemed surprised for a second and then matched her husband's camera-ready expression. Scott appeared to say something to her that made her toss her head back and laugh.

"Not surprising, is it?" Crys said. "The press seems to follow him wherever he goes."

"His campaign makes sure of that. That's what his PR team is for."

She noticed Evan Kruper, looking distinguished in a navy suit and blue tie, standing behind the cameraman and peering over his shoulder, as if checking the line of his shot. The cameraman was older and bald, not the same one she'd seen at the hospital.

Maggie touched her arm. "I see some journalists I know, Sue Banfield and Marta McMillan. They write for the *Tribune*, but I think they're in POW, too. Let's go say hello and see if they know anything about Jase Norman."

Halfway across the room, the crowd separated her from

Maggie. When she made her way through, Crys found herself face-to-face with Randy. The young woman in the colorful summery dress now hovered next to him like a tropical bird near a patch of questionable grass.

"Hey! I wasn't sure you'd come," he said, a wide smile splitting his face. "Great shindig. Lots of big money here." As an afterthought he added, "This is Carla."

"I'm Crys," she told the young woman, who gave her a tepid smile and a "Hi." When Randy elbowed her, she added, "Pleased to meet you."

Randy's gaze wandered beyond her shoulder. "We're going to press some more flesh before dinner. Doesn't hurt to network. Hey, I think I see some guys in the restaurant business. Catch up with you later."

Carla hesitated and then followed her date.

From what Wes had told her, Randy was probably working the room to find some investors in whatever new restaurant venture he was planning. It was a fundraiser, after all. Amazing that he'd bothered to bring a date, unless he didn't want to waste a free ticket for a good meal at a fancy venue. Carla didn't seem impressed.

She looked around for Maggie's green dress and spotted her talking to two women. After the introductions were made, Maggie said, "Sue was just telling me that she interned at the *Times* and met Jase Norman."

"I would just say that we were introduced," Sue said. She was a curvaceous strawberry blond with darkened eyebrows, whose navy dress emphasized the paper whiteness of her skin. Her blue eyes were sharp as she assessed Crys. "I understand you found him. Rumor is that he was trying to score an interview with the homeowner."

"Sue reports on sports," Maggie told her.

"I'm still curious," Sue said with a smile, "especially since I'd met the guy. It's not every day that a giant in our business falls." She turned to Crys. "Marta is the local reporter. She's the one your friend Maggie here should warn you about."

"That murder is old news," replied the other woman, a short blond also dressed in the standard LBD. "All that's left is making the arrest. Do you think she killed him?"

Crys held her hands up. "I've only known Farrah for about three weeks. I know the police are anxious to talk to her when she's able to answer questions."

Maggie rescued her from further interrogation. "Tell us about Jase Norman. I heard he won a Pulitzer or two."

Sue shrugged. "He was good, I'll give him that, but he could be really cold and intense. Not much of a team player. He was all about the story, and I heard he could be ruthless. I guess that's what made him a good journalist."

"From what I read, he covered international news. Any idea why he would be working on a story in Chicago?" Crys asked.

Sue looked at Marta, who said, "Possibly cutbacks at the *Times*. A lot of papers—those still in business—rely on the wire services or other sources for the international beat rather than paying for their own reporters to travel."

"I wouldn't be surprised if it was due to budget cuts," Sue said. "Or maybe he was looking for a change. I'd think he'd quit and write a book rather than be forced into an assignment he didn't choose. As I said, he could be ruthless, but he was also one of their top reporters. They'd want to keep him. He had the clout and the arrogance to write his own ticket."

"He sounds like more of a lone wolf, not someone who would mentor young female reporters," Maggie noted. "Come on, girlfriend. He looked really cute. I know you made a play for him. Don't tell me he was gay."

"You've got me there," Sue said, her grin widening. "And no, he was a straight shooter from what I heard. Even back then, he was a god at the paper, rarely seen, too, with all of his overseas reporting. Personally, I like my men to stay closer to home."

"That's why you married a professional baseball pitcher," Marta said, giving her friend a droll look.

"And divorced him," Sue replied.

"Oh, no. Too many fast balls and not enough sliders?" Maggie asked with a wink.

They all laughed.

"I've missed you, Maggie," Marta said, squeezing her in a one-armed hug. "Are you coming to the press club meeting next week?"

Crys was relieved to no longer be at the center of their conversation. There was nothing she could tell them anyway, and Farrah was entitled to her privacy. Until she could tell her side of the story, Farrah deserved to be presumed innocent.

She glanced around the crowded room. In the center, the group around Scott Danforth was still swelling. The camera must have been turned off as there was no bright light shining on his white teeth that flashed every minute or so as he greeted someone else or responded to a comment. There was still plenty of time before the program would start, so she excused herself. She headed to the back of the room and out through the double doors to find the nearest restroom.

The convention center hadn't spared money on the ladies' lounge. Crys found herself in what appeared to be a designer space with marble countertops, brass fixtures, and midnight-blue wallpaper with a Grecian key border in gold. Thick, folded paper towels were fanned on the surface for drying hands and accompanied by a bottle of an expensive brand of hand lotion.

When she emerged from the toilet, Crys recognized Laura Danforth washing her hands. The candidate's wife wore minimal makeup on her eyes and lips. With smooth and unblemished skin, she didn't need cosmetic enhancement. Her wavy, dark hair hung to her shoulders. A small diamond pendant on a fine gold chain was her only jewelry, other than her wedding rings. She glanced at Crys in the mirror.

"Mrs. Danforth, I'm Crystal Ward. Your husband was kind to give me tickets for tonight."

Laura Danforth turned and smiled. She had a slight overbite, Crys noticed, and standing next to her, she could see dark smudges under the woman's eyes.

"I'm glad you support him, or at least I hope you do. He's in this to win."

The words sounded automatic. Crys smiled at her and turned on the faucet. The water was instantly warm, unlike her home hand-washing experience. "I bet you attend these events all the time. Do you enjoy them?"

Laura reached for one of the paper towels. Her fingernails were cut short and unpolished. Her gaze met Crys's in the mirror, a pleasant but neutral expression on her face. "You're not press, are you?"

"No, I'm a mother trying to start a business as a professional organizer." She lowered her voice as if sharing a secret. "I'm not even a member of POW, although the friend who came with me is."

The other woman laughed. "Same here, although I'm not a professional organizer. And no, these dinners are not high on my favorite activities list, but don't tell anyone."

"Don't worry. Your secret is safe with me."

"I'd rather be home with the kids, especially tonight. My youngest is recovering from a bad cold."

"I'm sorry to hear that." A sick child probably explained the dark shadows under her eyes. She lowered her voice back to a conspiratorial tone. "You couldn't use that as an excuse to stay home tonight?"

"No, Allie is doing better and we have a nanny." She chuckled. "That sounds pretentious, doesn't it? I'm still not used to having live-in help, but it's wonderful. Anyhow, attending these events is the least I can do for Scott."

Before Crys could comment, Laura changed the topic.

"Tell me, what does a professional organizer do?"

Her interest seemed genuine, so Crys described some of the types of jobs she handled. "In fact, Farrah Compton is a client of mine. I understand that she works for your husband's campaign."

Laura Danforth's hands stilled. "I heard that she's in

the hospital. Scott said she's expected to recover?"

"That's what I've heard. I haven't been able to actually see her. They're still not allowing visitors other than family."

"Scott couldn't see her, either. He told me there was a policeman at her door." She resumed drying her hands. "That was horrible about that reporter being killed in her house. I hope she's not in any danger."

"I do, too." Finally, there was someone who shared her belief that Farrah hadn't killed Jase Norman. "I'm glad the police are there to protect her. She's a material witness, maybe the only person who can tell them what happened."

Laura studied her. "Now there's a legal term." Her eyes twinkled. "You aren't a recovering lawyer, are you?"

"Recovering...?" She laughed. "No, no. My husband is a detective. He's the only person in our household who knows something about the law, mainly how to enforce it."

Laura's smile disappeared. "Is he involved in Farrah's case?"

"No." *At least not directly.* "He's in the financial crimes unit—embezzlement, fraud, that kind of thing." She didn't mention Rick's big case last year that had made headlines. It seemed tactless to brag to a candidate's wife at her husband's glitzy event about how Rick had exposed a crooked politician.

Laura dropped her paper towel in the trash. "Financial crimes... That must keep your husband busy in this city. There's plenty of fraud and corruption here, especially in local politics. Not Scott, though. We run a clean campaign. Evan makes sure of that."

"Evan Kruper? I met him at the hospital with your husband."

"Yes, he's Scott's campaign manager. He keeps us all organized. He's on top of everything." She didn't seem to be aware that she was twisting her wedding ring. "Speaking of which, we'd better head back or he'll be looking for me. Dinner should start soon. The food is great here, I've heard."

She asked about Crys's children as they left and then talked about her own three little ones as they returned to the banquet room. People were still clustered in groups or walking around. A woman with a POW officer badge approached Laura with her hand outstretched to shake, so Crys left her. As she began to make her way to her table, she heard Maggie calling her name.

"Were you with Laura Danforth? Did you talk to her?"

"Yes, we met in the restroom. She seems really nice—down to earth and more open than I thought she'd be. She's doesn't seem to be a fan of politics, although she supports her husband's ambitions. She said—"

"Uh-oh." Maggie had been watching Laura. Crys turned to see that the candidate's wife was now surrounded by several people with microphones. The bright light of a television camera flashed on. It wasn't the same media crew who had been taking pictures of Scott earlier.

"Let's find out what's going on," Maggie whispered.

"That's not true!" Laura was saying. Her facial expression smoothed out as she calmed herself. "Scott and I both wish Ms. Compton a speedy recovery. Now if you'll excuse me—"

The reporters continued shouting questions: "So you're denying an affair?"

"What did your husband have to do with Jase Norman's murder?"

"Why was your husband at the Compton house that morning?"

Crys found herself following the reporters as they trailed Laura Danforth. At the last question, their prey turned back toward them, her face now pale, her lips a tight line.

"Mrs. Danforth has no more comments," Evan Kruper said smoothly, stepping in to take Laura's arm. "I believe dinner is about to start. Let's all enjoy tonight's program."

Crys felt like groaning along with the journalists. She wanted to know the answer to that last question, too.

Chapter Fifteen

"WHAT A NIGHTMARE!" Maggie said as they headed back to their table. "The campaign is going to have to do a lot of fast tap dancing tomorrow to fix that ambush."

"At least they have people to handle that. Farrah doesn't have anyone."

The announcement about the program beginning interrupted Maggie's reply just as they reached their table. As soon as she sat, Crys slipped off her heels and enjoyed the feel of carpet beneath the long, white tablecloth. She introduced herself to the couple on her left and two elderly women next to them. Two more women, both with gold POW nametags, joined the group. Randy and the still bored-looking Carla arrived last. Randy looked disappointed with their seats, but after craning his neck to look around, he seemed to realize his options for changing them were limited. The room was full, and most of the guests were now seated. At least the couple wasn't sitting next to her. She'd spent enough time with Randy, and Carla didn't seem chatty.

When the table introductions had finished again for the benefit of the late arrivals, everyone's attention turned to the stage, where a POW officer appeared at the microphone to welcome them.

Maggie whispered, "Did you catch what they were asking Laura—whether her husband was having an affair with Farrah?"

"Yes, and she denied it."

"No surprise there. The wife is usually the last to know."

Yet Laura had seemed more angry than shocked. She may have heard speculation before about her husband straying from the marital bed.

As the applause for the welcoming speaker died down, servers began to arrive offering complimentary wine and supplying bread baskets. Crys accepted a glass of chardonnay and unfolded her napkin, but her thoughts weren't on the speeches or food.

Laura had said in the restroom that she wasn't involved in the campaign, so Scott had probably spent a lot of time with Farrah without his wife around. And Farrah was separated from Wes. Was that because of Scott? Wes had noted Scott's charm, too, resenting the way the politician was able to befriend everyone. Yet Crys hadn't sensed that Wes hated Scott. It was possible, though, that Wes didn't know that his wife was having an affair, if that was the case.

The biggest surprise had been the last question about Scott visiting Farrah that morning. Laura had turned around to face the reporters at that point. Was she just angry that the press was continuing to hound her about Farrah, or was she about to defend her husband against an accusation of murder?

Had Scott Danforth been one of Farrah's visitors that morning?

Gary Zygman had observed the two cars. Mitch hadn't given her any details. Had he been able to trace the owners? She wouldn't put it past the neighborhood's self-appointed guardian to write down plate numbers. Perhaps there had been a leak to the press, and one of the cars had been traced to Scott Danforth.

She was distracted by her food arriving and realized she was hungry. The beef bourguignon, potato au gratin, and green beans (*haricots verts*, to the better dressed guests in the crowd) lived up to the Riverview's reputation for excellent food. The president of POW spoke about the organization's accomplishments and introduced a dozen scholarship winners, all female, who were attending local universities. As the cheesecake dessert was being served and studiously shunned by the diet conscious, Scott Danforth took the stage. His charisma beamed out across the entire room.

"I have to vote for him," Maggie whispered halfway into his speech. "Cute and caring, or so he seems. I hope he's not cheating on his wife. So many of them do."

"Innocent until proven guilty," Crys whispered back. She had been won over, too. The rumors of an affair had to be unfounded. Even so, Farrah was going to have a lot of questions to answer when she recovered.

RANDY AND CARLA left after the speeches and dessert were

finished. He tugged his date by the hand around tables, heading toward Scott Danforth, who was still standing near the stage talking to a group of guests. Crys tried to follow the details of the home remodel the couple next to her were describing. The next time she glanced up, Randy was talking to Evan Kruper, and they had moved away from the crowd swelling around Scott.

By the time Maggie finished her conversation with her neighbors, half of the guests at the table had left. They excused themselves and headed toward the Danforths to thank them. Scott was busy with a group of men, but Laura stood momentarily on her own, a smile fixed on her face. It became more genuine when she recognized Crys.

"You were right—the food was delicious," Crys said. She introduced Maggie.

"I was impressed by your husband's speech," Maggie said, "but I'm also impressed by what you do at the Chicago Center Legal Clinic. I've heard great things about the work there."

Laura's smile broadened. "That's all due to the founder, Martin Feinstein. Marty is amazing. He's been a mentor to me."

"I'm sure you've made important contributions. It's going to be a loss to Chicago when you move to Washington."

Her smile faded, but she kept her expression neutral. "Scott and I are still working out the details on that, but—"

"We have to get Scott elected first," Evan Kruper said, interrupting her and startling Crys. She hadn't seen him approach.

"Ah, Ms. Ward," he said turning to her. "Any news on Ms. Compton?"

"I haven't heard anything since we met at the hospital."

He glanced around. "I was just talking to her brother. He says her memory is expected to come back."

Laura Danforth fingered the gold chain of her necklace. "That's good news."

"Yes, it is. She's a brilliant woman," Evan continued, exchanging a look with the candidate's wife that Crys couldn't decipher. Whatever he communicated caused Laura to drop her hand from the necklace and straighten her shoulders. Her pleasant plastic smile returned to her face.

Evan turned his attention back to her. "It would be a shame to see her have any permanent damage to her mind. Have you been able to talk to her? Aren't you related?"

"No, I—"

"Crystal is a professional organizer. Farrah Compton is her client," Laura said, stepping again into the role of graceful hostess at her husband's party. Her smile became more genuine. "And a friend of hers, too. Isn't that right?"

"Yes, although I haven't known her that long." She wasn't sure why she'd said that. Friendships weren't necessarily dependent on how long you knew someone. She had only known Maggie about five years.

"Crystal's husband is a detective. Isn't that exciting, Evan?" Laura said.

His attention swiveled back to her. "Chicago PD?"

"Yes, but he's not handling the murder of—"

"Jase Norman." He frowned. "A Detective Burdine already talked to us."

"That could have been great publicity for your candidate, being profiled in a national story," Maggie said. "If he hadn't been murdered. Did you actually meet Jase Norman?"

Her wide eyes and flattering tone had the desired effect on her target. "Of course. The press have to come through me before they see Scott."

Maggie raised an eyebrow. Crys didn't say anything. Even she knew that most communications were normally filtered through a press secretary or PR team. Laura Danforth was watching Evan, too, but her expression was more troubled than surprised at his answer.

"I can handle reporters," he said to Laura, as if he expected her to voice a concern. "Even pushy ones from major outlets."

"Jase Norman certainly had impressive credentials and a reputation for being persistent," Crys said. "Could someone working on the campaign have given him Farrah's address?"

"I'd like to know that, too," Laura said. "Did Farrah's name come up in your conversation with him?"

Evan shot the candidate's wife a startled glance, probably remembering, as Crys was, that Laura was an attorney.

"No, of course not. Farrah's name never came up," he told Laura before turning to her. "I can assure you, Ms. Ward, the staff have been trained not to talk to the press, and they would never give out a team member's address. Farrah wasn't there when he came by, and I never mentioned her. Why would I?"

"I'm guessing he mostly wanted to speak to Scott anyway," Laura said in a conciliatory tone. "Was he there?"

"He talked to him briefly," Evan acknowledged. "We promised Norman an interview the next day after the Democratic Men's lunch. He didn't like being put off, but he'd gotten what he wanted—a meeting with Scott."

And that hadn't been the outcome Evan had wanted, it appeared. Laura still looked concerned.

"How did the interview go?" Crys asked to keep the conversation going.

They looked at her as if they had forgotten she was there.

"Norman never showed," Evan said.

"The interview was scheduled for the day he died," Laura told her. "That was the day of the men's luncheon Evan mentioned."

"He wasn't supposed to go to Farrah's that morning," Evan said. "I don't know how he found out that she was working with us. Like I said, he was pushy."

"He was also an investigative reporter. He could have read about her work on the campaign or seen her picture with Scott in the papers," Laura told him.

"Yeah, that must be what happened. She liked having her name and picture posted with his."

"That VFW groundbreaking," Laura reminded him.

Evan grunted.

"That photo was all over the local news," Maggie said. "It wouldn't be hard for a reporter to look up her home address or contact her through the university. Everyone's personal information is on the internet these days."

"Yes, and it's dangerous," Laura agreed, gazing at her husband still talking to his supporters. She fingered her necklace again.

Crys was still thinking about Jase Norman at Farrah's house. "So, you think he surprised Farrah that morning by showing up at her home?"

Evan's jaw tightened. "He wouldn't waste his time unless he knew she would be there. He probably contacted her first and set up the interview. All he'd have to do was flatter her or maybe mention that he wrote for *The New York Times*."

"Evan!"

"Well, it's true," he said to Laura. "She shouldn't have agreed to talk to him without consulting me."

"Maybe she didn't," Laura said. "That might not be what happened at all."

"That's right," Crys said. To defuse the tension she sensed between them, she asked Evan, "Did Jase Norman tell you what he was writing about?"

His laugh was like a sharp bark. "He claimed he was profiling four candidates running for the House who were expected to win, but he was digging for dirt, like they all do. He was out of luck, if that's what he was after. I run a clean campaign."

His answer about the reporter's assignment tallied with what Rick had told her. But even if Farrah had agreed to an interview that morning, why had Jase Norman been murdered? Had Wes returned early and caught them together? Or had someone else arrived, someone like Scott Danforth? He could have become furious, either as a jealous lover or as a shocked boss thinking she was betraying his confidence by agreeing to an unauthorized interview. Or both. Either man might have spared the life of the woman he loved. If, that is, Scott Danforth *was* her lover. The jury was still out on that rumor.

Maggie had stepped away to chat with an African-American couple she seemed to know. Evan's attention had wandered to his candidate, whose expression had become serious as he talked to an imposing man with a broad chest and lips poked out in apparent disapproval. He excused himself and moved swiftly toward Scott. Laura was greeted by three matronly women in similarly styled pastel sequined dresses. One of them gave Crys an apologetic half-smile.

Message received. Crys stepped away from the group, but she still caught Laura's glance at Evan's back as he headed toward her husband. There was an interesting dynamic between them. Evan was Scott's campaign manager, but he had to coordinate with Laura and manage her public appearances, too. In some ways it reminded her of her relationship with Mitch. They were like two legs of a three-legged stool, with the third being Rick. As much as they resisted and resented each other, pushing away or pulling together, they were both necessary for support. Both Laura and Evan would do anything to protect and support Scott. Neither of them wanted to cause that stool to collapse.

Unfortunately, Jase Norman's murder might do just that.

"You should consider joining," Maggie told her on the drive home. "They're a good group overall, even if they're a little pretentious and too suburban white for my liking. As their token biracial member, I can say that."

Crys smiled as she wiggled her freed toes. "At least I'd be joining an integrated group. I think I'll pass for now, though."

"Maybe when the kids are older," Maggie said kindly.

"I'm glad we talked to your journalist friends. I have a better picture of what Jase Norman was like."

"Ruthless and arrogant. If anybody could thaw that ambition, it would be Sue. Spoken admiringly, by the way."

"Sue said he was all about the story. That could explain why he never married or had children. Of course, we don't know if he had a partner."

"Or a woman in every port, like a sailor." She tossed an arch look as she stopped at a yellow light.

Crys smiled. "Do you think Sue was right about him possibly requesting to come back to the States?"

"I agree that with all the prizes he's earned, the *Times* would let him write his own ticket. He could have even suggested this story. If you're writing about politics, there's no place like Chicago."

"That's the truth. No outsider can fathom Chicago politics. Maybe that was the new challenge he was seeking. I can see the headline now: Chicago Politics Revealed."

"More like Pols Exposed. Tight and titillating. You'd

have to read the article to see what our beloved corruptocrats were caught doing this time."

Crys laughed. "I love this city, political corruption and all. You have to admit it has character."

"That it does. Speaking of politics, that Evan guy seemed to be grilling you." She honked at the car in front of them. The driver hadn't noticed the light had turned green. They began moving forward again.

"He did seem curious about my relationship to Farrah. He's trying to appear concerned about her, but I think his main interest is in keeping the campaign on track. That's his job, after all."

"And if that's the case, he should be worried that Farrah will be arrested for murder. That would be terrible publicity for the Danforth campaign."

Bad enough if Farrah, a senior advisor close to the candidate, were arrested, but disastrous if word leaked that Scott had been one of her visitors that morning. Maybe that was why Evan Kruper wanted to know about her relationship with Farrah. He would want to be prepared for damage control if Scott had been at the house or worse, had been having an affair. Anyone Farrah had confided in would need to be *handled*. Her denial of a close relationship may have reassured him that she knew nothing, which was exactly the case.

Maggie stopped at another light. "Of course, they could play down Farrah's role with the campaign. Just one of many volunteers—something like that."

"The rumor about an affair complicates that spin, doesn't it? Also, I'm guessing she's on the campaign payroll.

That makes it harder to brush her off as just a volunteer."

"Absolutely. It's a double whammy. If he were having an affair and embroiled in a murder… What a mess. That might mean the end of his run for the House."

"He'd be more than embroiled. He'd be a suspect in Jase Norman's murder."

Maggie glanced at her. "Not to mention cast off the POW speaker list. At least he enjoyed a delicious last supper."

"If you weren't driving, I'd give you an elbow for that one." She yawned. "I'm getting too old for these late nights."

Maggie laughed. "You're not exactly out partying all the time. Once in a while does a girl good, especially you, my hardworking girlfriend."

AFTER MAGGIE DROPPED her off, she tiptoed into the kitchen and set her handbag on the counter. She removed her cell phone, which buzzed in her hand. The screen lit up with the incoming message:

"Both in the Peace Corps 1987-88 Sudan."

The pizza man had delivered.

Chapter Sixteen

Saturdays were meant to be family days with Rick and the kids home, but Kurt and Dana now often had other plans. It was just as well that they took their parents' presence for granted. Knowing how close their father had come to dying five years ago could have resulted in a fear of losing him that wouldn't be healthy. Kurt and Dana bounced back from illness and injury. They probably assumed their dad was the same, even if he was now using a wheelchair. They had long ago embraced the new normal. Even Rick's mother had stopped calling every day or so to check on him. Too bad she hadn't stopped calling to complain about her life or ask for money, which Rick too often provided.

Today the kids were spending the morning at friends' houses, and Rick was in the other room reading the newspaper. Crys sat at the kitchen table, staring at the chipped side of the end cabinet where Rick's wheelchair had hit as he maneuvered in the narrow space. From her seated vantage point, she saw how high the upper cabinets must look to him, how impossible they were to reach. If only they had money for a renovation. Today, while he was relaxed and they were alone, would be a good time to talk to him about setting up a website for Organizing Chicago, but what was the point? He still considered Farrah the prime suspect for Jase Norman's murder.

She swallowed the last cold dregs of her coffee and rose to rinse her cup. From the window above the sink she watched oak leaves stirring on the brittle grass.

So the Danforths and Evan Kruper seemed to view Farrah as an outsider who had broken the rules and agreed to talk to Jase Norman. To make matters worse, Farrah was the other woman in rumors of an affair with Scott, who may have been one of the visitors to her house that morning. But if she had known Jase Norman from her service in the Peace Corps, that could explain why she had opened her door and let him in. Had Scott still been there? What about the other visitor whose car had been seen?

She sighed. If only Farrah could tell them what had happened, maybe this whole mess could be cleared up. There had to be someone who knew about Farrah's past. Not Randy. He hadn't said anything about knowing who the dead man was. Maybe Farrah had confided in Wes?

Crys dried her hands and picked up her phone. She stepped out into the backyard.

"I saw Randy last night," she told Wes after exchanging hellos. "He said Farrah was conscious."

"She's in and out. The doctor says she's doing better, though. The meds are working." He sounded depressed rather than encouraged by his wife's progress.

"That's wonderful! Does she remember what happened?"

"No. I'm not even sure she remembers who I am. She

keeps calling for Jase."

"The reporter?"

"Yeah, I guess." He hesitated. "She must have known him. That could be why she let him in."

"It could be." Wes didn't seem to know about the past relationship between Farrah and the reporter. She wasn't going to be the one to tell him. She pushed her disappointment aside and tried to reassure Wes. "I heard he was interviewing people at the Danforth campaign. Maybe that's why he came to see her."

There was silence. "Maybe." He didn't sound like he believed it.

There had to be a way to find out about Farrah's Peace Corps days. She started pacing around the yard as plan B occurred to her.

"Is there anything I can do to help? I let the university know Farrah will probably be out for at least two weeks. Does she have friends I could call for you? It might help her to hear from some of them, now that she's starting to come around."

"You don't need to do that."

"I want to, unless you've already let her friends know." She listened to dead air for a moment. "I'd want to know if my best friend were hurt."

"Her best friend lives in California. Hold on."

She heard footsteps retreating and then returning before Wes came back on the line. "Her name's Alana with an A—Alana Cortez-Portingal." He spelled it out for her and provided the woman's phone number.

"Great! I'll call her today. You take care, Wes."

"Wait. You still there?"

"Yes."

"I was thinking that maybe you should finish her office. Farrah will want to work there when she's back home."

Crys hesitated. She didn't want to go back to the house until Farrah could be there. However, her client would appreciate having her office ready for use and not greeting her as an unfinished project when she walked into the house. They could always tweak it when Farrah returned home.

"I'd be glad to finish it for her. I'll have to check my calendar, but I think I'm free Monday morning if that works for you."

"Sure. I'll be at work, but I can give you the door code." He provided the numbers she'd already memorized.

Something about the conversation or maybe the idea of being in that house alone made her regret her answer. "Wes, if you'd rather, I can come when you're there or wait until Farrah is back at home."

"No, that's okay. She'd want you to go ahead."

"Okay, I'll keep you informed. Take care of yourself."

There was a long pause. "I just want her back, you know?"

"I know." Hopefully, for his sake, Farrah would feel the same way about their marriage when she recovered.

"ALANA CORTEZ-PORTINGAL," A confident voice answered a few minutes later.

Crys introduced herself as a friend of Farrah Compton, who was in the hospital, and told her that Farrah's husband had asked her to call.

"Oh my god! I had a feeling that something was wrong. I usually hear from her once a week or so, even if it's just a silly text. You know, one of those emojis saying that she liked my comment or found it funny. I tried to call her yesterday and the day before, but she didn't answer or return my call. That's not like her."

"She's expected to recover. She's regaining consciousness, but she hasn't remembered much about what happened."

"What did happen?"

She hadn't meant to talk about the murder, but the story had made the news. She gave Farrah's friend a summary of what had been released to the public.

"Wait a minute—Jase Norman? I read about his death. She was the woman he was visiting, wasn't she? The news reports didn't say."

"Yes, that's right. Did you know him?" Crys shifted on the concrete step of her back porch and hunched forward, resting her elbows on her thighs.

"Not personally. I knew who he was because of Farrah. We were roommates when she was in graduate school, and I was doing law. That was…after she knew Jase. I can't believe he's dead. She didn't—the police don't think she—?"

"They're still investigating and hoping Farrah will be able to talk to them soon."

"Oh god," Alana said.

The wind kicked up, and oak leaves somersaulted

around their small, fenced-in yard. "Alana, did Farrah and Jase have a bad history?"

There was a pause. "You said you were a friend. I want to make sure that nothing I say will get back to the press. I wouldn't do anything to hurt Farrah."

"I'm not with the press, and I wouldn't want to hurt Farrah, either. I'm actually a professional organizer and a friend. I was helping Farrah rearrange her home office. I'm the one who found her, along with her brother, and called 911."

"And you said Wes gave you this number?"

"That's right. I know they've been separated, but he's devastated. He's been by her side at the hospital since it happened."

"I'm sorry for doubting you, but I have to be careful."

"No, I understand. I'm just sorry to be the bearer of bad news."

Alana sighed. "Farrah loved Jase at one time, but he broke her heart."

"Was that when they were in the Peace Corps?"

"You know about that? Yes, that's where they met. They were working in different villages in the Sudan. Once a month or so, they saw each other at team meetings."

The concrete step where she sat had become too hard and cold beneath her, so Crys rose and began strolling around the yard. "What else did she tell you about Jase?"

"She said he was unbelievably handsome and smart. He was clever at figuring out ways to help the villagers improve their water and food supplies, although he claimed he learned more from them than they did from him."

"And Farrah fell in love with him?"

"Yes, but he pursued her first. She didn't think they had much in common. He was from old New York money, and she'd grown up in a working-class family in Chicago. I think she was the first in her family to go to college. She didn't think he was serious, especially given the temporary nature of their Peace Corps jobs."

Crys had reached the back fence and turned around to head toward the house. "Did the relationship end when she returned to the States?"

"No, actually before that, while she was still in Africa. She said it must have just been a fling, at least in Jase's mind. He left without saying good-bye."

"It sounds as if Farrah was serious about him by then."

There was a hesitation. "Very serious. She believed he felt the same way she did, but as far as I know, she never heard from him again."

Until last week. "Maybe he decided to look her up. He was in Chicago doing a story on a political campaign she was involved with."

"Yes, their paths must have crossed, after all of these years."

More like two semi-trailers meeting head-on on a single-lane road. And only one driver had survived the impact.

"Everything okay out back?" Rick asked when she returned to the kitchen. He must have noticed she had her cell phone in her hand but didn't say anything about it.

Instead, he grabbed the plate she always left in the dish drainer within reach for him. There were only so many items that could be stored in the four lower cupboards or under the sink.

"Ready for lunch?" she asked. "There's some tuna salad in the fridge. I might have some cheese for a tuna melt."

"As long as you put pickles on it."

She wanted to tease him and ask if he was sour or sweet today, but she didn't. She was having trouble reading his mood this morning.

When they were seated at the table with their open-faced sandwiches, Rick asked her about the POW gala. It sounded like an ordinary conversational gambit along the lines of *how was your day, dear*. She stuck to describing the gathering and the menu. She was probably being paranoid, but something was bothering him about her going out last night.

"You always say Maggie knows where to find the best food," he commented, taking a bite of his sandwich. Half of the swiss cheese slice on top disappeared into his mouth. He chewed for a while watching her. "So, she wants you to join POW?"

"She says it's a good group, but I told her I have too much going on right now. Besides, it's a little out of my league." And her wardrobe. She reached into the potato chip bag open between them and munched.

"I heard that Scott Danforth was the guest speaker," Rick said, still watching her as he took another bite.

He heard that? Maybe there had been a story on the local television news. "Yes. He makes a good impression.

Very charismatic. Not a bad speaker, either. Maggie has become a big fan."

She broke eye contact, took another bite of her sandwich. When she finished chewing, she said, "I met his wife, too, in the restroom. She seems surprisingly normal—a working mom not caught up in her husband's politics. She's a lawyer. She works at a legal clinic downtown."

He reached for a napkin. "Danforth is the politician your client was working for, the one you asked me about. This wasn't a coincidence, you and Maggie going to hear him speak, was it?"

"She does want me to join POW, and it was fun—a girls' night out." She emphasized "girls," her subtle reminder that he'd gone out with Kurt and Mitch. It wasn't the same, though. She didn't have to admit it, but she wasn't going to lie to him about why she had gone to the event. There was no point, anyhow. He knew her too well. In her peripheral vision, she noticed that he'd put his bread down.

Here it comes.

"Mitch isn't going to be happy if he finds out you're prying into his case."

"It was a speech and dinner. Nothing happened last night that would affect Mitch's investigation."

"Don't try to bullshit me, Crys. You talked to those people. You just can't leave it alone, can you?"

"I know what I can and can't say about the investigation, Rick. I didn't grill them."

"I don't care. Farrah Compton is the chief suspect in a murder. Everything and everyone in her life, including

Danforth and his campaign, is Mitch's concern, not yours. He's the investigator, not you."

She gritted her teeth and enunciated each word clearly. "Farrah didn't kill him."

He leaned back in his chair and crossed his arms. "Okay, let's assume you're right. That means that whoever did kill the reporter is still out there. Who's to say it wasn't Danforth or one of his team? It wouldn't be the first time a politician crossed the line."

The reporters had questioned Laura Danforth about her husband being seen at Farrah's house that morning and raised the rumors of an affair. Rick didn't seem aware of those developments, but there would probably be speculation in the news soon, maybe tonight.

"His manager made a point of saying they were running a clean campaign." So did Laura. They had used the same words.

Rick gave her a skeptical look. "*Clean campaign* is an oxymoron. Who's the manager?"

"Evan Kruper."

"Kruper? You've got to be kidding. That's the guy who managed Dominick Ricci's run for mayor."

Her jaw dropped. Ricci had recently been sentenced to ten years for not disclosing donations. Rick had played an important role in uncovering evidence to prove the financial fraud. It had been his biggest case in the past year. "Evan Kruper wasn't charged with anything, was he?"

"Nothing we could prove, but he probably knew what his boss was doing." He turned away from her, his gaze unfocused and his fingers twitching on the arms of his chair. Then he turned his attention back to her, giving her a look that his subordinates probably knew well, a glare that brooked no argument. "I don't like you being anywhere near that campaign or this case. Let Mitch handle it."

The front door opened and their son bounded in, saving her from responding. "What's for lunch, Mom? I'm starved!"

Later, seated again alone at the kitchen table, she heard Rick and Kurt cheer at what must have been a good shot by the Chicago Bulls. She was too mad at Rick to go join them.

Let Mitch handle it.

Sure, it was Mitch's case and his job to solve it. She wasn't stupid. All she had done was attend a crowded social event and talk to some people there who happened to know Farrah. Mitch had already interviewed them. Even he would have to agree that there had been no harm, no foul in talking to them after his interviews were completed.

Or would he?

Truce or no truce, Mitch would take Rick's side.

Her familiar anger toward Mitch soured her stomach. Too bad he hadn't been at Rick's side when that bastard had shot him. It wasn't until Rick lay on the filthy pavement, his blood pooling around him, that Mitch had shown up.

How Rick could continue to be a friend to him—to trust him—she didn't understand.

Maybe it was because it was Mitch handling the murder investigation that she wanted to be sure her client was treated fairly. Rick might prefer that she stay out of the case, but until she was satisfied Mitch wasn't going to take the easy way out and arrest a helpless woman, she would continue to ask her questions. After all, Farrah couldn't speak for herself.

Not yet, anyhow.

Chapter Seventeen

"If you're looking for the people who live there, they're not home."

Crys looked up to see Gary Zygman with his hands on his hips standing at the end of his driveway across the street. She pulled the box of drawer inserts from the back of her van and set it on the Compton/O'Malley driveway.

"Hi. It's okay—Wes knows I'm here. You're Mr. Zygman, aren't you? We met—well, we didn't exactly exchange introductions—the morning the police were here."

He uncrossed his arms and approached her. "I remember you."

"Crystal Ward." She stuck out a hand. His handshake was limp, probably because his attention had been drawn to her van, which, she had to admit, looked like it had parked in the wrong neighborhood.

"I recognize your vehicle. You and the brother pulled up about the same time and went inside. After that, the cops came rolling in."

"You're very observant. I can see why you're the Neighborhood Watch commander."

He looked surprised. "Well, it's not the official Neighborhood Watch organization, but I formed something similar."

"That's really admirable. I bet the police were glad that you offered to help that day."

He pointed to his two-story, red brick house diagonally across the street. "It's hard not to see what's going on over here, if I'm outside."

Or looking out the window. His well-maintained yard had more mature trees and several islands of shrubs, none of them high enough to obscure the owner's view of his neighbors. The large, plate-glass window would ensure good views from inside, but Gary probably didn't want to sound as if he spied on Farrah and Wes.

"It must have been a shock to have a crime committed so close to your home and then have the police question you."

"They talked to all the neighbors, all the way down to the Allens on the corner." He pointed to where another street intersected. "That's what they do, you know, in case someone saw something—canvass the neighborhood."

"I remember you told the detective that you had some information for them."

His chest puffed out. "That's right. I told them about the cars I saw here in the driveway that morning, besides yours." He cast another dubious look at her van.

"Really? There were others?"

"Several, in and out. If I didn't know better, I'd guess Ms. Compton was running a crack house and business was booming."

"Oh, no. She's not like that."

"No, I guess not." His tone allowed for the possibility, even if it was unlikely. "Wrong time of day for junkies, too." His chest expanded again, and he shook his finger at her. "That stuff isn't coming into this neighborhood, not if I can help it."

"I bet you were very helpful, though. What kind of vehicles did you see?" Rick wouldn't like her questioning this witness, but too bad. Mitch had already shared the information about the two cars with her, even though their last conversation had ended before she could ask him for more details. Under the truce rules, they were working together on this case, a fact that she might have shared with Rick if he hadn't been acting like such a patronizing jerk.

At least Gary Zygman seemed willing to talk about the case. "There was a Kia Sorento, one of those big SUVs. I didn't see the driver. After that, some guy in a suit pulled up in a black Lincoln. Then there was the brother's car, that Jeep."

If it was a Sorento, it wasn't the cleaner's Kia. "Wow, you did see a lot. I'm sure the police appreciated all that information, especially if you gave them license plate numbers."

He frowned. "I didn't say I wrote down the plate numbers."

"Oh, I must have assumed that. You know what they say about assuming, but it doesn't always stop me from jumping to conclusions." She made a *silly woman that I am* face.

He seemed mollified. "It's too bad someone taped over the Mikkelsens' camera." He jabbed his thumb toward the house next to his. "Probably could have saved a lot of time. Here, too, I heard."

"Yes." She looked back at Farrah's house. "I noticed that. I thought it had to do with the signs." She turned back to him and ignored his scowl. "Farrah told me that someone had taken her Scott Danforth sign. She put two more up, but now they're gone. I don't suppose you saw anyone—?"

His face flushed, and he took a step closer. He was several inches shorter than she was, but she took a step back in the face of his anger. "I told her I can't be everywhere at once. I don't like that guy Danforth, but I wouldn't take her damn signs."

"Sorry. I didn't mean to upset you."

He huffed and blinked a few times. "This is a good neighborhood. We have all kinds here—liberals, blacks, commies for all I know. I checked the rules, and she's allowed to put up her election signs. Freedom of speech. If I catch the scumbag, I'll be the first to call the cops."

A door slammed behind him, and he jerked around.

"Hey, where are you going?" he yelled at the young man who emerged from the open garage wheeling a bicycle.

"Over to Ace's."

He appeared to be an older teen, dressed in jeans and a gray hoody with the hood down. His dark curls were untamed and would have given him a cherubic look if not for the thick eyebrows and deepened voice that suggested he was on the advanced side of puberty.

"No surprise there," Gary muttered. "Be back by noon," he yelled. "I have some chores for you."

"Is that your son?" Crys asked as they watched the youth pedal fast down the driveway and swerve into the street.

"Yeah, Mikey. He's my youngest, the only one still at home. The girls are married."

Crys lifted another box from the van.

He didn't take the hint that she needed to get to work. "Are you a cleaner? Must have been a hell of a mess inside. Wes didn't mention anyone coming today."

"I'm an organizer."

He shrugged, universal for *whatever*.

"Tell the O'Malleys I'm keeping an eye on the place." The stern look he gave her underscored his comment—he was watching her comings and goings, too.

Maybe Gary Zygman should keep an eye on his son. Mitch might have something to say about the florescent stripes on the back of the boy's shoes.

THAT EVENING THE doorbell rang as they were watching a movie. Crys glanced at Rick, who shrugged at her unspoken question. The kids were upstairs, so she rose to answer it. Through the peephole she saw Mitch gazing over toward Connie's house.

"Come on in. Rick's in the living room."

"Actually, it's you I need to talk to." He was still dressed in work clothes. The blue shirt beneath his sports jacket looked rumpled, and his eyes looked as if they'd seen too much and worked too hard to still be on the job.

The television became silent. "It's Mitch," she announced.

"Hey," Mitch said as he entered the living room. "I have a few more questions for Crys about the Norman murder."

"Have a seat. You want me to leave?" Rick asked.

"Not as far as I'm concerned."

They both looked at her. Rick would hate to be excluded from a conversation about this case.

"You can stay," she told him. Maybe he would realize that Mitch wanted her help.

She offered Mitch a drink, which he refused, saying he was only going to be there for a few minutes. That made her nervous. She hadn't told Rick about today's return visit to reassemble Farrah's office, but she didn't think Mitch was aware of it, either. She'd worked alone in the house, unpacking boxes and replacing items on Farrah's built-in shelving unit and only occasionally looking over her shoulder when a noise in the house startled her. The new desk hadn't arrived yet, so she'd need another visit to finish the job.

Maybe Rick had told Mitch about the POW dinner, or he'd spoken to Laura Danforth or Evan Kruper and her name had come up. Mitch wouldn't be happy about that, but it was a free country. She settled on the sofa at the end nearest to Rick. Mitch considered his seating options and then pulled an armchair closer, facing them.

"We're looking for Randall Compton," he said, speaking to her. "Have you seen him?"

"Randy? That's Farrah's brother," she told Rick, "the

one who—"

"Arrived when you did and let you inside," he finished. "I remember. He's disappeared?" he asked Mitch.

"Or he's running. His neighbors say he hasn't been in his apartment for a few days, but we don't have a search warrant yet."

"Is he a suspect?" she asked. Randy had seemed shocked at the murder and couldn't bear to look at the bloodied victim. A guilty conscience, or had his queasiness been an act?

"I'd say he's a person of interest, officially."

Rick massaged his right thigh with both hands. "What do you have on him?"

"He was at the house before you arrived on the morning of the murder," Mitch said, looking at her. "The camera footage we have from Zygman showed his Jeep circling the block a few times prior to your arrival at ten."

"He pulled in the driveway a minute or so after I did. He said he had a quick question for his sister."

"We saw that on the video, too." Mitch leaned forward and rested his forearms on his thighs. "We need to talk to him since he didn't tell us the full story about that morning."

"What about his work?" Rick asked, switching his massage to his other thigh. "Have they seen him?"

"Not since Friday, when he showed up to collect his paycheck. They didn't seem worried—said he's usually out on his own selling restaurant equipment and only checks in when he feels like it or is collecting his pay. Apparently, he doesn't have a checking account for direct deposit."

Given what she'd heard about Randy's money issues, that wasn't surprising. "So he could be on the road, maybe out of town?" she asked.

"His neighbor saw him leave Friday night. She said he was dressed up in a suit. Something about a green jacket." His skeptical expression suggested he couldn't believe any man would choose that color. "He told her his luck was going to change, and he was finally going to be able to launch his new restaurant. She says he always talks big, and she didn't buy it."

"He was at the POW gala Friday night in a green jacket," Crys said. "He was networking, probably looking for some investors. He said there were some big names in the food business there."

"POW?" Mitch asked. "As in Prisoner of War?" He reached in his jacket pocket for his notebook and pen.

Rick chuckled. "If you're a man. I think it stands for Plenty of Women."

"Professional Organization of Women." Crys enunciated each word to discourage further joking. "Maggie is a member, and we went to their event Friday night." She told him where the banquet had been held.

"Where did *he* get tickets to that dinner?" Rick asked, frowning at her.

"From Scott Danforth." Better not volunteer that's where she obtained her own tickets. "Danforth was the guest speaker," she told Mitch.

Mitch was watching her, but his expression gave nothing away. "That helps," he said after a moment. "When did the party end?"

"Maggie and I left around nine. I think Randy left before us. With his date, Carla," she added.

"Can you verify that's when he left?"

She could feel Rick's eyes on her. "Not exactly. He and Carla were seated at our table. They left as soon as the program ended and headed toward Danforth. There were a lot of people around him. I didn't see him after that. Oh, except that he also spoke to Evan Kruper, the campaign manager. Probably thanking him for the tickets."

Mitch jotted a note. "You said he was with a woman named Carla? What's her last name?"

"I don't know. He just introduced her as Carla." Now she felt bad about ignoring Randy's girlfriend. She didn't know anything about her, not even her full name. At least when Mitch asked for a physical description, she was able to provide it.

"I thought you were still considering Wes O'Malley as a suspect," she said. "Or did his alibi hold up?"

Mitch finished writing and pocketed his notebook and pen. "He's moved down the list, but not off of it."

"His trip to Wisconsin checked out?" Rick asked. "I thought there was some time that he couldn't account for."

"He gave us some names for his personal time. His alibi isn't what I'd call ironclad, but I have a feeling he's telling the truth."

She wanted to ask more about the nature of Wes's *personal time*, but Rick wouldn't appreciate her having more than a casual interest in the investigation. And Mitch didn't seem inclined to share that information, as he was now rising from his chair.

"Sorry to interrupt your evening. I'll see you tomorrow," he told Rick. He motioned to them to stay where they were.

"It sounds as if Farrah is no longer the only suspect," she said after the front door closed.

"I wouldn't count her out." Rick looked thoughtful.

"It makes sense, though. If she saw her brother murder"—she almost said *her former boyfriend*—"him, then that could explain her catatonic state. She was shocked to the point that her mind couldn't cope."

He tapped the remote control on his thigh and then used it to resume playing the movie. "It's Mitch's case. He'll handle it."

His expression darkened as he watched the screen, a sure sign he was thinking of the real-life murder mystery and not the romantic comedy she had picked. She folded her legs beneath her on the sofa, although she wanted to kick him. He used to enjoy talking to her about cases. Was it because Mitch was the lead on this one or because Rick's overactive protective nature wanted to keep her away from this homicide?

Screw his paternal dictate to let Mitch handle the investigation. Many hands make light work, according to one of her mother's favorite sayings. That maxim applied to any task, including solving crimes. Weren't the police always asking for help from the public?

Besides, she had a personal stake in solving the case as quickly as possible, especially if a killer was still out there. And then there was Farrah, her client. The poor woman had no one to represent her interests or defend her in the investigation in her current confused state. Mitch and Rick should welcome help from any source to solve this case and bringing the murderer to justice. That was the happy ending they all wanted, wasn't it?

The movie was in the predictable second act, where misunderstandings and hurt feelings threatened the couple's destiny to live happily ever after together. Or so the viewer was meant to believe, even though a happy ending was inevitable. Too bad life didn't always work out that way, or at least not in the short timeframe of a movie.

As communication broke down between the couple onscreen (and would continue to do even after their marriage, she wanted to tell them), her mind strayed back to the murder investigation. Why had Mitch come to the house instead of calling her? The only explanation that made sense was that he wanted to see her reaction to his questions. A chill ran down her spine. She was used to cops, but she'd never been interrogated about a murder. Maggie had asked if she was a suspect, but the idea was crazy. Even Mitch wouldn't seriously consider her as Jason Norman's killer.

So why did she sense that Mitch was suspicious of her?

Probably because she had talked to Wes O'Malley after she discovered he wasn't the victim. She had also learned that Farrah had been involved with the Danforth campaign before Mitch had told her. She grimaced. She hadn't called him immediately to share that information, but his investigation had led him to that discovery at about the same time. He didn't need to hear it from her.

She also hadn't told him about Friday night, but she

hadn't learned anything important at the POW gala. She'd only heard rumors about Scott Danforth and Farrah. Mitch had already interviewed Danforth and Evan Kruper. Probably others at campaign headquarters, too. She had networked, as Randy had described it. That's all.

Mitch had reason to suspect she might have kept in touch with Randy, given her conversations with others involved in the case. That's why he had come over tonight. Maybe Rick was right about Mitch not being happy with her investigating on her own. Would he have said anything about her staying out of the case if Rick hadn't been there? Or would he go through Rick to stop her from asking questions? It was all confusing, including Rick's own interest in the investigation. He had asked more questions than she had.

But what had happened to Randy? Was he at Carla's, stretching his weekend? Or was he running from a murder charge? Mitch had said that Zygman's camera had caught him driving around before he stopped at the house. What had he been doing? Was he waiting for someone like her to arrive to *discover* the man he'd killed earlier? But what motive would Randy have for killing Jase Norman? Randy didn't seem to be a hothead, and why wait until now to seek vengeance for his sister being dumped all those years ago? Would Farrah have even told him about her past romance or Jase Norman's planned visit, assuming he'd called her before dropping back into her life? Randy didn't seem like his sister's confidant.

Gary Zygman had also mentioned seeing Randy's car, and not in the context of arriving when she had. She still needed to ask Mitch about the Kia and the Lincoln Zygman had reported seeing. Had the owners been traced? Despite his denial, Zygman had probably written down the license plate numbers and was the one who had leaked Scott Danforth's name to the press as the driver of the Lincoln. Either that or he'd recognized the candidate's face from the signs in Farrah's yard.

When the movie ended with a kiss between the two now (temporarily, no doubt) happy lovers, Rick called it a night and headed to their bedroom. She checked upstairs to make sure Kurt and Dana had turned out their lights and then went to the kitchen to check the back door.

Her phone lay like a silent invitation on the countertop.

She picked it up and texted Austin.

"Can you find out what type of cars Scott and Laura Danforth drive?"

She waited and then saw the dots that indicated he was typing.

"No problem. $20?"

"Deal. BE SAFE!!!"

She hoped he'd know what that meant. She couldn't afford bail money if he was caught hacking into the DMV.

Chapter Eighteen

CONNIE'S FRIEND BETTY had been more than willing to donate her late husband's clothes and clean out his side of their shared closet. It wasn't a large space, and Crys suspected that Betty was looking forward to having more room for her own clothes.

"I don't have sons like Connie," Betty said. She had a soft, shy voice. "No one to give these good suits to, and it's not worth the price of dry cleaning to take the cigarette stink out of them. I wouldn't hand them over to anyone I knew without doing that."

"Don't worry—someone will appreciate them." Crys removed a pair of navy slacks from their hanger and folded them. Ed's taste in clothes had been traditional, mostly blues and tans, so maybe he had been more conventional than the loud and boisterous man she'd imagined.

She had initially suspected that Betty smoked, given the cigarette smell that had caused her to sneeze when she'd entered the house last week. But Ed had been the culprit, and the odor of his tobacco habit had outlived his departure. The clothes reeked. Betty was right—they might have to be aired out before they could be given away, even to strangers.

"Does your church have a resale shop?"

Betty reached her hands in the pockets of a plaid summer blazer. "I don't want those old biddies pawing through Ed's clothes." She pulled out a store receipt and looked at it before crumpling it. "Cigarettes. And him a fireman. You'd think he'd know better."

Judging from the gentle brush of her hand on the jacket as she folded it, Betty had more regret than resentment for Ed's vices.

"Why don't I take some of these hangers, too? Charities or dry cleaners can always use them."

Betty agreed to part with half of them. Crys didn't push her, even though most people had at least twice as many hangers as they would ever use. She was always happy for any victory this early in the purging process. Her clients tended to gain confidence in parting with belongings as they saw the positive changes made in lightening up the first space they tackled.

With four black garbage bags of Ed's clothing donations sitting in the back of her van, Crys headed to a nearby Goodwill donation center. They could sort out the cigarette smell. She'd spent less time at Betty's house than she'd planned.

The helpers at Goodwill handed her a receipt to fill in for the donation, in case Betty wanted to claim it on her taxes. While she was out, Crys also deposited the check Betty had given her for her work.

She considered visiting Farrah on her way home, but she had a lot to do before the kids finished school. She also wasn't sure if Farrah was allowed visitors other than family.

And with Randy missing, even if she could see Farrah, today might not be the best time.

The weather had stayed mild but windy, and being out with other people enjoying a beautiful autumn day filled her with positive energy until she sneezed. Damn those cigarette smoke-infested clothes! She rolled down both front windows. That was better. She stuck her fingers out to wiggle them in the balmy, fresh air.

MAGGIE STOPPED BY to pick up her daughter at five thirty.

"What's cooking, good looking?" She hugged Crys. "Can you break for a glass of wine? If you have some, that is."

"We only have our special reserve, but I'll share it with you."

"I deserve the reserve," Maggie said as she followed Crys into the kitchen. "I signed a new account today—Mueller's Hardware, no less!"

"Congrats! That's huge. Don't they have several stores around the city?"

"Five, to be exact. The founder died last year, and his successors want some guidance to be able to compete with the big box stores. They were impressed with my proposals to build on their image as a friendly, family-oriented neighborhood store by sponsoring local events. That swimming pool is looking a lot less like a mirage in my backyard."

The pool was the latest reward Maggie had promised

herself. She'd already remodeled her master bath and added a sun porch as she met her goals. Crys listened to the details of the new account as she poured two glasses of inexpensive pinot grigio, the so-called *special reserve*. It would be nice to have her friend's drive and confidence, not to mention a relatively uncomplicated life.

"Did you see the news?" Maggie asked after she'd inquired about Crys's day and listened to her describe her newest job at Betty's house and need for a car air freshener. "Scott Danforth denied that he'd had an affair with Farrah Compton. He didn't answer a question about visiting her house the morning of the murder—he just repeated that the rumors were false. I couldn't believe he didn't sound more indignant or shocked. I'm afraid it's becoming a scandal that's going to hurt his campaign, big-time."

"Even if he's innocent, he looks guilty."

"Guilty as sin." Maggie took a sip of wine. "Come on—don't you think it's true? I like Laura Danforth, too, but he's sure a good-looking guy. Mmm mmm."

"I don't know. He could have had a campaign-related reason for stopping by her house that morning. I just have a feeling there's more to it." She didn't want it to be true, either. She liked the Danforths, or at least their wholesome image.

"It would be a shame," Maggie said, echoing her thoughts. "I really liked what he had to say Friday night. He had me believing he was the hope for a better future for Illinois politics."

"Speaking of Friday night, did you happen to talk to Carla, the girl in the floral dress who sat at our table?"

"The one with your buddy Randy?" Maggie rolled her eyes. "I sure did, although it wasn't the most stimulating conversation I've ever had."

"Did you catch her last name?"

She tapped her fingernail on her glass. "No, but she works at the Midwest Steakhouse on Dennison Drive. She made a point of telling me that she was the hostess. I guess she didn't want me to assume she was a waitress, as if being the hostess is a more important job."

Crys rose to check the spaghetti sauce simmering on the stove. "Be careful with that opinion or you'll find yourself seated in a corner by the kitchen at the next restaurant you visit."

"Not me, honey. No hostess would dare."

That was probably true. Crys smiled as she gave the sauce another stir and then turned off the burner. "Maybe that's where Randy met her. He's in the restaurant biz, or was."

"Was? He's unemployed? That doesn't surprise me. He struck me as the type who has a higher opinion of himself than his employer might."

She slid back into her chair across from Maggie. "You could be right about that, although I think he's still employed. Mitch has some more questions for him, but he hasn't shown up at work or at his apartment for a few days."

Maggie's hand jerked her wineglass, nearly causing the small amount left to slosh out. "Do you think something has happened to him? What if he's the killer and he used you as his alibi that morning? You saw him arrive at the house after Jase Norman was dead."

"He's probably with Carla, but I didn't know her full name to tell Mitch. I bet that's where he'll find Randy."

She could see her attempt to sound casual wasn't working. Maggie's skeptical look was replaced by an excited gleam. "We could find out. No harm in going out to lunch tomorrow, is there?"

The idea was tempting, but would she be interfering in the investigation if she questioned Carla before Mitch did? Assuming Carla was hostessing when they had lunch.

"I don't know, Mags. Rick wasn't happy about us going to the POW dinner. He realized that it wasn't simply a girls' night out when he discovered Scott Danforth was the guest speaker. He knew that Farrah worked for the campaign, so it wasn't hard for him to figure out why we were there. He's a detective, Maggie. He'll find out, or Mitch will."

She arched an eyebrow. "His disapproval of you investigating didn't stop you asking me if I knew Carla's last name."

Crys sighed. "There's a difference in talking to you and questioning Carla about Randy at her workplace."

"I suppose you could just let Mitch know what I've told you. He could check out the steakhouse himself when he gets around to it or have one of his minions do it. Of course, he doesn't have an unofficial, nonthreatening relationship with Carla like we do that might encourage her to talk."

Maggie must have sensed she was wavering. "Isn't Rick's concern about your safety? Going to a restaurant at lunchtime isn't exactly dangerous, unless their food is terrible. If we can help Mitch solve the murder, wouldn't that make Rick feel less stressed and more open to expanding Organizing Chicago? I'm not forgetting about that website, girlfriend."

"If I can help Mitch solve this case, I'll feel less stressed. Rick will, too." And she could continue to do the work she loved if she could prove to Rick that he could trust her instincts about her clients. "I guess if you're willing to risk bad food, I can risk my husband's displeasure."

She clapped her hands together. "Great! At least we can find out Carla's last name. Who knows—maybe we can find Randy and present him to Mitch on a platter."

Crys moaned and rested her head in her hands. "How would I explain that? We happened to choose a restaurant where Carla happened to work, and after she told us where Randy was as we ate our steaks, we just happened to go find him?"

"Okay, I'm not saying we chase Randy down. You could tell Mitch that you asked me if I knew Carla's last name, which you did, and I remembered it. Anything else she tells us—well, we'll have to see how to spin that. They don't have to know that we visited her at work."

More deceit. She was going to go to hell or its earthly equivalent, divorce court, at this rate, but what Maggie was proposing could save Mitch time in solving this case. Most likely, Carla would know where Randy was. As Maggie had said, what was the harm in going out to lunch?

Chapter Nineteen

THE MIDWEST STEAKHOUSE had many culinary cousins across the country. When she thought of a steakhouse, Crys pictured this exact décor: a square, brick building with charcoaled beams framing the entrance and leaded windows. As she parked her van, she could already picture what the restaurant would look like inside. There would be red booth seats and captain's chairs at wooden tables, as befitted an old-world, masculine eatery.

After reading reviews online of the restaurant's service and cuisine, Maggie had consented to ride in the van, claiming that she didn't want anyone to recognize her or her red car.

"You can always have a salad," Crys said, watching Maggie reluctantly emerge, her nose wrinkled beneath her sunglasses. "They can't mess that up, can they?"

"Brown lettuce with poorly cut raw, spotted veggies, anemic tomato slices, and stale croutons drowned in an oily dressing?"

"Point taken. I promise never to mention I brought you here."

"Thank you. Fortunately, we're not here for a five-star dining experience. When I called before we left to see if we needed reservations, the woman who answered identified herself as Carla."

Crys smiled. Their trip hadn't been wasted.

"Are you referring to *the* hostess?" she asked as she opened the outer door and held it for her friend.

Maggie lifted her chin. "I am. And I'm sure she'll find us a great table and summon the waitstaff to serve us in style. I expect no less, even in a dump like this."

The dimly lit interior of the restaurant had a few tables occupied by diners who either hadn't read the reviews or didn't care if their steaks were "tough as pack mules and not nearly as tasty." Carla was at the bar talking to a young bartender with a man bun and tattooed forearms displayed beneath rolled-up white sleeves. She glanced at the door when they entered and did a double take.

Maggie removed her sunglasses and laid it on thick by exclaiming, "Look who it is, Crys—Carla from the POW dinner. I tell you, it's a small world. My goodness mercy!"

"You're right." Crys smiled at their hostess and waved. "Hi, Carla!"

"Hi." Carla left Man Bun and headed toward them. Today, Randy's date was dressed in a white, button-down shirt and a black skirt that hit mid-thigh. Flakes from her caked eye makeup dotted the skin beneath her eyes. Crimson lipstick emphasized rather than enhanced her thin lips. "Two for lunch?"

No *glad to see you again*. So much for social graces. They followed her to a table in the middle of the dining room where she stopped.

"If you asked me where I'd like to sit," Maggie spun her

finger in the air, "I would choose... that table over there."

Carla's gaze followed Maggie's finger now pointed like an arrow. "Would you like to sit by a window?" she asked.

"Perfect," Maggie said with a smile.

Crys slid into the booth and accepted the oversized menu handed to her.

"How are you, Carla?" Maggie asked. "I hope you enjoyed the event Friday night. I'm a member of POW, although not an officer or anything like that. You remember Crys, here, don't you?"

"Sure." She shifted on her feet. "Your server will be—"

"How's Randy?" Crys asked, afraid she would leave before they could question her. "I'm a friend of his sister, Farrah. She was hoping he would visit her again in the hospital."

Carla's face clouded, a rare show of emotion. "I don't know. I haven't seen him."

Crys lowered her voice. "Did the police come ask you about him? A detective came to my house a few days ago. He said they need Randy's help with the murder investigation."

Carla's eyes had widened. "Police?" She glanced around. None of the other customers or the bartender were looking their way. "They won't come here, will they? I could lose my job."

"Have you seen him since Friday?"

"No." She shook her head. "He dropped me off and promised to call Saturday. He said he had to meet someone. He never called."

"He didn't give you any idea who he was meeting or

where he was going?"

She shook her head again. "He said it was family business, but I didn't believe him. He seemed real excited, like he'd hit a jackpot. He said our problems were gonna all be solved and he'd have me outta here soon."

"What did he mean by that?" Crys asked.

"He's been promising he'd make me the manager of his new restaurant, but I don't think that's ever gonna happen."

"Big plans, huh?" Maggie said. "I know guys like that—all talk but no action."

"It wasn't just talk," Carla said, flushing. "There's nothing wrong with having a dream of owning your own restaurant. He had one before, but he couldn't get a liquor license in time to make enough money. You have to have connections for that."

The last part was probably what Randy had told her. "Did you work for him then?"

"Yeah. He was a good boss." She glanced around again. A middle-aged man was standing next to the bartender watching her. "If you ladies don't have any more questions," she said more loudly, "I'll leave you to look at the menu. Your server, Kendra, will be with you soon."

"Thank you," they chorused with smiles to reassure the presumed manager.

Kendra's friendliness was a point above Carla's, but she brought Maggie the wrong soft drink and told them the house Caesar Crys ordered was *dope*. Maggie's worst-case salad description was an accurate forecast of the soggy lettuce bowl she received. Maggie's grilled chicken sandwich looked more appetizing. Before she bit into it, Maggie confirmed that the grill marks were authentic and not painted on the meat.

"Not bad," she said, to Crys's surprise.

When Kendra returned later to see if they wanted dessert—predictably, a choice between cheesecake or a chocolate brownie with vanilla ice cream—Maggie declined for both of them and told Kendra how delicious her sandwich had been.

"Your service has been excellent, Kendra. I'd like to write a note to your manager, if that's okay, and tell him what a great job you do."

Kendra beamed as if she'd won the lottery. "That would be nice."

"You should mention Carla, too," Crys said, playing along. "She was very accommodating in finding us a good table."

"I sure will," Maggie said. She asked Kendra for her last name and Carla's and then obtained the manager's name as well. With the promised note to their boss and the generous tip they left, surely they had managed to be elevated to favorite-customer status.

On the way out, Crys left one of her cards with Carla, who sat up straighter when they approached her station. Kendra must have told her about being included in their praise.

"Here's my phone number. If you hear from Randy, will you call? I'd like to know if he's all right. His sister needs him."

Carla's expectant expression faded. "He'd better show

up. I loaned him half of my last paycheck. He promised he'd pay me back this week."

Crys nodded. She doubted that Randy's and Carla's initials would be carved with a heart on a tree anytime soon, if ever. "Take care of yourself and good luck."

The hostess was going to need it.

"That went well," Maggie said, looking smug as they settled into the van. "Now we know Carla's last name is Shore, she hasn't seen Randy, and she's very gullible."

"Are you really going to send a note to the manager?" Crys started the van. Catching a whiff of cigarette smoke lingering from Betty's Goodwill donations, she rolled down her window.

"I think I will. Imagine working all day in a dark place like that with the boss man watching your every move." She shuddered. "If it makes them smile, I can afford a few minutes, a little ink, and a stamp."

"You're a kind person, Magenta Townsend."

Maggie retrieved her sunglasses from her purse and put them on. "Thanks, but I'm never returning to that place, even if they treat me like royalty next time."

Crys pulled into an opening in traffic. "You deserve it. You were terrific in there, and that was a brilliant way to tease out Carla's last name."

"Oh hush. She probably would have just told us."

"I don't know. She seemed afraid of being questioned by the police or anyone in front of her boss. I wonder if she's hiding something, although she doesn't seem to know where Randy is."

"Maybe, but she doesn't strike me as particularly clever. Whatever she's hiding, it isn't her Friday night date. She seemed genuinely surprised that she hadn't heard from him."

Crys sighed. "We're still not any closer to finding Randy. Who could he have been meeting?"

"Someone he talked to at the POW event? Carla sounded as if she expected him to spend the night, so I take it his plans changed during the evening."

"That was my impression, too, although he may not have shared his plans with her until he dropped her off. They don't seem like a couple. More like work friends."

Maggie glanced at her. "Boyfriend or not, that girl back there thinks he's her ticket to a better life."

"True." She stopped at a red light. "We know he was looking for money for his restaurant venture. Every time I saw him Friday night, he was talking to someone else. I think he networked with everybody in the room."

"There were a lot of rich folks there, but they wouldn't set up a meeting late at night. That's not how business is conducted."

"Legitimate business, you mean. He was desperate for money and not above borrowing from loan sharks." Carla's description of him being excited about his appointment didn't jive with a meeting with a leg-breaker. And what had he meant when he told her it was *family business*? Did it have something to do with Farrah?

Maggie made a disapproving noise. "That's a mistake

and a half. From what Carla said, he expected to obtain the money he needed to solve all of their problems. I don't think it was with his past lenders. He'd be avoiding them, if he didn't have the cash to pay them back, and they'd be unlikely to give him more."

"You're right." She accelerated when the light turned green. "It had to be someone new to tap for cash."

"He wasn't going to get any more from Carla—that's for sure."

AT HOME, CRYS texted Carla's last name and place of employment to Mitch. She told him that Maggie had provided the information, which was the truth. She had just started her computer in the basement to begin working when he called her.

"Carla Shore, huh? How come Maggie didn't get her home address?"

His chuckle annoyed her. "You're welcome. I told you where she works—isn't that enough?" Mitch could easily look up Carla's address. If she'd asked Randy's girlfriend where she lived, she would have sounded more like a cop than a concerned but nosy friend of Farrah's.

"Are you going to question her about Randy?"

"Probably."

She heard his chair squeak and what sounded like chips being munched. What was it with him calling her while he ate lunch?

The crunching stopped. "Anything else? Did she know

where he was?"

"She said she hasn't seen him since he dropped her off Friday night at her place."

She realized too late that Mitch's question had been a trick.

"So, how's the food at the Midwestern Steakhouse?"

"Order the grilled chicken sandwich. Avoid the Caesar salad."

He laughed until he started coughing. It would serve him right if he choked on a chip.

"What's your read on her?" he asked, coughing again. "Did you believe her?"

He was asking her opinion? At least he wasn't jumping all over her for interviewing Carla. He was probably just trying to avoid questioning her himself, taking the easy way out, as usual.

But isn't that why you talked to Carla—to save him time?

"I think she was telling the truth," she said reluctantly. "She said he'd promised to call her on Monday and owes her money. Of course, he could be avoiding her for that reason."

"Either that or he's feeding the fish in Lake Michigan." He crunched again, underscoring the image by sounding like the great white shark in *Jaws*.

"You think he's dead?"

"Let's just say a little birdy told me he'd borrowed 50K from a loan shark known for his persuasive methods in enforcing timely payments. Randy Compton strikes me as a guy who thinks he can talk his way out of any problem, but he may have met his match. Those guys don't have any patience for excuses."

"I hope he's okay. Poor Farrah has enough to deal with. Any word from forensics?"

His chair squeaked again. She heard a sigh in the pause. "Look, Crys. I appreciate your help, I do, but there's only so much I can share. I'll let you know when we make an arrest. Okay?"

"I was just wondering if you'd matched any fingerprints in the living room or found any blood that didn't belong to the victim."

"I can't talk about it. But thanks for the information today. Just"—his hesitation warned her that he was choosing his words—"just let me handle it."

Rick's words. Her cheeks began to burn.

"Wait. I thought we had a truce, that we could talk about this case. I am involved, you know."

His voice was lower. "That's exactly the point. You are involved. You could have walked in during a murder. Now you've met with this Carla chick and questioned her. I promised Rick—"

"Oh, so that's what this is about. Don't you think you've done enough, Mitch?"

There was silence on the line.

"Let me handle Rick and forget about your one-sided truce." She couldn't stop her voice from shaking. "It's not worth the paper it should have been written on."

She ended the call and resisted the urge to throw her phone across the room.

Chapter Twenty

THAT EVENING, KURT invited Rafe to stay for dinner.

"That's okay, isn't it, Mom? I told him you wouldn't mind."

Rafe was watching her. Shadows smudged the skin under his eyes.

"It's fine with me. Rafe, is it okay with your mom?"

"She won't care."

"Well, you'd better call her to check. If it's okay with her, it's okay with me." She didn't know if he had his own cell, but he could use Kurt's.

"Okay." He jerked his head to motion to Kurt. They headed back outside.

A few minutes later, she heard the basketball thudding against the backboard.

RAFE SEEMED TO like her meat loaf and potatoes, helping himself to seconds. His eyes grew big when she brought out warm brownies and ice cream for dessert.

Rick, who had said little since he'd come home, had at least registered the teen's appetite for her cooking. "You boys must have played hard today."

"Rafe is really fast on rebounds, Dad. I think he'll make the team. I sure hope I do."

"If I can, you can," Rafe said.

Rick nodded approval. "Either way, practice is what it takes."

"And believing in yourself," Crys added.

"Like you, Mom," Dana said.

"Why, thank you, honey." She was touched that her children were proud of her starting her own business.

"You didn't believe you had time to make brownies when you agreed to let Rafe stay for dinner, but then you said you could do it. And you did!"

Her husband's lips twitched as he gave her an amused glance. At least he wasn't mad at her, which must mean that Mitch hadn't relayed their conversation about her meeting with Carla. She was still mad at herself for falling into the trap he'd laid to trick her into revealing that she'd visited Randy's girlfriend.

After the dinner dishes were done, she found Rick nodding off in front of the television. She woke him to tell him that she was leaving to drive Rafe home.

"Where's he live?" he said, stretching.

"On Mulberry." It was only a few streets over, but she didn't want the boy to walk home in the dark. "Kurt's coming with me."

"Okay."

She wanted to encourage him to go to bed early. Working a full day and commuting challenged his endurance more than he would admit. Instead, she resisted the urge to mother or nurse him. Rick was a proud man. She bent over to give him a kiss on the cheek.

"Back in a few."

The boys sat in the back, as if her van were a taxi, which essentially it was. They talked about the basketball tryouts, wondering how soon they would know who was chosen. She didn't miss those days of being picked for teams, not that she had ever been chosen last. Her height made her a natural for volleyball, and she'd been on her school team in Wisconsin for three years. She hadn't been a star, but she was a good server with the ability to spike the ball when her opponents weren't expecting it.

"It's right here, Mrs. Ward," Rafe said. "The one with the lights on."

She pulled up in front of a nondescript single-story house. The yard had a few ancient shrubs and the neglected air of a rental property. Cars were parked along the street, so she pulled across the end of the drive. There were two pickups, an old Chevy, and a small Toyota sedan in the short driveway. Both interior and exterior lights illuminated the front yard. Music with a deep base throbbed like a heartbeat behind the walls.

"Thanks for the ride and the dinner," Rafe said as he opened his door. "Later," he said to Kurt, giving him a fist bump.

"Does Rafe have any brothers or sisters?" she asked Kurt as she watched the boy shoulder his backpack and head up the driveway, weaving his way between vehicles.

"He has a sister and some brothers. They're a lot older."

"What about his parents?"

"They're divorced. His dad's still in Florida, I think."

She watched Rafe open the front door and disappear inside. "He lives with his mom?"

When Kurt didn't answer, she glanced in the mirror, expecting to see him on his phone. Instead, he was looking at Rafe's house.

"Kurt? Something wrong?"

He met her gaze. "Mom, it's just…"

"What, honey?"

"Nothing."

From the music and the glimpse inside she'd had when Rafe opened the front door, it looked like a party in full swing. An adult party that he either didn't know about or had chosen to avoid by eating dinner with them. Maybe partying was a regular event. No surprise that the poor kid looked tired. She probably should have asked if he wanted to spend the night, even though tomorrow was a school day. Unless the party ended early, he was going to have a late night.

Back at home, Kurt was out of the van and dashing inside before she could remind him to put out the trash and recycling bins for tomorrow's pickup. She should call him out to do it, but she couldn't be bothered. She'd just do it herself.

Crys locked the van and headed to the side of the house where they kept the bins. She reached for the handle of the first one.

A hand covered her mouth and jerked her back into a tight embrace.

"Don't scream. It's me, Randy."

She nodded and he released her. She turned around and kicked his shin.

"Oww!"

"Don't scare me like that! Where have you been? The police are looking for you."

Her voice was at stage-whisper level, but he still shushed her. "Look, it doesn't matter. I need to know how Farrah is doing."

"It does matter! The police need to talk to you. What's going on? Is somebody after you?"

She recognized the leather jacket as the one he'd worn that morning at Farrah's. His face looked pouchy and his beard was scruffier. She could smell a sour body odor, the kind you got from wearing the same clothes for several days. At least he wasn't still dressed in the outfit he'd worn Friday night. He must have been able to return to his apartment sometime after the POW dinner.

"I owe some guys some money, but I'll have it for them tomorrow. How's Farrah?"

"Wes said she was talking a little, so she seems better."

"That's good. What's she saying?"

Her heart was still racing from the shock of being ambushed. "You couldn't just call Wes?"

"He won't talk to me." His gaze jumped behind her as a tree branch brushed against the house. "Has she said anything about what happened?"

"I don't know."

He reached for her arm, but she jumped backward. "Hey, I'm not going to hurt you, but I need a favor. Please. Go see her and find out when she's going to be released. I'll come back tomorrow night."

"Randy, you need to talk to the police. Then you can go see Farrah yourself."

"No, you don't understand. I tried that, but Wes told me to f—Never mind. You can see her, though."

"Okay, but you don't have to lurk around outside and scare me half to death. Just come to the front door." On second thought, that wouldn't work when Rick was home. "Come in the afternoon, before five. But you have to promise me that you'll contact the police."

His face and shoulders twitched. "What do the cops want?"

"I think they have some more questions about that morning. Is it true you were circling the block before I arrived?" She hadn't intended on blurting out that question.

His gaze came back to her. "How do they know that?"

"Cameras. You know—like your sister's doorbell camera."

"But it was taped up."

She narrowed her eyes and studied him. "Did you tape it?"

"Me? No." He took a step toward her. She gave him a warning look, so he stopped. He held his hands out palms up. "You gotta believe me. I didn't hurt Farrah or that reporter guy. Yeah, I drove around. There was another car pulling in there, so I decided not to stop. I wanted to talk to Farrah alone."

It made sense if he was planning on begging for money. "What kind of car was in the driveway?"

He rubbed his face. "I dunno. One of those Japanese cars. Used to be everybody drove a Chevy or a Ford. I thought maybe Sis had her housekeeper there."

It was probably the Kia Sorento Gary Zygman had noticed. "Okay, so you didn't stop then. What did you do?"

"I had breakfast at McDonald's, the one up on the highway. Then I decided to go back. There was another car in the driveway, a Lincoln. I figured maybe that one wouldn't stay long, either, so I cruised around. Third time's a charm, right? Then you pulled in just before I did. I didn't want to keep driving around all day."

"Did you tell Detective Alvarez about the cars you saw?"

"She didn't ask. All she wanted to know was when I arrived and what happened then."

She sighed. "You didn't tell the whole truth about what you did that morning, and now that they've seen your Jeep on security footage, it looks suspicious. You have to talk to the detectives to clear this up." She reached in her shoulder bag for her phone. "If you want, I can call Detective Burdine—"

He grabbed her arm. "No. I can't right now. I have to meet with someone tonight."

"Randy, if you care about your sister—"

Next door, Connie's garage door started to rise. She was probably going to pull her bins out to the curb for trash pickup.

Randy had released her arm. She turned back to him, but he was gone.

"Randy?" she whispered.

A crack of a foot stepping on a branch in the shadows of the backyard drew her attention to a man-sized form moving away from her. He disappeared into the darkness. She heard the muffled bark of a dog inside the house behind hers as he crossed their yard.

CRYS WAS STILL shaking after she rolled the trash and recycling containers to the end of the driveway. In the kitchen, she pulled her phone from her purse and noticed a text had come in.

"*2018 Kia Sorento.*"

Chapter Twenty-One

WHEN CRYS STEPPED out of the hospital elevator doors, the chair and the police officer occupying it were missing. For a moment she thought she'd punched the wrong floor number, but, no, there was a large 4 on the wall. Maybe Farrah had been moved or even released. She glanced inside room 417 to check and recognized the woman awake in the raised bed.

Farrah's gaze shifted to her as she entered the room.

"Hi. I'm so glad to see you awake."

To her relief, Farrah smiled. "You're the organizer."

"Crys Ward. Yes, that's right."

"We're going to do my office. I remember." She seemed proud. Her speech was hesitant, though, and unlike the confident client who had articulated detailed plans of how she wanted to arrange her work space for maximum efficiency. Even her word choice was simpler: *do* her office?

"It's going to be wonderful, exactly the way you planned it. How are you feeling?"

Farrah shifted in the bed. Crys tried not to wince. She may have had a catheter inserted while she was unconscious. Rick had hated it, even though he couldn't feel it.

"I'm bored," Farrah said after a moment. "I have a television, but it's all mindless dribble." She frowned. "That's not the right word, is it?"

"Drivel?"

"That's it. Wes promised to bring me some books today. Maybe if I read, I'll feel sharper." She gave a single nod, as if satisfied she'd found the right word.

"Is there anything else you need?"

Farrah's eyes teared up. "No." She shook her head vigorously. "No!"

Crys reached for her hand. "Farrah, what is it?"

She turned her head. "I-I think I'm just—" Words seemed to fail her.

"You've been through a lot." She stroked Farrah's hand, watching her grow calmer. Her children and even Rick had always responded to being stroked in this way.

Farrah touched her temple. "The doctor says I'll be fine and not so foggy soon." She gave a strangled laugh. "I can't stand not remembering what happened. I thought I'd had a miscarriage when I woke up."

Crys's hand stilled. "Are you pregnant?"

"No. The doctor said no. Wes and I want children, but we haven't been able to." She teared up again. "I'm sorry, I'm so—" She pointed to her wet eyes. "Maybe it was a dream, a nightmare. That's what the doctor said. My mind is playing tricks on me."

"Of course you're emotional. They say it's better to feel those emotions than keeping them in. It's okay to cry."

At least that's what a nurse had told her when she'd suffered a miscarriage two weeks after Rick had been shot. By then, they knew he was paralyzed from the waist down and would have to depend on a wheelchair for mobility. She didn't know how she would have managed a baby that year, but she had wanted it badly, especially when she knew Rick's condition meant it was unlikely that she'd ever become pregnant again.

"Don't be sad." Farrah squeezed her hand. "I'm glad you're here."

"I am, too." Her gaze shifted to the table next to the bed. A navy cap with Danforth stitched in a cursive script in red thread rested on top of a tissue box.

"Have you had any other visitors?"

"Wes comes every day. He should be here soon. Is it lunchtime?"

"Almost."

If Danforth or the police had come, Farrah didn't seem to remember. More sobering, she didn't seem to understand how she had come to be in the hospital in such a confused state. Crys wasn't going to risk upsetting her by mentioning Jase Norman's murder.

"I hope my brother comes today," Farrah said. "I need to ask him something, but I can't remember it."

"Maybe Wes can find him. I like your husband. He seems to really care about you."

Farrah's puzzled look of worry was replaced with a relaxed smile. "He said he'll take me home soon. Then you can come help me fix my office. I have work to do."

"Yes," Crys said, releasing her hand. "I hope you're home soon, too." Now she was convinced that Farrah hadn't remembered the murder. What would she feel when she walked into her living room? Would the memories come back then?

She shifted her handbag on her shoulder. "Take care of yourself, and cry if you feel like it."

"Let it all out!" Farrah said in a singsong voice. "Wasn't that a song or something?"

"Just good advice, I think. 'Big Girls Don't Cry' was a song, but we'll ignore that one. I think it was written by men. What do they know?"

Farrah's smile was fading. Her eyelids drooped. "Yes, let's ignore that one." Her forehead wrinkled for a moment as if a thought had escaped her, and then she closed her eyes.

WHEN THE ELEVATOR doors opened to the lobby, Crys spotted Wes heading her way. He didn't seem to notice her as he hurried toward the open elevator door.

"Wes! Do you have a minute?"

It seemed to take a few seconds for him to place her. "Oh, it's you. Have you been upstairs to see Farrah? How is she?"

"She seems a little confused, but she remembered me."

He looked relieved. "That's okay, then. She didn't say much yesterday. I wasn't sure she wanted me around."

"She does. She told me you were coming today. She's looking forward to seeing you." She stepped aside to allow more room for a nursing assistant with a cart. "She doesn't seem to remember what happened or why she's in the hospital."

He looked alarmed. "You didn't tell her, did you? The doc said we should give it some time."

"No, no. We didn't talk about that. I was only with her for a few minutes. She remembered I was organizing her office, and then she seemed to be ready to sleep."

He glanced behind her at the elevator doors, which were now closing.

"Wes, she told me she'd had a dream about having a miscarriage. She woke up thinking that's why she was in the hospital."

"A miscarriage?" He looked at her in shock. "She never was pregnant. We tried, but…"

"That's probably what her brain was sorting through. You know how dreams are."

"Yeah, right. I guess so. Well, I gotta go. Thanks for coming to see her."

He pressed the button, but he would have to wait for an elevator to return. The second elevator was already on its way down, so she didn't have much time. "She said she wanted to see Randy. I told her that maybe you could find him."

Wes's face darkened. "Not gonna happen, not if I can help it."

She lowered her voice. "The police want to speak to him. Wes, is he blackmailing you?"

"What?"

"Is he asking for money to keep a secret or hide something from Farrah or someone else?"

His expression became thunderous. "Look, I don't like him, and Farrah knows how I feel. He wouldn't dare try that. I'd beat the crap out of him."

He turned away from her and headed through the elevator's open doors.

IN THE PARKING lot, Crys noticed a black Lincoln signaling to turn into a vacant space. The rear bumper had two SCOTT DANFORTH FOR CONGRESS bumper stickers. She detoured into the aisle where the car was parking.

The man who emerged was dressed in khaki chino pants and a blue nylon windcheater. The ball cap shading his face had the Cubs's *C* on the front.

"Hi, Evan. Have you come to visit Farrah?"

He stopped. "Ms. Ward. I'd guess that's what you've been doing. How is she?"

"I think she's napping right now. Her husband's with her. It may not be the best time to visit."

"Is she talking?" he asked her.

"She's struggling to remember words, but she recognized me."

He jiggled keys or coins in his pants pocket. "When do they think she'll be better? I'm surprised they haven't released her."

"She said she hopes to be released soon."

"That's good news," a familiar voice said behind her. "I think we've met, haven't we?"

She hadn't heard Scott Danforth approaching. He must have been in the car, which had darkened windows.

"Yes, we—"

He snapped his fingers. "I remember—right here at the hospital. You're Crystal."

He certainly had the memory for names necessary for a politician.

"That's right."

He took her hand and clasped it. "And didn't I see you at the POW dinner? You have to love that acronym. It's so powerful, no pun intended." He laughed, and she couldn't help but join him. "Anyhow, I think my wife was talking to you."

"That's right." Smiling back at him came naturally, like turning her face to the sun after a long, gray winter. He still hadn't released her hand, as if he were reluctant to let her go.

Evan broke the spell. "Ms. Ward says Farrah's sleeping and her husband's there."

"I'd like to talk to him," Scott said, releasing her. He gave her the full *Scott Danforth for Representative and someday President* smile. "It's great to see you again, Crystal. Evan here is my point man. He was going in first to make sure there were no press in the lobby. Did you happen to see any reporters?"

"Press?" His blue eyes pinned her in place. "No, but I wasn't looking for reporters." It seemed unlikely. Farrah and the murder had vanished from the news the last few days, although there was always the possibility of a leak about the candidate's visit or a reporter hoping to catch Farrah's alleged high-profile lover showing up.

"I'll go check," Evan said with a grim expression, as if he were girding his loins to run a gauntlet. In the Middle

Ages, he probably would have tasted Scott's food for him before he ate, in case it had been poisoned. From what she'd observed, he would do anything to keep the candidate and the campaign safe from threats.

"No, that's okay, Evan. Relax. We can go in together. There shouldn't be any reporters. We didn't announce a visit."

"Someone could have tipped them off. You know they'll be all over you with questions."

"And I'll answer them. I have nothing to hide."

Evan didn't look reassured by his reply.

"Thanks for your help, Crystal," Scott Danforth said. "I'll tell Laura I ran into you."

Feeling ridiculously like a teenager in the company of an idol, she shook off his magnetic pull. She needed to find her car. She looked at the Lincoln with the campaign's bumper stickers. The Danforths didn't have a Lincoln registered to them, but Evan had arrived in this car or a similar one Friday night at the POW event.

She pulled out her phone and texted Austin: *"Any cars registered to the Danforth campaign? STAY SAFE!!"*

Chapter Twenty-Two

Rick had accused Crys of being obsessed on several occasions during their marriage. There had been the time when she'd shopped for her current van. She'd spent hours researching models online and then calling dealers with used vehicles for sale that matched her specifications. She was convinced that she could find a van with low miles at the price she wanted to pay, even though the Honda model she wanted was in high demand. She even had her brother Andrew looking for her in Wisconsin and texting back pictures of vans for sale.

"Look for an older model or another make. How about this one?" Rick had said, showing her an ad for a 2012 Toyota Sienna.

She wouldn't give up, though, and finally had found exactly what she wanted right here in town, although the price and mileage were a little bit higher than she'd hoped. Not by much, though.

She had also been obsessed trying to find Rick a study to join to help him to walk again. They'd fought about it. He was being released from rehab, and his only desire was to return home. She stubbornly persisted. She only stopped after calling a doctor in Boston about a research program there. He asked her if she was calling for herself or her husband.

"For him," she replied. "He wants to walk again, and he'll do anything to help make that possible."

There was a long pause. "Then have *him* call me, Mrs. Ward."

She cried that night. She had known her hopes for him to walk again were probably unrealistic. Rick's doctors had explained that no current treatment or cure for his spinal cord injury existed. He had already accepted his new reality. Her own first steps along that path of acceptance had started then.

She wasn't sure she had yet reached her destination.

Crys knew she was crossing the line between curiosity and obsession when she drove back to Gary Zygman's house. Across the street, the white concrete expanse of Farrah's empty driveway shimmered in the late morning sun. On the shady side of the street, Gary's pavement looked gray. His drive had an uphill tilt that was probably treacherous in winter. She parked at the bottom for an easier departure, or a quick escape, if needed.

Zygman's garage door was open. He emerged from the shadows inside and approached her as she opened her door.

"I was just leaving. Oh, it's you."

"Hi, Mr. Zygman. I won't keep you. I just have a quick question."

"I thought you weren't the police." Today he was dressed in gray slacks and a pale blue shirt. His black windcheater was unzipped, allowing his low-belted waistline to assume front-and-center position.

"I'm not, but as a friend and employee of Farrah's, I'm concerned about security at her place. I thought you could help."

"As long as it's quick. I have to get back to my business."

He must be referring to the auto parts store franchises Mitch had said he managed around town.

"It's about those cars you saw the morning Jase Norman was killed. I think I saw one of them when I was here the other day. Do you remember if either the Kia or Lincoln had bumper stickers?"

He frowned, probably thinking she was neurotic or nosy or both. "Yeah, two of them, both the same, for that Danforth guy. I figured it was one of her liberal buddies or maybe Danforth himself. He's been to her house, you know. Can't understand why anyone would mess up a new Lincoln with that crap. Stickers are hell to remove, you know."

All Crys could do was nod. "You also saw a Kia in their driveway—"

"If you're talking about the maid, I don't think she has a sticker, unless it's one of those Guatemalan flags. Or maybe it's Mexico."

"Yes, but she drives a Kia Forte. Didn't you say you saw a Kia Sorento parked there on the day Jase Norman was killed?"

"Yeah, that's right. It wasn't the maid's car, or I would have said so."

Crys resisted the urge to sigh. How did Rick and Mitch find the patience to interview witnesses like this? "Right.

Did the Sorento you saw have any bumper stickers?"

"I told you. Danforth stickers, two of them, on both cars—the Kia and the Lincoln. Look, I have to go." He indicated Farrah's house with a nod of his head. "Tell them that they're safe. I'm keeping a sharp eye on the place for them."

CRYS BACKED OUT of Zygman's driveway and headed out of the neighborhood in the opposite direction she usually traveled. The street intersected a busier road, with a McDonald's on the corner. This was probably where Randy had gone, provided he was telling the truth. His breath had reminded her of fast-food hamburger, she recalled.

She pulled into the parking lot. Why not eat—she was hungry and it was lunchtime. She decided to pick up a salad, despite her recent disappointment with the soggy Caesar. The drive-through was backed up about six cars, so she parked and went inside to order.

After she purchased her salad with grilled chicken strips and dressing in a separate packet to go, she noticed Gary Zygman's son sitting in a booth with another young man, whose back was toward her. Mikey appeared to be wolfing down a Quarter Pounder and hadn't noticed her. His dark, unruly curls were held back by a bright blue sweatband. Both boys wore faded jeans and sweatshirts.

"Hi, Mike," she said, stopping at their table. His father had called him Mikey, but she suspected he'd grown out of that name. He wore a small earring that looked like a diamond chip in his left ear. Definitely no longer a Mikey. And it was doubtful that Gary approved of the look.

She smiled at both boys. "I'm Mrs. Ward. I'm helping Ms. Compton across the street from you, and I was wondering if you could do me a favor."

Young Zygman's Adam's apple bobbled as he swallowed. He glanced at his companion, whose spotty, oily face and chunky frame suggested that salads weren't his go-to menu item at Mickey D's.

"Uh, sure?"

"You know Ms. Compton has been in the hospital?"

"Yeah." He wiped his hands on a napkin. She pointed to the corner of her mouth, and he took the hint and removed the drop of ketchup on his face.

"Well, she's probably coming home soon, and I was hoping you could help locate two signs that are missing from her yard. I've seen you out on your bike. I'm guessing you notice things going on in the neighborhood and have sharp eyes, like your dad."

He glanced at his friend, who had started coughing as if he'd swallowed the wrong way. His companion reached for his milkshake and sucked on the straw as if he were drawing a life-saving elixir from it.

Mike avoided looking at her and reached for his fries. He shook half a dozen out of their envelope onto his burger wrapper. Selecting one, he dragged it through ketchup and took a bite. He chewed for a moment and said, "I don't know anything about those signs."

"I'm not saying you do. I just think it would cheer up

Ms. Compton if the signs could be found and returned. It would save the police some work, too."

"The police?" His friend removed his lips from his straw and looked up at her. She could tell from the pink milk on his lower lip that he'd ordered a strawberry shake. "No way!"

"Way," she said. "I hear they have a lead—a young man in a hoodie wearing those fancy sneakers with the orange florescent stripe around the heel. He was captured on camera. You know, the footage your dad gave them to see what was going on the night before the murder. Those stripes sure do show up well in the dark. He shouldn't be hard to identify with those shoes."

She avoided glancing down as Mike/Mikey shifted his feet farther under the table and away from her.

"Dude," his friend said with some urgency. He set his shake down. His half-eaten Quarter Pounder had been abandoned on its wrapper.

"Of course, if the signs are returned," Crys continued, "the police won't look any further. I'm sure they'll just assume it was a prank. Anyhow, it would be a good deed, but I understand if you can't help, Mike. I know you're busy with school and other things." *Like petty theft.* "Good to see you. Enjoy your lunch, guys."

She waited until she reached the door to look back at them. Mikey was bent over the table, his head almost touching his friend's. She didn't have to be a fry on his greasy wrapper to guess the topic of their conversation.

MITCH STOPPED BY at dinnertime as they finished dessert. He declined a brownie.

"Don't want to spoil my dinner," he said, watching her warily. It was the same look Kurt gave her when he knew he had misbehaved.

His khakis, checkered shirt, and sports jacket didn't look like they'd had to survive a day in the life of a Chicago detective. His blond hair glistened with something wet in an attempt to tame it, and she could smell his mild cologne. For some reason it annoyed her. It had the clean scent of sand and surf with a whiff of sandalwood. Not exactly the cowboy cologne she'd expect of him, but what woman would want to be wooed by eau de horse?

"Dinner date?" Crys asked, forcing herself to make conversation.

His mouth curled in a lazy grin. "Dinner and dessert."

Rick snorted. She was sorry she'd asked.

"May I be excused?" Kurt was already standing and holding his plate to take into the kitchen.

Crys nodded.

"Put your dishes in the dishwasher," Rick told him. Dana lingered for a moment, finishing her last bite, and then followed him, taking her father's plate as well as her own.

"What's up?" Rick asked, relaxing against the back of his chair.

"We have forensics back." Mitch had taken Kurt's seat and leaned forward with his forearms resting on the table. He glanced at Crys. "Your client's fingerprints were the only ones on the murder weapon, that statue. That should be enough for the DA's office to issue a warrant and charge her, as soon as we turn the case over to them."

"What about motive?"

"We have that, too. They knew each other. Turns out they served in the Peace Corps in Africa together when they were in their twenties. Could have been some bad blood between them. It doesn't really matter since the forensics all point to her killing him."

"Sure it matters! It could have been self-defense."

"He was hit in the back of the head, Crys," Rick said. "Even if he was threatening her in some way, she hit him with enough force to kill him."

Mitch nodded. "I'm not saying it'll be first degree murder, but it looks like she'll be charged."

"But you haven't heard her side of the story, have you? Shouldn't you interview her first?"

Rick raised an eyebrow and turned toward Mitch.

"Her doctor still hasn't let us talk to her, but the doc said she's making good progress. She asked us to wait until next week, to give her a few more days."

Poor Farrah. Had she still been angry at Jase Norman after all of these years? Or had he told her something that upset her? Crys still couldn't picture the well-dressed college professor braining her old lover in her living room. She knew Rick wouldn't agree that a professional woman would be above murder, but there were still too many missing pieces for her to accept their assessment that her client was guilty. Farrah needed to tell her side of the story, if she could remember what happened. There was still time for her to avoid a murder charge.

"Looks like we won't be needing your help anymore," Mitch said to Rick. "There don't appear to be any financial connections to the killing."

"One less case for me then." Rick didn't sound pleased. He exchanged a look with Mitch, communicating something they didn't want to discuss in front of her.

"Did you talk to Randy?" Crys asked.

"He never turned up," Mitch said. "He was probably just circling the block, working up his nerve to hit up his sister for more money."

"But what about the other cars Gary Zygman saw?"

Mitch picked up the saltshaker, not meeting her eyes. He placed it next to the pepper at the end of the table. "They've been eliminated."

"What do you mean?"

"Let it go, Crys," her husband said. "I know you don't want to believe this woman you worked with is a killer, but all the evidence points to her."

She could feel her cheeks flaming. Two against one again. For now, though, she didn't argue, for Rick's sake. Also, there was still time to prove the evidence and Mitch wrong.

LATER, CRYS FOUND herself listening for Randy as she sat by Dana at the cleared dinner table, reading a story her daughter had written for school. Rick was watching television, and Kurt was using the computer upstairs.

"Mom, I asked you about the horse. Would it really

bite someone, or should I change that part?"

"Sorry, honey." She focused again on the story. "You print so neatly."

"Mom!"

"Okay, yes, that's fine. Horses do bite. They have big teeth. Sometimes they nip to get attention."

"I wish I could have a horse, like Uncle Squeak."

"I'm sure you do, but horses cost money. They need a pasture, food, equipment, vet care—more than your allowance would cover. And who's going to muck out the horse's stall every day? I don't see you doing that, and I'm certainly not volunteering."

"I could do that."

She shot her daughter a skeptical look. Dana's sweatshirt cuffs were rolled up just so, and her hair was pulled back from her long face in a tight ponytail that lifted her eyebrows and refused to allow any hairs to stray. She was an immaculate child, but she had an inner toughness that would serve her well, even ankle deep in horse manure.

"For now, you'll have to settle for visiting Uncle Squeak's horses. We'll have to go see his new colt soon."

Dana chatted about the colt, and Crys only half listened. How would she handle the situation with Rick if Randy rang her doorbell? He should have come this afternoon. She had waited, cleaning and using her phone to research online instead of her computer in the basement. At least he hadn't arrived when Mitch was here—or had he recognized him and left? She looked up when lights from a passing car shone through the crack in the dining room curtains. Taillights glowed red as it continued down the street. Dana was watching her, still waiting for her feedback.

"Do you have any other homework?"

"No, it's all done."

"So's this. Good job, honey." She handed Dana the story that she'd tried to read. She wasn't sure she had finished it, but she trusted Dana's writing skills would be sufficient for a good grade. They always were.

When Dana left the table to put her assignment in her bookbag, Crys followed her and opened the front door. "I need to check to make sure I closed the lid on the trash bin earlier. Don't want raccoons getting in and making a mess."

She never should have told Randy that he could come back. If Rick or Mitch found out he'd showed up here, she'd have to lie to protect him or tell the truth about Randy's ambush last night. Neither option would be good. She didn't want to lie, but if she admitted that Randy had tracked her to her home, then Rick would argue that her work was exposing her and potentially their family to too much danger. At least Mitch no longer considered Randy a suspect. She didn't believe he was dangerous, either, but Rick didn't trust her instincts.

The trash bin lids were both closed, as she already knew.

She checked around the side of the house.

"Randy?" she called in a hoarse whisper, stepping into the darkness of the backyard.

A breeze sighed through the oak trees. She jumped when an acorn hit the roof near her.

Hugging her arms to her chest, she walked into the backyard. Their security light came on as it detected her movement. An intruder would have to stay by the fence to avoid triggering the light. There was no one between her and the property line.

She waited in the shadows at the side of the garage for a few minutes longer. The security light in the backyard switched off. She could see light above her in the bedroom where Kurt was using the computer, and she heard faint voices from the television in the living room where Rick sat. It was time for her to go back inside to her family.

She closed the front door behind her and locked it. No one seemed to have missed her. She settled near Rick on the sofa. The talent show they both enjoyed was about to start.

Randy never came.

Chapter Twenty-Three

RANDY DIDN'T CONTACT her all weekend, which was a relief with Rick and the kids home. Rick didn't sleep well Friday night and decided to go back to bed for a nap after breakfast the next morning. She took the kids to her brother's farm, taking carrots for Dana to feed his horse and new colt. Kurt and Rafe, who had shown up, were given feed for the chickens. Kurt showed Rafe where to look for eggs, and they found four in the henhouse.

"Seems like a nice kid," Gregg said as they watched all three heading to the back pasture to see the goats.

"I think he's adopted us." He might prefer the relative quiet of the Ward home. With parties in full swing on school nights, who could blame the poor kid?

With a day's rest, Rick seemed better on Sunday. They drove to St. Charles for the Scarecrow Fest, which they had missed last year when Rick had a urinary tract infection that kept him in the hospital for two days.

"I'm too old for that," Kurt had complained when she'd told the kids about the outing.

"Well, I'm not and neither is your father," she said. "You can bring Rafe. Why don't you see if he can come?"

Despite Kurt's objection, the boys enjoyed the festival

as much as Dana, who brought Annie with her. Rafe seemed amazed at the pumpkin carving demonstration and the variety of complex faces and creatures that had emerged from the orange squash.

"Are you artistic, Rafe?" she asked him as he had bent down for a closer look at a pumpkin carved to show a spider in a web.

He blushed as he straightened. "Sometimes I like to draw. I could do that if I had the tools."

"I admire you. That's detailed work, and it takes a vision. They say Michelangelo could see David in the block of marble before he carved him."

His brow furrowed. She was about to explain when Kurt pulled him away to show him a magician.

Rick seemed depleted by the time they returned home. Her stomach clenched at the sight of his gray-tinged face. Instead of settling in the living room to watch football, he went to bed. She had to wake him for dinner. She was tempted to let him sleep, but he'd asked her to rouse him then. He returned to bed two hours after they ate.

The next morning his color looked better, and he'd joked with the kids as they all prepared to start a new work and school week. He told her he'd slept well. Crys was relieved. If he hadn't felt better, she was going to insist he go to his doctor.

After Rick and the kids left, she prepared for her appointment with a potential new client, Steve Hartley, a cousin of one of her first customers. "Terry said you helped her get rid of stuff," he'd told her when they'd talked on the phone last week.

The exterior of his bungalow, a few blocks from her street, needed work and more than a coat or two of paint to spiff it up. The gutter was drooping, and the roof appeared to be near the end of its life. Shingles were loose or missing, and the roof had darker places where patches had been made. The garage door was closed but looked to be in decent shape, other than its row of dirty and cobwebbed square windows. She could see what might be rot or termite damage splintering away the edges of the wood framing the garage entrance.

She parked in the driveway next to a pickup truck with a dented front fender and an odd assortment of equipment in the back. Old lumber, a folded square of canvas, and some kind of table saw were stored in the bed of the pickup. The fact that the truck was parked outside was also a bad sign, assuming it belonged to him. Why not park it in the two-car garage? The answer had to be that there was no room.

Steve had more than a nodding acquaintance with *stuff*.

He was friendly and wore the usual abashed look of her clients who had (or thought they had) messy houses. He was dressed in wrinkled khakis and a green polo shirt with his first name embroidered on the pocket. He had mentioned working at a garden center in sales.

He invited her into the living room. A brown sagging sofa and recliner in the open and extended position claimed most of the room's small space. They faced what was probably a nonworking fireplace. A television the size of a broad door on its side was mounted above it. In front of the sofa was a coffee table hidden beneath stacks of video games, controllers, and headsets. Piles of boxes and odd chairs lined one wall, and there were also tools, electronic parts and cords, keyboards, and old computer monitors filling floor space around the perimeter. The room had a smell like Kurt's unwashed gym socks with an undertone of pizza.

"I know it's kinda messy. Terry keeps telling me I need to get rid of some stuff."

"What do you think about that?" she asked. It was always better when clients were ready to let go of their accumulated belongings.

He shrugged. He was clean shaven with a full head of brown hair and about fifty pounds of excess weight, mostly in his midsection. "She made it sound like I have a problem, like one of those hoarders on TV. I guess I do have some things I should move out of here." He gestured vaguely at the living room. It was the first space visitors would see and probably the last. It didn't encourage them to stay.

"I'm guessing you like to shop at yard or estate sales?" He smiled and nodded, then she asked, "You seem to like tools and computers. Is there room in the garage for them?"

"Uh, no. It's full."

No surprise there. She carefully stepped around a few boxes to peer into the kitchen, where pizza boxes were stacked on a table. She didn't want to see any more. She was beginning to itch.

"Steve, I have to be honest with you. You're offering me a bigger challenge here than I can take on."

"Oh. That's okay." He seemed relieved. "Terry says

you're good. I bet you're really busy."

"It's not that. You need to be ready to reduce the amount of stuff you have, seriously reduce it. And when you're ready, it will take a lot of work to clear out your rooms, including the garage. Do you have a basement?"

"It's pretty bad," he admitted. "I don't go down there much."

She hadn't even looked in the backyard, but at least he didn't have clutter in the front. "I don't think you're quite ready to let things go, are you?"

He looked around. "I could get rid of a few things. Maybe have a yard sale."

"It's going to take more than selling or giving away a few things. The goal is to make a lasting change in your relationship with stuff and learn to manage your shopping habit so all of these extra items don't come back and take over once they leave. You have to decide if you're ready to make that change. It won't work if you do it for Terry or for me. It's like quitting smoking. You have to be ready to quit for it to take."

He jiggled keys or coins in his pocket. Maybe a handful of parts he'd collected. "I never smoked."

"That's good." A dropped ash in his home could mean an instant inferno with all of the newspapers, magazines, cardboard boxes, and paper bags. "It's hard to change habits like smoking or hoarding." She deliberately used the word that frightened him. "I can give you some names of people who can coach you through the process of changing."

"No, that's okay. I'll figure something out." He looked

deflated, as if a small bubble of hope for a better life had been popped. At least he seemed to know he had a problem. That was the first step to being able to start solving it.

"I'm glad I met you, Steve. I hope that one of these days you'll call me back for another walk-through. I'd enjoy working with you."

His grin returned. "Maybe I will. Soon as I figure out where to put everything."

AT HOME, CRYS washed her hands thoroughly, even though she hadn't touched anything but the doorbell at Steve's house. He hadn't even invited her to sit down, which had been a relief. Hoarders fascinated her, but they needed more than organizational help to make a permanent change. Also, she drew the line at cleaning out messes that could be biological hazards. She would text Terry to thank her for referring her cousin and tell her that she was unable to help at this time without explaining why. That would be up to Steve to explain. She was going to text him the name of a psychologist he could contact.

She fixed herself a sandwich with the leftover roast chicken they'd had for dinner last night. After turning on the small television in the kitchen, she settled at the table to watch the noon news as she ate.

She had begun to tune out the reporter's litany of crimes, traffic accidents, and local politics when a new story began about a man's body being found in LaBagh Woods. Murders were so common in Chicago that they usually didn't make the news unless several people or a celebrity had been killed. The man found floating in a pond in a popular nature preserve was unusual enough to merit a few minutes of the local noon news. The police hadn't released details of his injuries but said his death was considered suspicious. As no identification had been found on him, police had released an artist's sketch.

Crys stopped chewing. She set her sandwich down and grabbed her cell phone from her purse. Her fingers fumbled on the keys. When Mitch answered, she told him what she'd seen. He took a minute before responding.

"Are you sure it's him?"

"I'm not positive, but the sketch sure looks like Randy Compton." Especially the scruffy beard and scar by his eye. The description of the victim's clothing also matched what Randy had worn the night he'd surprised her as she'd fetched the trash bins. She wasn't about to tell Mitch about that meeting.

"I'll check it out. We have to officially confirm that it's him, though."

That's what she had expected he'd say. "Farrah will be devastated. Have you interviewed her yet?"

"No."

She heard a crunching noise. "Are you eating again?"

"Mmm-hmm."

She compressed her lips, although it was noon and she'd been eating lunch until she'd lost her appetite. "Is the doctor still telling you to wait? And why isn't there a guard on her door? I thought you were ready to cuff her and haul her off to prison."

"You've been to the hospital again." It wasn't a question.

She silently swore. "I visited her last week."

There was a loud *squeak*, probably his chair. "You didn't talk to her about the murder, did you?"

"No, I was careful. I didn't want to upset her... or step on your toes."

He sighed and then the chair squeaked again. "Okay. Just checking."

Okay nothing. He should know by now that she wanted to help Farrah, not hurt her or his case. How could he expect them to work together if he didn't trust her? No wonder their truce hadn't lasted five minutes.

"We had to remove the guard," Mitch continued. "Orders from above. Not enough manpower to keep one at the hospital. Plus, she doesn't seem like a flight risk, at least not in her current condition." He didn't sound happy about it. "She's still our chief suspect though. If her doctor gives me the green light to question her before the DA issues an arrest warrant, I'll talk to her."

She bit back a sarcastic reply. Mitch must have changed his mind about questioning Farrah after he'd come over to talk to her and Rick. She had no doubt which one of them had influenced him on that point. In any case, alienating him would end the call, and she wanted to know more.

"What about Randy, assuming he has been found? Do you think his death had anything to do with his sister's case?"

He chuckled. "So there is something you don't know? I bet you already have a theory on that."

She held her phone out and counted to five. "If I had to guess," she said in a tone she would use with a preschooler, "I'd say it's quite a coincidence that he died so soon after a murder at his sister's house."

"I have to agree with you there, but again, we'll have to confirm the ID and see what the autopsy shows. He could have killed himself, for all I know at this point."

"Randy? No way. He had big plans. He thought his ship was about to come in. I bet your partner would agree that he didn't seem the type to kill himself."

"I'll ask her. In any case, the autopsy should tell us how he died."

And possibly link his death to Jase Norman's, although grabbing a statue and hitting him on the head seemed more opportunistic than the modus operandi of a killer.

"I guess you'll be tracing his movements since the POW event." Hopefully, there were no cameras on her street, but there should be no reason to suspect that he'd contacted her.

"That's what we do, if and when a homicide is assigned to my team. You said Scott Danforth gave him tickets?"

She described how she'd been at the hospital when Danforth had shown up with Evan Kruper and the reporter and cameraman. "Randy came then and introduced himself. We were each given two tickets."

"And he brought Carla Shore as his date." He emphasized her last name, no doubt a subtle reminder of him tricking her to reveal her lunch at the Midwest Steakhouse. "We may have to talk to her if he was murdered. Didn't you say the grilled chicken where she works was okay? I wonder if I can get fries with that."

"I'd suggest the Caesar salad."

"Uh-huh. Well, I'd better get back to—"

"You might want to talk to Wes O'Malley about his brother-in-law. Randy wanted to borrow money from his sister or anyone else who would support his latest restaurant venture. He may know something about Randy's lender."

"Did he hit up O'Malley for money, too?"

She hesitated. "In the past. I'm not sure when." Wes had seemed angry at Randy the last time she had talked to him. Could he have been the *family business* Randy had told Carla about? But Wes had denied that Randy was blackmailing him. That was several days ago. Maybe Randy had gone back to Wes as a last resort. Would Wes have been angry enough to kill him?

"Anything else I should know about?"

She couldn't tell if he was being sarcastic. "No, I think you'll figure it out."

Silence. She guessed it was his turn to be pissed off.

"I guess I will," he drawled. "Thanks for supporting your local police. Y'all have a good day, ya hear?"

She pressed the red button to end the call. "You, too, Tex," she muttered.

THAT AFTERNOON SHE couldn't concentrate enough to work, so she grabbed a jacket for a walk. The street was quiet in the early afternoon. Most of her neighbors were either working or catching a nap while preschoolers slept, as she used to do this time of day. She wasn't sure what the retired folks did. Some of them, like Connie, were active in card groups, volunteering, or checking up on less-healthy friends. She liked the mix of people and ages on her street. It was a place where residents stayed for years, and both she and Rick wanted that for their family.

She turned the corner, feeling better with each step. The autumn air was crisp with the smell of nature's seasonal decay. Her shoes scuffed fallen leaves as she waved to Mr. Canady, a retired plumber who was out raking his yard. His house was one of the few similar in style to hers, although it had a newer roof and paint.

Like many Chicago neighborhoods, this one was a hodgepodge of architectural styles, with 1960s split-levels rubbing lawns with craftsman cottages, and 1930s bungalows mingling with newly built Victorians arriving late to the party. Older, small houses were being replaced by larger two-story homes. She had no desire to sell their house and buy a more modern one. She couldn't imagine not having Connie next door, Maggie close by, or the other neighbors who shared her small-town, Midwestern values and looked out for each other.

After she circled the block, she headed toward her driveway. Connie was sweeping her front walk. Her neighbor waved her over.

"I heard you were over at Betty's," Connie said, broom on pause.

"Yes. I'm going back tomorrow."

"Your ears must have been burning. She said she

couldn't believe she finally got rid of Ed's clothes."

"We cleaned them all out. I think she was ready to say good-bye to them." Not to mention the cigarette stink.

"Says she has plenty of room now in the closet and plans to go shopping. I haven't seen her this excited since her banana cream pie went for thirty dollars in the church raffle. That was before Ed passed on. He was proud as punch for her."

"I'm happy I can help her. A new outfit or two will make her feel like she's starting a new chapter in her life."

"Huh," Connie said, not disagreeing. The broom was still upright in her hand. "Something I want to ask you. Have you noticed anyone cutting through your backyard at night? I thought I heard someone out by my shed a few nights ago."

She must have heard Randy. "A friend stopped by on Thursday and cut through my backyard. I'm sorry if he scared you."

Connie shook her head. "No problem. Just glad it's not a peeper."

"You could install a security light in the back, one with a motion detector."

Connie waved her hand. "You sound just like Pete Jr. I don't want a light shining in my bedroom waking me up when some squirrel decides he needs more nuts for the winter."

"It would only come on if someone was back there, although I guess an animal could trip the sensor." She had to admit that they didn't pay much attention to their light coming on anymore after realizing their nocturnal intruders were likely to be animals, not humans.

"That's all I need," Connie said. "A deer in the headlight." She made a wide-eyed shocked face and laughed. With a wave, she resumed sweeping.

Crys returned inside. She pulled her phone from her jacket pocket and noticed a text had come in:

"2 lincoln town cars 428 9712, 428 9834"

Chapter Twenty-Four

THAT EVENING RICK was quieter than usual. He barely acknowledged Kurt's news of the high school coach coming to his middle school basketball tryouts to scout the eighth graders. Dana accused him of not listening to her story of the science teacher's bad jokes about rocks, to which he commented, "Piled it on, did he?"

Kurt suggested the teacher was probably stoned, and Crys had to remind him that he shouldn't even joke about teachers doing drugs.

Their jokes made Dana angry.

"Think of your own joke," Crys said to encourage Dana to join in. Sometimes she worried that her daughter didn't have a sense of humor.

Dana's forehead wrinkled. She glanced at Kurt, who was playing an air guitar. "Mr. Watkins was a—" Her face cleared. "Mr. Watkins was a rock star!"

Crys applauded, and Rick stirred enough to give her a thumbs-up.

"Geez, it took you long enough," her brother said, "but I was going to say *rocking the jokes out*."

They both turned to look to Rick for approval, but he was taking a bite of his hamburger.

"Good one, both of you," Crys said to cover his lack of attention.

Later, in bed, she snuggled close to her husband. He was stretched on his back, covered to the waist with the sheet and blanket. She flattened her hand on his exposed chest, taut and powerful from his upper body workouts.

"Hard day?"

He crooked his arm and rested his head on his wrist. "You could say that."

"A case?"

"Come on, Crys. You know which case."

"I thought Mitch told you that you could stop your research on the Norman murder."

"Hard to let go of that one, especially when my wife is involved."

She wasn't sure what to make of that comment. Had Mitch told him about her visit to the hospital? Had someone reported that she'd been back to Farrah's house? Or was he more worried about her safety with a murderer on the loose than she realized? Something had been eating away at her husband all evening.

"Mitch said you called him today and identified the floater found in LaBagh Woods." He turned his head to look at her. His eyes were dark. "Why didn't you tell me?"

"I called Mitch because he'd been looking for Randy. They showed the artist's drawing on the noon news. I'm sure it was Farrah's brother."

He turned his head away as if her answer had disappointed him and gazed up at the ceiling. "Yeah, the one who was with you when you discovered the reporter. Now he's dead, too."

Please don't let him start arguing again about how dangerous her career had become. It wasn't fair—all she'd done this time was recognize an artist's drawing shown on television.

"I'm sorry. I should have told you, but you haven't exactly been in a chatty mood tonight." It was no more than a token apology and an open invitation to argue. She didn't care. He wasn't the only partner in this marriage who was frustrated and not only about this horrible case. What did they say in marriage counseling about arguments having to do with more than which way the toilet paper roll was put on the holder? Sometimes it was just too painful or scary to confront the deeper issues.

Rick was silent. Stretched out on his back with his gaze still focused above him, he lay like a corpse. His exposed chest was pale in the darkness of the room, although his skin was warm beneath her palm. His facial muscles seemed relaxed. There was no trace of anger, which made his silence more unsettling.

"Was Randy Compton one of the people you were investigating?"

He remained silent. She was about to turn away from him when he said, "He'd borrowed money from some loan sharks we've been trying to nail." His voice was calm and factual. "His name had already come up in that investigation."

It took her a minute to register that he was willing to talk about the case with her. "Could they have killed him?"

"Anything's possible, but I doubt it. That's not how

they operate. They want their money repaid with interest, so killing the borrower is a losing proposition—until they grow tired of chasing him."

She resumed stroking his chest. "I think he wanted to borrow money from Farrah that day. He kept asking, 'What am I going to do now?' like he was in a real bind."

"He probably was. You don't skip payments with those guys. They'll break your legs or beat you to a pulp. No delinquency letters in the mail to kindly remind you to pay up."

She shivered. "No one deserves to die like that."

Randy had seemed hapless, but he had believed in himself and his dream of having a successful restaurant. He reminded her in that sense of her brother. Gregg had taken years to find work that suited him and paid a living wage, but he'd always believed that one day he would have his own farm. Gregg had the patience of a poop-encrusted statue in a park filled with pigeons, unlike Randy. He would never borrow money from loan sharks to finance his dream. At least, she hoped not.

"You always say there's often a financial motive in homicides where nothing else fits. Were you close to a breakthrough on Jase Norman's murder when you were told to back off?"

He turned his head to look at her.

"I know. I'm not supposed to be interested. It's Mitch's case." She sighed and rolled onto her back.

She was surprised to hear him chuckle.

"I know by now how stubborn you can be when you decide to investigate something."

She turned back on her side and raised up on her elbow. "So you're not mad?"

"Cryssie, I just worry. That's all." He sighed. "And I feel so damned helpless. This case... I want to be a part of it. There's something more going on. I can't figure out what it is."

"Aha! You don't believe it's a lover's quarrel turned violent."

"Too pat. They may have been lovers once, but there's no evidence that they'd had any contact in almost two decades. We're still missing a motive, even if she did kill him."

"I could tell that you weren't happy that Mitch hadn't interviewed Farrah."

"He would if he could. There's still a possibility of talking to her, although she may never remember what happened."

"So, what can we do about it?"

He fingered the faded blue T-shirt she slept in. "*We?* You heard Mitch—I'm off the case."

"Because he's convinced Farrah killed Jase Norman?"

He shook his head. "It's all about politics and money, babe. The bosses want this murder solved ASAP. As soon as your client's fingerprints turned up on the murder weapon, extra resources, including my team, were cut. It wasn't Mitch's idea."

That also explained the withdrawal of Farrah's hospital guard.

"Were you close to discovering anything?" she asked again.

"No. We hadn't gotten very far, but nothing suggested a financial motive for Norman's death. Everything has changed now, though."

"With Randy's death."

"Yeah. There's gotta be a connection."

Her hand stilled. "Didn't you just say you have an open case on those loan sharks?"

"Yeah." A smile slowly spread across his face. "Randy Compton's name had already come up as a customer of those guys."

"If the two deaths are connected or if Randy was Jase Norman's killer, you may solve a murder—or two." She told him about Mitch's discovery that Randy had been doing drive-bys before she had arrived that morning.

"I hadn't heard about that," he said.

"There's something else, too." She told him about the two cars Gary Zygman had observed. "Wes O'Malley had received three notifications of the doorbell being rung that morning. We know Jase Norman arrived by taxi, so he could have been the third visitor."

"I don't suppose Zygman happened to notice the plate numbers on the cars?"

The twinge from her conscience wasn't strong enough to make her reveal the source of her information. "The Kia belonged to Scott and Laura Danforth, and the Lincoln was registered to the Danforth campaign." The cars' ownership was still only a guess, but a good one, given that the models matched and two DANFORTH bumper stickers had been seen on both vehicles. "Mitch told me that they had been *eliminated* as suspects."

He raised an eyebrow. "Interesting. Could be politics. Mitch could have been told to back off since Danforth is a candidate in a highly visible federal campaign."

"And Mitch would back off? Just like that?"

"More likely, their alibis checked out."

Her hand slid to his cheek. Her thumb stroked the rough bristles there. "Could you find out what happened? Why Mitch eliminated them?"

He frowned. "Crys—"

She stopped the motion by grabbing his jaw. Raising up on her elbow, she forced him to look her in the eye. "Don't you dare say *Let Mitch handle it*! I'm not the one stopping him. There's a killer out there, Rick, and I know you want to catch him—or her—as badly as I do."

He raised his eyebrows. "I should have known you wouldn't sit quietly on the sidelines."

Her hand returned to his chest. "Don't you want to know? I mean, isn't it interesting that there's a connection to a high-profile campaign, a campaign with a manager whose previous boss was caught with his fingers in the funds?"

"There's a big difference between fraud and murder. We couldn't prove that Kruper knew what was going on."

"But the campaign links all of them. Jase Norman was writing a story about it, and Farrah was one of Danforth's inner circle. That may be why Jase came to see her, although I suspect he recognized her name. He could have confirmed it was his former girlfriend with a little research. Her picture was online. Farrah wasn't supposed to be talking to him, according to Evan Kruper. That leads to several interesting possibilities." She tapped her finger on his chest. "One, Scott Danforth, according to rumor, was her lover. He shows up and surprise! There's another man visiting her, a former lover who happens to also be investigating his campaign. Whack—he's dead."

"Watch it, lady." His grin widened. "You're turning me on."

She gave his chest a kiss where she'd lightly swatted him and then she tapped the same place again. "Two, Laura Danforth could have been there as a jealous wife if her husband was having an affair. Jase Norman tries to protect Farrah and whack!"

He grabbed her hand. "Hold on. Wouldn't she finish off the other woman while she's at it?"

"No. She was too horrified at what she'd done."

"Yeah, but Farrah's prints were on the murder weapon. The killer was cool enough to frame her."

She made a face. "Maybe Farrah grabbed the statue after Laura whacked him. When she realized he was dead, she dropped it and blanked out."

"Or maybe Farrah had already gone into her catatonic state when she witnessed the murder, and Laura was cold-blooded enough to frame her." He gazed at their entwined hands. "You said the Lincoln arrived after the Kia left. Wouldn't Laura Danforth have been driving the Kia?"

"Okay. I'll have to think about that one." He released her hand with a sly grin. His eyes had darkened with arousal. "Is there another theory coming here, or are we finished with the foreplay?"

"Third," she said, poking him, "there's Evan Kruper,

who follows Laura around, drives a Lincoln registered to the campaign, and has a need to prove himself after a certain financial crimes whiz of a detective had his previous candidate arrested and convicted for fraud. He makes up some excuse to find out what Laura or Scott discussed with Farrah and discovers the ace reporter interviewing her." Her hand hovered over his chest. "And then—" Her hand wavered...

Rick raised his head at the same time he reached for her. Their kiss became heated, melting months of frustration. When it ended, he pulled her to his chest, which rose and fell with his breath. She could feel his accelerated heart rate beneath her palm.

After a few moments, he said, "There could have been two people in the Kia, Danforth and his wife, or in the Lincoln, but you're right, there is a strong connection to the Danforth campaign and its top players. Lover's quarrel." He snorted. "Lover's triangle is more like it."

A smile swelled up from deep inside her heart. Rick was with her on this obsession, investigation, whack job—whatever they wanted to call it.

He stroked her hair and neck. "Two murders now. I don't like you being caught up in them, but I know telling you to stop talking to these people isn't going to work."

"Randy's cause of death has been confirmed?"

"Not officially, but he was bashed in the head."

"Just like Jase Norman."

"Maybe," Rick said. "We'll have to see what the autopsy report says."

She liked that *we*. She snuggled against him. "Don't

worry. My name wasn't in the paper. Those loan sharks don't know me."

"But the killer might." His hand stilled on her back. "You don't have to protect me, you know. You or Mitch. Promise me that you'll tell me what you're doing."

The rare vulnerability behind his words caused sudden tears to burn her eyes. She closed them. "I promise," she said against his chest.

His hand resumed circling on her back, but he didn't say anything. When she raised her head to look at him, he added, "I couldn't live without you."

"I couldn't live without you." She didn't need to remind him of how close she had come to facing that reality five years ago and several times since then.

"It could happen, you know. Paras don't live long lives."

She placed her palm on his cheek. "The kids need you, Rick. I need you. If you weren't here, who would they share their terrible jokes with?"

He groaned. "They were terrible, weren't they? Okay, I promise to be your rock, or maybe I should say your rolling stone."

She moaned. "Now I know where they get it from."

She giggled as he reached for the hem of her T-shirt and began touching her in places that had been missing him, aching for physical release. Later, when her body was still tingling and they both were exhausted, she closed her eyes and slept with her arm across his chest.

Chapter Twenty-Five

THE NEXT MORNING, she saw Rick off to work with a kiss that almost rekindled the lingering glow from their lovemaking. The kids hadn't come downstairs yet for breakfast, so they didn't have to explain Rick's quip about feeling bushwhacked or her comment that she would work on more theories to share with him. She had told him her plans for the day, none of which involved anything or anyone related to the two murders.

Her client today was Maddy Swain, who had hired Crys to help her sort through her collection of her grown children's childhoods. They carried eight plastic containers from the attic to the spacious living room. Soon piles of onesies, tiny hats, and bibs—many stained—occupied part of the gray sectional. Her client was hesitant, picking up one item and putting it down again as she tried to select what to keep.

Maddy was what Crys called a *clinger*. She wanted to hold onto her past by clutching the baby memorabilia that represented happy memories tightly to her chest. Crys envied her marriage of thirty years, spacious home, and loving family. At least Maddy appreciated what she had. But her client appeared to have an underlying fear that she didn't deserve her happiness or that it could be snatched away at any time. People were complex, and it was Crys's job to help her clients sort their shoes, not walk in them. Even so, she couldn't resist trying to understand Maddy's motivation for clinging.

"I might want to keep more than three of these for grandchildren. They're so tiny. Wouldn't it be okay if I kept a few more?"

Grandchildren. Rick had reminded her that his was likely a shortened lifespan. If only they could reach this point in their life together—Kurt and Dana grown and on their own and maybe married, the two of them anticipating having grandchildren. Was it too much to hope for?

"Crys?" Maddy said. "Are you okay?"

She wore a headband around her straight, shoulder-length hair. Her face looked younger than her fifty-five years, thanks to smooth skin with only a hint of wrinkles by her eyes when she smiled. Crys pictured her with the same hairstyle and headband in a school picture circa fourth grade. Definitely a clinger.

"Sorry, I was just remembering when my own children were little," she lied. She laughed. "I wasn't sure I would survive all those feedings and sleepless nights." *And fears of Rick dying.* But she had to put her worries about their future aside for now.

"And no, you don't need to keep any of these. Think what fun you'll have shopping for new ones when you have grandchildren."

Maddy sat down, still clutching the handful of onesies she'd been examining. "If only Brad hadn't accepted this transfer to Dallas."

Crys silently completed her client's thought: *Then you wouldn't be here making me throw things away.*

She scooted closer to Maddy. "You don't have to part with any of them. You can pack everything back in the boxes and haul them to Texas. Or—" She drew out the word.

"Or I can help children who need clothes now by donating them and create new energy by clearing out things I no longer need. You really believe in this energy thing, don't you?"

"I do. I think everything has energy, and we need to keep positive energy flowing by releasing things we no longer need. That creates space for new opportunities."

Practice what you preach. She was such a hypocrite. Now wasn't the time to tackle her conscience's demands. Maddy was listening to her as if she were a wiser soul, so she focused on her client's needs. "Remember Miss Havisham in *Great Expectations*? That's a great example of negative energy that's become stuck."

"She was still wearing her bridal gown, wasn't she? I remember the wedding cake sitting there moldering after all those years." She shuddered.

Crys touched one of the little outfits. "I know these have happy memories attached to them." She had seen quilts made of ties and T-shirts—why not baby clothes? But Maddy didn't sew and wasn't into crafts, so she wasn't going to suggest memorializing them. That idea would just provide a new excuse to hold onto them. She had to come up with another strategy to encourage Maddy to let go.

"Here's what we're going to do. I call it the fire drill. I'll give you one minute to select three of these to keep."

Panic filled Maddy's eyes. "A minute?"

"One minute." She pulled out her cell phone and clicked into her timer.

Her client's eyes narrowed. "Just the onesies?"

"Yes. We'll start there." And then she'd move on to the hats. She would save the bibs until last, betting that they would all go into the trash.

Maddy took a deep breath. "I know I'm being ridiculous."

"You really won't miss them. Didn't you tell me it had been five years since you last looked in these boxes?"

"Yes, when Alexis turned twenty-one." She hugged the clothes to her and then placed them on her lap. "Okay. Three children, three onesies. I'm in."

As she had expected, Maddy's ability to part with her baby clothes improved after the first few fire drills. Now she looked at the bibs and picked one up as if it were a nasty rag. "These can be thrown away. They've served their purpose." She thumbed an orange stain. "Aww, strained carrots. I remember—"

Crys held out her palm. With a mere nod, her client handed over all of them.

Later, driving away with more bags for Goodwill and grateful that babies didn't smoke, Crys thought of Farrah, crying over a miscarriage that had probably never happened. Did Farrah's dream about losing a pregnancy indicate she had regrets about being childless? There was so much help these days for women unable to conceive or carry a pregnancy to term. The first step, though, would be fixing her marriage, if she wanted a child with Wes. Maybe Farrah's close call with death would bring about a reconciliation.

At a stoplight, Crys watched a mother and three children holding hands cross the street. Had Farrah been told about her brother's death? The police would notify family as soon as his identification was confirmed. Wes would probably be the one to break the news. From what he'd said about his in-laws and their lack of visits, Farrah's parents weren't that close to her. Crys couldn't imagine losing any of her four brothers. In fact, she needed to check in with them.

In the past, she would be heading to Wisconsin this time of year for a family reunion with her parents, brothers, and their families. She and sometimes Rick would take the kids to her parents' farm over the long teacher's planning weekend at the end of October. Dad would hook up the horses to an old wagon for hayrides and carve pumpkins with Kurt and Dana and their cousins. Fall had been his favorite time of year. God, she missed him.

Since her father's death four years ago, which had happened during the time Rick was finishing rehab, she hadn't made the trip in October. She couldn't imagine being at the farm in the fall without her dad. Her brothers and mother had felt the same way, and the tradition had died with him. Now she drove the kids to Wisconsin in the summer, leaving them with her mother for two weeks. The farmhouse wasn't wheelchair accessible for Rick, and his pride prevented him from depending on others to carry him up the porch stairs to access the first floor. It was just as well. Crys suspected the doorways were too narrow for his chair to navigate. Her father had been making plans to build a ramp when he suffered the massive stroke that killed him.

Sending Kurt and Dana to spend time with their grandma and cousins in the summer gave her and Rick time together alone. Rick would take a few days off work, and they would explore places in the city together, even daring to talk about plans for the future. True, they only talked about a year or two ahead, but it was a special time together creating new memories that she cherished.

"You don't have to protect me, you know," he'd said last night.

Maybe not, but she would have to break her habit of doing just that.

Back in her basement office that afternoon, she turned on her computer and tried to ignore her own clutter. Her guilt always caught up with her when she returned home after working with a client. She had used every persuasive argument in her arsenal to coax Maddy to clean out her attic treasures. Why didn't those same logical reasons work for her in her own cluttered spaces, especially the basement and their bedroom?

You're only human. A flawed human nonetheless in denying reality and procrastinating tackling a dreaded project. Maybe she needed to hire an organizer. The thought made her laugh. Sure. She would just tell Rick she was working to earn money to pay for her own professional help to declutter their space. That would do wonders for his confidence in her abilities. Besides, it would take money, unless she could swap spaces as a professional courtesy with one of her peers. That was another unlikely scenario. Who in this business would admit to having trouble organizing their own space?

The furnace didn't distract her today once she focused on updating her notes and accounting spreadsheet. Her income promised to increase this month, despite having to turn down the job with Steve Hartley. Farrah's account could yield another pay day, if she recovered soon. Their work was almost finished, but she'd have to wait for her client to come home and check out what she'd done. Poor Farrah—she had enough to deal with right now, including her brother's death.

Crys's hands stilled on the keyboard. There had to be a connection between the two murders. All of the signs pointed to that. Maybe Rick would have some answers this evening.

Chapter Twenty-Six

"Before you ask," Maggie said, pouring her a glass of pinot grigio, "I wrote that letter to Carla's boss. She and Kendra will be the new stars of the Midwest Steakhouse when he reads it."

It was after five. Their daughters were playing upstairs in Annie's room, so they had Maggie's kitchen to themselves.

"That's great."

Maggie frowned. "You don't sound like you think it's great. Did something happen? I haven't mailed it yet."

"Randy Compton was found dead." She told her about the discovery of his body and how she had recognized him from the artist's drawing shown on the news.

"I can't believe it! Poor Carla. I'm glad I did write her boss a note. She'll have to figure another way out of that steakhouse job."

"I don't think she was seriously counting on Randy rescuing her."

"True. She did seem like a realist about the odds of him paying her back, too. Now she definitely won't see that money again." She started to raise her glass to her lips and then stopped. "You don't think she killed him, do you?"

Crys hadn't considered that possibility. She pictured Carla, first as a glum date in her floral dress at the POW dinner and then as a hostess at a depressing steakhouse. She seemed more of a victim than a violent killer. "No, I don't see it. Mitch thinks he could have been killed because he couldn't repay the loan sharks." Rick didn't, though, and she agreed with him.

"Mitch? He's sharing information about Randy's case with you, too?"

"I called him when I saw the artist's sketch. He hadn't heard about the body being found."

"But you two are still operating under the white flag?"

"It's fairly tattered and trampled at this point. He didn't hold up his end of the bargain about sharing information about Farrah's case." Or at least not as much as he could have.

"Uh-oh. Just when I thought there may be progress on the forgiveness front."

Her fingers tightened on her glass. Forgiveness? No. Tolerating Mitch being around was all she could handle, and only for Rick's sake. Besides, Mitch had cut her out of the case. No, she wasn't ready to forgive him, and she didn't know if she ever would be.

"Okaaaay." Maggie passed the etched glass dish containing chocolate-dusted almonds in front of her. "Let's say Randy was networking for investors, either to pay off his old debt or start a new venture, or maybe both. If he was meeting someone Friday night, who was it? *Family business* could refer to him or his sister."

"Or Wes. Whatever the business was, it would solve

Randy's financial problems as well. He'd found a source of income—or a payoff."

Maggie lowered her wineglass and raised an eyebrow. "Blackmail?"

"That's what I thought. I asked Wes if Randy had tried to extort money from him, but he denied it."

"Wes wasn't at the POW gala, although I suppose he could have called Randy that night to set up a meeting. Remember, Carla expected Randy to stay with her after the dinner. Something changed that evening."

"You're right, but we still don't know who he was meeting with. He set up a meeting with someone for later, possibly a person he'd talked to at the event. If he received a call or text… I could ask if they've checked his phone records." She would ask Rick. Outgoing calls after Friday night would help pinpoint time of death, so the police probably would request his cell records. At least Randy had never called her.

"The police may question you and everyone who was at the POW dinner. They'll want to determine when he was last seen and what he was doing before he died."

Maggie arched an eyebrow. "Is that when they think he died—Friday night?"

"They haven't said, but he was…seen a few days later. So far, it looks like he may have been killed as recently as Thursday night or maybe the next day." If luck was on her side, the investigation—and possibly the cell phone records—would uncover other proof he was alive at least until Thursday so she wouldn't have to confess she'd talked to him that night. She might have to give Mitch the information, though, to help the police pinpoint the time of death and find Randy's killer. Rick wouldn't be happy to find out she'd been keeping the incident from him. He'd be more unhappy realizing his wife had been approached outside his home by a murder suspect while he was inside watching TV.

Maggie startled her out of her thoughts. "Wait a minute, though. If he was killed several days after the POW dinner, doesn't that lift suspicion from his activities that night? I may not have to be grilled by Chicago's finest, darn it."

Crys smiled. "Poor Mags. You could be right, though. Whoever he met after he dropped Carla off Friday night wasn't necessarily his killer, given the fact that several days passed after that."

When it came to borrowing money, Randy had been like a squirrel looking for nuts. If one oak didn't have them, he would have found another. But what if he'd found an entire forest? Probably not the best metaphor. Maybe she shouldn't think about the case while she was drinking wine.

Maggie raised her glass. "May he rest in peace. Not to speak ill of the dead, but Randy was sexist. He was mostly buttonholing men that night. At least, that's what it seemed. I happened to know several women in that group who have connections in the hospitality industry, not to mention moi, of course." She took a sip of wine. "He did talk to one woman: Laura Danforth."

Crys shrugged. "He talked to Scott Danforth, I think, after dinner, or he was headed that way. I saw him with

Evan Kruper, too."

There was nothing unusual in Randy making the rounds at the party. He had seen the tickets as an opportunity to network and had been open about his intention that evening. Scott Danforth would have been a valuable contact, giving Randy a name to drop to impress others and appear to have important connections. That could explain him chatting with the candidate and his wife, even Evan.

"Kruper had his eye on Laura the whole evening. That seems odd to me," Maggie said. "You'd expect him to be glued to Scott's side or talking to potential donors himself. There was some big money in the room for their war chest."

"True. He came to her rescue when those reporters were crowding around her to ask about rumors that Scott was having an affair. I think he wanted to protect her from the press. Her husband was too busy socializing with donors to do that."

"Muzzle her is more like it." Maggie licked chocolate from her fingers. "Laura strikes me as a woman who speaks her mind, and you said she didn't want to have a role in the campaign. She might not like her husband's political ambitions, even if she says she supports him."

"She didn't seem to want to move to Washington."

"Maybe a move is what she needs to save her family."

"Do you think Scott is having an affair?"

Maggie made a face. "I know you don't want to hear this, but my journalist friends say your client is at the top of the list of possible *other women*."

"I don't want to believe it, but that doesn't make it a lie. On the other hand, Laura Danforth seemed quite confident of her husband's fidelity."

"The wife is the last to know?"

"Or the wife knows her husband best. But if there was an affair, maybe Randy knew about it. He could have been trying to blackmail Scott." At the hospital, Scott and Evan had seemed anxious to talk to Farrah as soon as possible—perhaps to ensure she remembered the need to remain quiet about her lover?

"Pay up or I'll tell your wife or the press?" Maggie slid off her stool to grab the wine bottle. Crys declined the proffered refill, but her hostess gave herself another splash of the pinot.

"Blackmail makes sense," Maggie said, "if Randy somehow found out about the affair. Also, the press claimed Scott was at Farrah's house that morning. Has Mitch said anything about that?"

"He didn't say Scott Danforth had been there, but one of the cars a neighbor saw in her driveway that morning was a Lincoln registered to the campaign." Or he could have come in the Kia Sorento, which was the same model as the car registered to the Danforths.

Had blackmail been Randy's forest of acorns, his lottery jackpot win, as Carla had described it? He, too, had observed the cars arriving at his sister's house. Maybe he had seen the killer and tapped him for money to keep quiet. Unfortunately, Randy was no longer alive to ask. The other visitors might know something. Mitch had made that cryptic comment about the owners of the Kia and

Lincoln being *eliminated*, so what would be the harm in talking to them again?

"If I could go to another event, maybe I could talk to Scott, Evan, or Laura. Somehow the campaign is tied in to what happened to Farrah. It links all of them with Jase Norman." She would have to tell Rick, though. She had promised to tell him what she was planning.

Maggie's reaction lacked the enthusiasm she expected. "I'm not so sure that's a good idea. If you're right, one of them could be a killer. Maybe you should talk to Mitch first."

Let Mitch handle it. That's what Rick would probably say, too, when she told him. He wouldn't want her taking any risks. Two men had died, and Farrah was still in the hospital.

Crys reached for an almond and popped it in her mouth. Mitch was convinced that Farrah was guilty. He was ready to arrest her. She doubted he would listen to her, especially since she had no proof. Even if he did, Mitch had been warned off investigating the campaign by his bosses. He would need more than a theory to confront the Danforths again.

Footsteps coming down the stairs announced that the girls were approaching. "I know you're mad at him, but Mitch will listen to you," Maggie said, nearly whispering. "You're very persuasive, you know. Think of how you convince your clients to throw out a lifetime of belongings. Pick up that tattered truce flag and march on, girlfriend. Just don't do it alone."

"I won't." She stretched to give Maggie a hug. "I love

you. Put those nuts away so we have some next time."

She laughed. "You know, I can just buy more. Besides, Gray is the one you should be worried about. I have to hide these from him."

"Mom, are those Dad's nuts?" Annie asked, her brown eyes huge.

Dana followed her into the kitchen. "Can we have one?"

"No," Maggie said, with a wink at Crys. "You'll spoil your dinner."

THAT NIGHT, CRYS was washing dishes when a motion in the darkness outside the window caught her attention. She bent closer to the glass as Connie appeared waving her arm in the pool of light shining from the kitchen. Crys waved back and pointed to the front door. Connie shook her head. She crooked her index finger and then pointed toward the garage.

"What's up?" she asked her neighbor a minute later on the driveway.

Connie put a finger to her lips and motioned her to follow. She was carrying a large tactical flashlight, similar to one Rick had. It was the same long, heavy model the police and fire departments used—useful as a weapon as well as for illumination. She hadn't turned it on, so they walked through the darkness into her backyard. Connie's white sneakers were easy to follow in the blackness of the moonless night. She zigzagged from time to time to avoid obstacles and a tree branch that had fallen. Crys matched the movements of the white sneakers as her eyes adjusted to night vision.

The shed where gardening equipment was stored soon loomed ahead of them. If someone had broken into Connie's shed, they should call the police, not risk confronting the intruder themselves. Crys jogged forward to catch up with her neighbor, but Connie turned around and again put her finger to her lips. She then made a circular motion for Crys to approach the shed from the left.

Crys held her hands up in a *what-the-heck?* questioning manner.

Her neighbor frowned and circled her finger more emphatically. She then turned her back and headed to the right. Crys stepped cautiously toward the left of the shed. Maybe Connie had already called the police or Pete Jr. Or maybe she had a reason not to.

The shed door was open a crack, revealing a strip of feeble light from inside.

Connie pointed her powerful flashlight at the gap. "Whoever you are, come out now."

Chapter Twenty-Seven

THERE WAS NO response.

Crys heard a scraping sound inside the shed. Something fell with a thump.

"I'm armed, and I'm not going to tell you again," Connie said firmly.

The door widened.

"Don't shoot!" a young male voice pleaded. His voice cracked on the second word. "I'm unarmed!"

The flashlight didn't waver in Connie's hand. "Come out with your hands up."

The door creaked open wider. Rafe appeared blinking and squinting in the flashlight beam directed at his face. His trembling hands were held high.

"Oh for Pete's sake," Connie said, pointing the light to the ground.

"Rafe!" Crys said. "What are you doing in Mrs. Byrne's shed?"

He blinked at her. "C-can I lower my arms?"

"Yes," Crys said while Connie answered, "No."

He jerked his arms up higher and looked from one woman to the other.

"Answer my question, Rafe." Crys lowered her voice to

calm the poor kid and Connie. "What are you doing here? I know you're not gardening."

He glanced at Connie as if he didn't trust her not to attack him. His arms lowered a few inches. "I'm sleeping here."

"You're sleeping in my shed?" Connie was still using her police voice.

Rafe's arms jerked up again. "I-I didn't think anyone would notice."

"What?" Connie exclaimed, pointing the beam of light into his eyes. "You didn't think I'd notice you prowling around in my yard? Thought I was an old fool, did you?"

Rafe hung his head, although whether he was ashamed or trying to avoid looking into the flashlight's beam wasn't clear. Probably both.

"Why are you sleeping here, Rafe?" Crys asked. "Are you in trouble at home?"

"No." He hesitated. "I just wanted some space."

No wonder, if people crowded into his home to party, like the night she'd dropped him off. Kurt had said he had older siblings. Were they all living there? The house only looked big enough to have three bedrooms.

"What do you mean? You can lower your hands."

Connie had stepped into the shed. Her flashlight beam was bouncing around behind the boy.

Rafe glanced back at his temporary shelter and then moved closer to Crys. "At home I have to share a room with my sister's kids."

"She lives there with you and your mom?"

He nodded.

"How many kids does she have?"

"Three."

If it was a three-bedroom home and his mother and sister each had a room, there would be some sharing going on.

"Does anyone else live there?"

"My brother, Marco."

Connie emerged with a large backpack and some sort of blanket. "He's set up camp in there. This yours?"

Rafe nodded.

"Does your mother know where you are?" Connie said.

He stepped closer to Crys. "You're not going to call the police, are you?"

Connie dropped the bag. "I should. Sleeping in my shed—humph! You didn't take anything, did you?"

He dropped his head again. "I used some matches I found in there and a screwdriver to open a can."

"Baked beans," Connie said to Crys. "The can's still there, full of ants." She turned back to Rafe. "You didn't answer my question, kid. Does your mother know where you are, or does she think you ran away?"

His eyes flickered to Crys's face and then down again. "I told her I was staying with the Wards."

"And that's where you will stay tonight," Crys said, "but tomorrow we're going to talk to your mom. Maybe we can figure something out together."

THE NEXT MORNING, breakfast had to be awkward for

Rafe, although he acted cool and unconcerned in the face of Dana's questions.

"But why did you come so late?" Dana said. "We're not allowed to have sleepovers on school nights."

"There are exceptions to every rule, if there's a good enough reason," Rick told her as he rolled into the kitchen. He was dressed for work and had a healthy glow after a good night's sleep. He stopped and grabbed his lunch bag from the counter. "Love you guys. Don't be too hard on your teachers today, especially you, Dana."

"Bye, Dad," they chorused. Even Rafe smiled and gave a wave.

Crys bent over for a kiss. She inhaled his aftershave and noticed more gray hairs around his temples. She'd told him what was going on last night after she'd taken Rafe upstairs to Kurt's room. His only comment had been, "He practically lives here anyhow, doesn't he?"

Her son hadn't seemed surprised by Rafe's appearance. Perhaps he'd known what was going on. She would talk to him later.

At her suggestion, Kurt had offered Rafe a sweatshirt and clean socks this morning after he pulled rumpled clothing from his bag. She didn't suggest an underwear exchange. Whether he'd packed any or not, he'd be okay wearing the same ones an extra day. She reminded him to come home with Kurt, and then they'd go together to talk to his mother.

In the quiet of the house after Rick and the kids left, Crys sat at the kitchen table, enjoying a second cup of coffee. She hadn't talked to Rick last night about the case or shared any new theories later in bed. By the time she'd organized Rafe and finished the dishes, Rick was yawning and ready to call it a night. He must have fallen asleep right away, and she was glad. He'd looked so gray and drawn last weekend that she had feared he was becoming ill. This morning he had looked more like his former self. Tonight was soon enough to ask if he'd had a chance to find anything out about the case or Randy's death.

Maggie had urged her to call Mitch, but that seemed pointless. He wasn't going to look into the campaign or consider another suspect.

She stared at her phone. If only she could talk to Laura Danforth. She had denied that her husband was having an affair with Farrah, but she probably knew why Scott had been at Farrah's house that morning. Whatever the reason, the drivers of both vehicles spotted in Farrah's driveway had been eliminated as suspects, according to Mitch. Or was that because of who they were, not what they had or hadn't done?

She jumped when the phone began to ring. Mitch's name appeared on the caller ID.

"The DA has agreed to press charges against Farrah Compton," he said. "I thought you'd want to know."

Her stomach dropped. "Did you talk to her?"

"Yes." He sounded defensive. She heard a horn beep; he was in his car. "She claims she doesn't remember. She admitted that Jason Norman was her former lover, but then her lawyer told her not to answer any more questions."

"How is she? Is she still in the hospital?"

"They were going to release her, but she had a setback. The doc says it's not uncommon with catatonia."

"Oh no." The events that morning must still be too traumatic for Farrah to face. Mitch wasn't the type of cop to bully a suspect, even if a lawyer hadn't been present. He'd cooperated with Dr. Park and respected Farrah's fragile mental state. She couldn't fault him on that.

"Anyhow, the warrant should be out tomorrow."

His tone was flat. She heard what sounded like a blinker noise. He would end the call soon, but she wasn't going to let him hang up without an answer.

"Mitch, why did you say the owners of the Lincoln and Kia had been eliminated?"

"Their alibis checked out. They left before Norman was killed."

She knew evasive when she heard it. "*You* checked them out?"

He hesitated. "Yeah."

"Personally?"

There was a pause that answered her question. "I told you that I can't share everything. Sometimes information is sensitive."

Politically sensitive, he meant. He was told to back off, and that's what he did.

"Let me ask one more thing. If the two visitors driving those cars weren't people whose alibis were *sensitive*, would you have eliminated them as suspects, based on their alibis?"

He was silent. She listened to the myriad sounds of city traffic and the occasional crackle of a police radio on low.

She'd gone too far, but she didn't care. He was the lead detective on this case, damn it! She should have known that Mitch Burdine would follow orders. Rick had always said he was a good cop that way. He wasn't a maverick. She shouldn't expect him to suddenly be someone else, someone like Rick, who was willing to take chances.

Hot tears stung her eyes, as unexpected as the jolt of realization that struck her.

Mitch followed orders. Rick was the one who was willing to take chances.

In the hospital waiting room after the shooting, she'd kept silent, shaking from fear for Rick and from a cold anger at Mitch, her husband's partner and the person she'd trusted to have his back. It had taken every ounce of her strength to stop angry, hateful words from exploding from her. When she'd started shaking so hard that her teeth rattled like machine gun fire, he had wrapped his arms around her, hugging her so tightly that she couldn't shake.

"Hey, it's okay. It's going to be all right," he'd said, as if he knew more than the doctors who had told her that Rick had suffered a traumatic spinal injury.

"No." Her voice had been muffled by the scratchy wool of his jacket. "Let me go!"

But he hadn't. She had smelled his guilt and even fear, along with that stupid sandalwood scent of his aftershave. Happy-go-lucky Mitch, the laugh-it-off, life's-a-joke partner of Rick Ward, husband and father of her two young children. His arms had clasped her like iron bands.

He'd murmured something then.

Don't say it, don't say it! She couldn't cover her ears with him pinning her arms. *Don't say it!* She couldn't even utter her objection to those words he had no right to say to her. She'd begun to gasp, her own fear and anger choking her. She'd screamed then, the fear and frustration inside her erupting into a single strangled cry that burst from her as if he'd squeezed it out in his unrelenting embrace. His arms had loosened then and dropped to his side.

"I'm sorry" he'd said to her that day as he'd held her. "I'm sorry."

Even in that dark moment in the hospital waiting room, she hadn't called him incompetent or irresponsible—a bad cop. And he hadn't been, she realized now. Mitch had just been Mitch. Rick had gone into the alley alone. Rick hadn't waited for the backup that Mitch had called. Mitch had followed procedure or maybe Rick's order to split up, even though it meant leaving his partner's back exposed to the bullet that had shattered his spine and his family.

"Crys—" Mitch started to say now into the silence between them.

Tears clogged her throat. "Thanks for letting me know about the arrest warrant." She disconnected before he could respond.

Chapter Twenty-Eight

CRYS HAD HER second session with Connie's friend Betty later that morning. She still felt confused and disturbed after her call with Mitch. Maybe it showed on her face, because Betty surprised her with a hug. She smelled of lavender and Aqua Net hairspray and reminded Crys of her grandmother. She hugged back, blinking back tears in the comfort of the older woman's arms.

Betty released her with a little laugh. She looked as if she'd shed ten years since they had cleaned out her late husband's wardrobe. Her white hair appeared salon styled in soft curls around her flushed face. Her clothes also seemed more youthful. She wore slim blue jeans beneath an oversized old shirt appropriate for their cleaning project. Had the shirt belonged to Ed and escaped the donation pile? At least it didn't smell of his cigarettes.

Crys cleared the emotion from her throat, determined to give Betty her full attention. "You look like a new woman."

"I haven't worn jeans since I was a teenager," Betty said with a shy smile. "I was afraid Ed would have a heart attack if I bought a pair for myself."

"They look terrific. Good for you!" Her own mother

lived in jeans, but she had a farm to run and her life was a lot different from Betty's. She suspected the two women would be friends. Betty was easy to like.

The garage had a tool bench, car fluids and cleaners, and yard equipment. It would be a dirty and physical job, exactly the sort of challenge Crys needed today. The first obstacle was moving the car out of the space to make room for them to work. Betty admitted that she'd never learned to drive.

"Never?" Crys couldn't hide her surprise.

"No. I married Ed right after I graduated from high school. He always drove me wherever I wanted to go, or a friend would pick me up. I can walk to church and the library if the weather's good, and my neighbor drives me in Ed's car once a week to the grocery store."

"Do you plan on selling the car?"

Betty ducked her head. "I know I'm probably crazy, but I thought I might take driving lessons. Ed tried to teach me once, but he didn't have much patience. He'd just say *Put your foot on the gas pedal and go!* and then he'd yell at me when I suddenly had to brake. I ran the car up on a curb once, and that was the end of our lessons."

She could see Rick having the same kind of patience issues. Crys would have to teach Kurt to drive in a year or two, or maybe her brother could do it. It was going to be hard for her to accept him being old enough to be behind the wheel.

"Sometimes it helps having someone you don't know teach you skills like driving. I have a feeling you'll do well, Betty. It just takes practice like everything else."

The Honda Accord started right away. With the car out of the way, they sorted through half of the garage, quickly identifying rusty rakes and broken parts for the trash. Crys packed a box of chemicals, paint, and car fluids that Betty wouldn't be needing to take to the recycling center for safe disposal. Betty asked to come along, so they put the box in Ed's car and took it for an outing.

"I can sense Ed with us," Betty said, sitting in the passenger seat. "I don't think he'd mind that we're cleaning out the garage."

Crys could smell Ed's cigarettes. She chose to believe the odor was left over from his past driving days and not a sign that he was with them in spirit.

CRYS WAS HOME in her kitchen and debating what to have for lunch when her phone rang. She fished it out of her handbag, afraid it might be Mitch. She wasn't sure what she would say to him after this morning's conversation. She was relieved when her caller ID told her it was Alana Cortez-Portingal, Farrah's friend in California.

"How is Farrah doing? I've been trying to call her and Wes, but they aren't answering."

"I haven't seen her in a few days," Crys hedged. "I heard that she's still in the hospital."

"Oh no. Is she still catatonic?"

"She had been awake but there was a relapse. I wish I had better news for you."

"Maybe I should come to see her."

Crys winced. If Alana came, she might see Farrah being arrested.

"I don't know what I could do," Alana continued, "but maybe another familiar face would help her to recover."

"I would give it a few more days, Alana. Let me check up on her, and I'll give you a call back. If she's better, maybe she can call you."

"I would appreciate that. I have two cases I'm prepping for court, although I could ask for a continuance if she needs me."

"I'll keep you informed." Before Alana could end the call, Crys said, "There is something I was wondering. You were telling me about Farrah's relationship with Jase Norman."

"I talk too much. I should know better as an attorney. I guess it was the shock of hearing that he was killed in Farrah's home."

"From what you told me, it did seem strange that they had reunited after so many years. Before her relapse, she told me that when she woke up, she thought she'd had a miscarriage. I was wondering if it was a dream or whether she'd had one in the past."

There was a silence that lasted long enough for Crys to ask if her caller was still there.

"Yes, I'm here." She sighed. "Let's just say that sometimes dreams are based on truth."

"Did it happen in Africa or after she came back?"

"If you're asking if Jase Norman was the father, I'm not sure. She told me once that she'd had a pregnancy that ended in a miscarriage. She didn't know how she would have coped, being a single mother and pursuing her education, or how her family would have reacted. She said she'd been incredibly lucky that the pregnancy terminated before she was showing, but she had still been sad to lose the child."

Lucky wasn't a word that Crys would use about her own miscarriage, even though having a baby with Rick paralyzed and two children needing her would have been a huge challenge, perhaps more than she could have handled at that time. The loss of that child was still painful, and Farrah's miscarriage also could have been a wound that had never completely healed. If Jase Norman had been the father, the wound might have reopened when he reappeared in her life. Her mind had replayed the memory of her miscarriage in her catatonic state.

"Thank you for telling me," Crys said.

"And now I have a question for you. I read about the rumors of Farrah having an affair with a politician, Scott Danforth. Is it true?"

Crys hesitated. "I don't know about an affair. She was working on his campaign. I've met him, and he's very attractive. Lots of charisma. I could understand any woman falling for him. She never mentioned him to you?"

"No. I didn't even know she was involved in his campaign."

Crys detected a note of frustration. As a good friend, Alana would expect to be trusted as a confidant and be told about affairs or scandals. Maybe Farrah wasn't a confiding sort of friend, though.

"I thought it might be why she and Wes separated,"

Crys probed.

"Pfft! Wes is a nice man but not Farrah's intellectual equal. I'm surprised the marriage lasted this long. It seemed a case of opposites attracting."

And sometimes opposites complement each other. "Scott Danforth and his wife seem happily married. This rumor may just be an attempt by the press to create a scandal where one doesn't exist. The Danforths are denying it."

Alana didn't take her bait to comment on the likelihood of an affair. "I have to go, but please keep me informed about her condition. If you talk to her, remind her that I'm here as a friend—and as a lawyer."

She hung up before Crys could respond.

WHEN THE BOYS came in from school, Rafe went upstairs to change back into his own clothes. Crys told Kurt to stay home. No sense in overwhelming Mrs. Canales with two of them visiting. Besides, she wanted some time alone with Rafe. Perhaps he'd drop the Mr. Cool act and open up more in the car if Kurt wasn't with them. Dana was at Annie's house, and she would pick her up on her way back.

Kurt hesitated at the kitchen door. "Mom, there's something you should know."

Her son was almost her height, she noticed with a shock. His face seemed longer, more angular. The baby fat that had rounded his cheeks was disappearing, and she could see the cheekbones that reminded her more of her brothers than Rick.

"What is it, honey?"

"Rafe doesn't have a phone. You know that night he stayed for dinner and you told him to call his mom? He didn't call her. I said he could use mine, but he said he didn't need it. I just thought his mom didn't care, like he told you."

"Did you know he was staying in Mrs. Byrne's shed?"

He shook his head. "I would have told you that, even if he got mad at me."

It was her turn to nod. "I'm glad you told me about the phone. We'll figure out how to help him. Don't worry."

"Thanks, Mom." She heard his footsteps as he pounded up the stairs. Whatever had happened to the patter of little feet?

"How was school today?" she asked Rafe when he was settled in the van next to her. He'd started to climb into the back, but she had insisted he sit in the front.

"Okay."

He was slouched in the seat and staring out the side window.

"Rafe, do you want to live at home with your mom?"

He shrugged.

She wasn't sure how to ask what she really wanted to know—was he safe? Had something bad happened? He hadn't run away very far. Maybe he only needed his own space, as he'd said.

"Would you want to live there if you had your own room?"

"I guess." He sounded as if the possibility were unimaginable, like Michael Jordan showing up to shoot a few baskets.

When she pulled up to his house, there was only one car in the driveway. She should have made sure his mother would be here. Maybe he'd known all along that she wouldn't be home for this visit.

"Is that your mom's car?"

"Yeah. She works the early shift."

Great. The poor woman might be sleeping.

She followed him into the house. Two young girls were sitting close to a television, gazing up at it with their mouths slightly open. Colorfully dressed adults sang and danced on the screen.

"I'll go get her," Rafe said, leaving her with the children, who still hadn't seemed to notice the stranger in the room with them. Having people flowing in and out of their home and lives must be normal for them.

The woman who returned with Rafe was taller than Crys had expected. Her long, brown hair pulled back in a loose ponytail was mildly peppered with gray, and her face was youthful for a woman probably in her forties. She wore jeans and a long-sleeved, V-neck maroon T-shirt. She carried a chubby baby boy who was playing with the small silver crucifix she wore around her neck.

"Rafael has told me you drove him here." She smiled. "Thank you for inviting him to your home." She said something in Spanish to him that included the word *gracias*.

"Thank you for letting me spend the night," Rafe said, not meeting her eyes.

"*Sí*," his mother said. "Many nights. It is very kind of

you." She nodded toward the two girls watching television. "My grandchildren and daughter are living with me and my sons. It is sometimes too much for this one."

"Actually, I wonder if I could help, Mrs. Canales."

"Alicia, please."

"Alicia, I'm an organizer. I help people to better arrange their homes. Would you mind if I looked at Rafe's room?"

Rafe told his mother something in Spanish.

"Ah," his mother said. "You are welcome to look at my home. It is not very *ordenado*, er, neat."

"I have two children, so I understand," Crys said with a smile. Not that Kurt and Dana were responsible for most of her clutter. The baby started to fuss, so she said, "Rafe, could you show me around?"

He took her to a bedroom with a twin bed and a full-sized blow-up mattress on the floor. There was a small desk against a wall and a closet with sliding doors. The desk chair had children's clothes stacked on it. Stuffed animals, toys, and baby blankets littered the mattress and the floor.

"Is this your room?"

"Yeah." He had his hands in his pockets and was looking at the overwhelmed room as if he didn't recognize what it had metamorphosed into.

She didn't blame him. There was no sign of Rafe in this children's bedroom that doubled as a playroom. The twin bed was probably his, but that was it. He was a teenager and still technically a child, but having to share with the little ones would seem demeaning.

At her request, he took her on a quick tour of the other rooms. A smaller bedroom, his brother's, held the other twin bed, a nightstand, and a metal coatrack tree with clothes hung on it. The master bedroom, shared by his mother and sister, had a queen bed and a crib. The hall bath was surprisingly neat, despite the toys around the tub and a towel count befitting a large family. After she'd been led back through the living room to a galley kitchen and laundry by a rear door, also freshly cleaned, she asked, "Is there a basement?"

"Yeah." He led her back toward the living room. There was a door she hadn't noticed by the entrance to the kitchen.

The basement was only as large as the main rooms upstairs, although there might be crawl space under the bedroom area for plumbing. There were cardboard boxes everywhere and furniture pieces stacked in the center as if they had been brought downstairs and not carried a foot farther than they had to be. There wasn't room enough for a bed, not without moving some of the items being stored.

She pointed to the collection of furniture and boxes. "Who does this belong to?"

He shrugged. "Mostly Dora. Some of it's Marco's, too."

She edged around between boxes and chairs. There were windows with light and the basement seemed dry. She couldn't smell any dampness.

"I don't mean to pry, Rafe, but do you think Dora is going to stay here for long, or is she planning on moving out any time soon?"

He sighed. "She broke up with her boyfriend. That's why we moved here, so Mama could help her with the kids."

That had been at least several months ago. Rafe had been in Chicago in August when school started. "Any chance she'll go back to him?"

He shook his head vigorously. "No way. He dumped her for another girl. They're living together. Dora heard she's pregnant."

"Okay. I have two ideas. One, you could share a room with Marco."

He shook his head, as she had expected. "He won't let me. Besides, he comes in late and snores."

She suspected there were other reasons, but she didn't press him. Marco was a young man who needed his own space, too.

"Okay. My second idea is that we create a space for you down here."

He wrinkled his nose and looked around. "Where?"

"Don't worry. We'll make space," she said, and led him back upstairs.

Chapter Twenty-Nine

"He'll be staying with us until his sister clears out the basement?"

Rick reached for the pan she had rinsed and began drying it. He was keeping her company in the kitchen after dinner so they could talk. The three kids were watching television. Between that noise and the sound of the dishwasher running, they had some privacy.

"That's the plan. Mrs. Canales—Alicia—thinks her daughter will be willing to sell her furniture in a yard sale, or, if not, she's going to insist she move it out, even if she has to pay to store it. She wants Rafe to have his own space and not feel like he's being kicked to the curb."

"Or become a ward of the Wards."

"Ha-ha. He's a good kid. We could do worse."

"Hey, I'm not complaining. I always wanted another son."

For a moment the conversation faltered. She'd never told Rick about the baby she'd lost.

She reached for the skillet she'd used to cook hamburgers and wiped grease out with a paper towel. "Anyhow, I offered to help set up a makeshift bedroom for him in the basement after the furniture is gone. Of course, he'll still have to share a bathroom with the others. He seems okay with that."

Rick rolled backward to open the lower cabinet where the pans were stored. Crys glanced down when she heard him grunt. He struggled at an awkward angle to stack the pan inside some others, but he managed. She rinsed the fry pan, pretending not to have noticed.

"I'm just glad that his mother agreed to the plan," she continued. "She had no idea why he was staying away so many nights. He never complained to her. I think he was being protective. Rafe knows that she works hard trying to take care of all of them. He didn't want to create another problem for her."

After Rick took the pan from the drainer to dry, he asked, "How will you do that—make a bedroom in the basement?"

She looked at him in surprise. He'd never shown much interest in her work before. "My plan is to use some screens and boxes to set up walls and give him some privacy. Maybe I can find a tall bookcase or two at a resale shop. There's a corner of the basement with a window that will be perfect, and we'll only have to create two walls." She pictured the corner space and another solution came to mind. "Or I could rig a curtain on one side at least. That could be his door. Maybe put hooks in the ceiling? I'd have to run that by Rafe and Alicia."

"Or use one of those semicircle curtain tracks."

"Yes!" She turned to Rick. "You should have seen Rafe when I described what we could do. His face lit up!"

She loved thinking about the rare smile their *adopted*

son had given her when he began to picture his new room. He'd looked so proud when she'd pointed out that he would have the biggest and coolest (in both senses of the word) bedroom in the house.

"You're amazing." Rick smiled at her. "You love doing this, don't you?"

"I do. I mean, a lot of it is common sense. Sometimes people just need to hear from someone else that they need to get rid of things when they've known that all along."

"Nope. Not buying it."

"What do you mean?"

He set the pan he'd dried on the countertop and pulled her down to his lap, wet hands and all. Then he wrapped his arms around her and started drying her hands. "Remember when we met and you were working at the bank? You told me the best part of your job was figuring out how to help people—what loan might help, how they might improve their credit rating to qualify for a loan, whether they should refinance."

"That *was* the best part."

He took her other hand and began to rub the towel around each finger. "You're doing the same thing now, helping people organize their lives."

"Well, their space anyway."

"Uh-uh. Don't be modest. You help them to become unstuck, to see things differently. Like Rafe and his mama. They didn't see the possibility of using the basement that way until you suggested it." He raised her hand and examined both sides as if it were a dish or pot he was drying. Then he laid it gently on her lap. "You're good at what you do."

Tears burned her eyes. "That's the nicest thing anyone has ever said about my work." And it meant the world coming from him.

His voice was close to her ear. "Look, Crys, I know I haven't been supportive."

"You haven't stopped me."

He laughed softly. "As if I could. There's a difference, though, between tolerating something and supporting it."

"I understand. I do. You worry about me, about the people I might be dealing with when I walk into someone's home or business." She clasped his hands in hers. "I just want you to have more faith in my instincts and judgment. I may make mistakes—one or two—but I am a good problem solver, and I know how to persuade people to see things differently, as you said. And there's something else."

His hands squeezed hers. "What's that?"

"I have you." She pulled their hands apart so she could turn around and straddle his legs. When they were face-to-face, she said, "I've realized since we talked the other night that I haven't included you in my business. I mean, sure, you're my husband and whatever I earn or spend is ours, but I want you to be a part of this. We're a great team when we work together."

"Yeah, right." The gleam faded from his eyes. "There's not much I can do to help you in this." He patted his chair arm. "I can't help you reorganize Rafe's basement. Hell, I can't go into my own basement."

She cocked her head. "There's a lot you can do. You're not just a pretty face, you know." She patted his cheek, making him laugh. She wasn't going to allow him to wallow in self-pity tonight. "I've been thinking about it."

"Uh-oh. Does it involve whacking?"

She burst out laughing. "Actually, it does, but not the type your dirty mind is considering. What about moving your workshop from the basement to the garage? I think there's room if we hang the bicycles from the ceiling and reorganize a few things. The boys can help with the moving. Then you can whack away with your hammer to your heart's content and maybe build a few things for me."

He raised an eyebrow. "Not to mention it would save Gregg a few steps, too, when he's fixing something around here."

Ouch. "I've also been thinking about putting you to work running background checks on my potential clients, if it would make you feel better."

"I can't use my access with the department. You know that."

She waited as he thought about it. He would reach the same solution she had.

And he did, nodding thoughtfully. "I see where you're going. We could subscribe to one of those online services and do it as private citizens. There's no rule against me using public access to records or subscribing to a private service on my own time."

"Exactly! And it would be a business expense we could write off. Not every potential client would have to be checked. Connie's church friend Betty, for example, doesn't even drive."

"Hmm, just because she goes to mass every day and

twice on Sundays doesn't mean she hasn't committed any sins. She might do phone sex from home or sell marijuana brownies."

"Not likely." Poor Betty would be shocked to know that people even did those things.

He slid his hands around her waist. "I suppose I could trust your judgment on that one, though."

"Good. Now let's talk about *our* client, Farrah. Did you find out anything about the drivers of those two cars and their alibis?"

"Not much. Mitch was called to another homicide before I was finished. Laura Danforth was driving the Kia. She admitted she went to talk to Farrah Compton about the rumors of an affair between Farrah and her husband."

That made sense. "What about the Lincoln?"

"Scott Danforth was driving it. Same reason. He drove separately, but they both arrived to meet with her together."

Crys frowned. Gary Zygman had said the Kia was there and then the Lincoln. She hadn't pictured them arriving together. "So they were there at the same time, but in separate cars?"

"That's right. Danforth denied an affair, but they wanted to talk to Farrah about how to handle the rumors. That's all I learned before Mitch was called out."

"Do you believe them?"

"Without being there when they were interviewed, I can't say. It's still only one side of the story."

She told him about Mitch's call and what she'd asked him. "I probably went too far," she admitted, "but who these people are shouldn't matter. They came to see Farrah that morning, and Jase Norman was killed."

"I think Mitch has his own doubts. He wasn't happy to be told to lay off the Danforths."

There had been reluctance in Mitch's tone each time she had asked him about the eliminated suspects. She had questioned his ethics, his professional duty to follow orders, and his loyalty to her and Rick. He hadn't deserved that.

"What?" Rick asked.

Good question—what was she going to do, other than apologize? That didn't mean the Danforths should be off the suspect list, though.

"Anything new on Randy Compton's murder or the loan sharks you were investigating?"

"Still ongoing. There's no talk on the streets about a whack job on Compton, which is interesting. His murder has been assigned to Mitch's team because of the victim's relationship to Farrah. Not that they need another case."

"Maybe they do. Mitch said they're ready to arrest Farrah."

"Yeah." He didn't seem happy about it. "She'll need to get a good lawyer."

That shouldn't be a problem. Farrah had money and Alana to help her find someone in Illinois. She shouldn't need to do that, though. Not if she was innocent.

"Mitch did interview her, you know," Rick said.

"He told me. He said she didn't remember what happened."

"She remembered a few things, like waking up and checking her calendar. She remembered that she had an appointment with you at ten that morning. Mitch said she seemed shocked when they asked her about Jase Norman coming to see her. She said she hadn't seen him in years. She didn't remember him being killed in her house, and she couldn't explain why her prints were on the statue used to kill him."

"No wonder she relapsed." Shock upon shock. Farrah's brain seemed to be trying to protect her, but from what—the trauma of bludgeoning her former lover? Or the memory of someone else killing him minutes after he'd surprised her, years after they had parted? Jase showed up on her doorstep and then—

"Yeah, they had to end the interview. The doctor said they could try a higher dose of the medicine that brought her out before, but it's risky."

"Poor Farrah." It wasn't the news she'd hoped to relay to Alana when she called Farrah's friend back.

She met his gaze. "I want to talk to the Danforths again, Laura in particular. Everything keeps coming back to the campaign."

Frowning, he unclasped his hands behind her and rested his palms on her thighs. "I don't think that will help, babe. You said she's a lawyer. She's not going to open up to you, particularly if we're right and her husband is in this up to his eyeballs."

"But it can't hurt, can it? Mitch's investigation is over."

"The case isn't closed, though."

"But talking to her wouldn't hurt, would it? I can find another campaign event and take Maggie with me, if she's willing. We'll be at a public gathering."

"I don't like it. If you're right, one of them could be the killer."

She placed her hands on his shoulders. "If I'm right, *we'll* be saving an innocent woman from prison."

He swore. "I'm beginning to regret telling you not to protect me."

Chapter Thirty

Reassured by Rick's consent, Maggie was thrilled to go on another fishing expedition that included food.

"Of course I'll go! I love sleuthing with you," she told Crys the next day on the phone. "I can't believe you told Rick about it. You didn't talk to Mitch?"

"I talked to him, but not about this. He's been told to lay off the Danforths. Too politically sensitive."

"Ah, so what he doesn't know won't hurt him. Well, at least we have Rick's go-ahead."

Maggie offered to look for an event to attend. After a moment of tapping, she said, "Here's one, and it's in Wheaton, Saturday night. He's the speaker at a fundraiser dinner for a women's coalition, and it says his wife will also be there. Perfect!"

"What kind of coalition?"

"Democratic Women's Action Group, Mothers Against Drunk Driving, Wheaton's LGBTQIA+ Democrats Alliance, Seven Sisters of Wheaton—"

"Seven Sisters?"

"You know, graduates of the seven women's colleges out east—Vassar, Barnard, Radcliffe, Smith."

"That's four."

"Wait—Wellesley! I can't think of the others. They're not my sisters. Maybe if they had football teams, we'd know them all."

"Or presidents as alumni. How do we get tickets? We don't have time to earn a degree from Vassar in two days."

"It's open to the public. I can buy tickets online. It starts at five thirty. Is that okay?"

"Perfect." Rick would be home and awake, in case she needed him. Maybe they could even make an early night of it. "Let's do it, sister."

Maggie clucked. "Don't *sista* me, girlfriend. More than likely, with you as my date, they'll be thinking we're from another one of those groups."

"Well, I am a mother and I'm against drunk driving."

"Good. You can be our designated driver."

THE WOMEN'S COALITION event was far less glamorous than POW's gathering. Held at a hall instead of a hotel, the meet and greet had the air of democracy at work. This wasn't a crowd of large donors in cocktail attire, but everyday women with moderate incomes who cared about politics. Maggie's red Lexus wasn't alone in the luxury class in the parking lot, though. Common interests cut across all economic levels, and women's issues seemed to be the solder welding tonight's groups together.

They registered at the entrance and filled out nametags. Inside the large meeting room, signs were posted above the heads of the crowd with local and state candidates' names and the races they were in. There were a dozen or so, but Scott Danforth and his opponent, a Republican woman named Marilyn Page, appeared to be the only ones running for a federal office. They also had the largest crowds around their signs. Evan Kruper stood on the outside of the knot of people under the DANFORTH banner. The bald man in a sports jacket and turtleneck talking to him was shaking his head and frowning. Whatever Evan was selling, he wasn't buying.

"Who do you want to talk to first?"

"Laura, if we can find her."

"If she's in that mosh pit with Scott, we'll need to throw ourselves on top and see if we can be passed bodily to the center, unless you have a better idea."

She gave Maggie a droll look. "I always suspected you were a wild child, despite your sophisticated tastes."

Maggie's laugh was full-hearted. Evan turned around and spotted them. He clapped the head shaker on the arm, ending their discussion, and headed toward them.

"Ms. Ward. I see you made it to another of our events."

"I don't know if you were introduced to my friend Maggie Townsend last week. She's very active in the community."

"It looks like a great turnout," Maggie said.

He looked around as if checking the crowd for the first time. He appeared satisfied with the number of prospective voters present. "Yes, mostly Democrats, I suspect. Most women are."

"I wouldn't assume that," Maggie said, taking offense. "The women I know are independent thinkers. Besides, your opponent is a woman."

He laughed. "Point taken." He gave Maggie an amused look. He was probably reassessing his opinion of her. Crys had seen others do the same. There was a lot more to Mags than her beautiful face.

Evan turned back to Crys. "How is our mutual friend Farrah?"

She wasn't sure later why she lied. Perhaps it was to protect Farrah's job with the campaign, or maybe she just wanted to be positive and hopeful for her recovery. In any case, she was surprised to hear herself saying, "She's doing much better. She regained consciousness."

He appeared startled. "Really? That's terrific news, although the police must have some questions for her about that reporter's death."

"She's starting to remember that day. I'm sure she'll be able to give the detectives some answers soon."

"She might not want to remember. Well, it was good to see you again, and you, Ms. Townsend. Enjoy your evening."

"Not as charming as his candidate," Maggie said as they watched him disappear into the crowd surrounding Scott. "Much lower wattage. Then again, he isn't the shining star."

"No, but he's the one who makes sure that star is shining where people can see him." And Evan's skills included knowing how to make his way through the mob without resorting to body surfing.

"Let's see if we can pull Laura away from her protector," Crys said as they approached the group gathered under the DANFORTH sign.

They spotted Laura farther away from her husband's crowd chatting with two women, whose gazes kept sliding over to Scott. His head of wavy hair was now visible over the heads of his mostly female admirers. The shining star was the main attraction, and Laura was their second choice. She was probably used to it.

"Crystal! How lovely to see you again," Laura said as the other women departed. A small crease appeared in her brow. "And a surprise, too."

She probably thinks I'm stalking her.

"Hi, Laura. It's good to see you, too. You remember my friend, Maggie."

"Of course. So nice of you to come. I hope you'll both vote for Scott. Please go say hello to him." She had shifted into campaign wife mode. They had to break through before Evan or Scott reclaimed her.

"Laura, I came to talk to you. I heard the reporters ask you at the POW event about Farrah Compton. Besides working for her, I was the one who found her and Jase Norman that day."

She looked startled. "That must have been terrible."

"It was. I know you were at her house earlier that morning and so was Scott."

Her eyes appeared huge in her pale face. Her gaze shifted toward her husband's back. "I can't talk about that," she said firmly. "No comment. Now if you'll excuse me—"

"Here's what I think," Crys said. "You told me that you trusted your husband, but you wanted to let her know about the rumors." She was guessing, but Laura and Farrah were both intelligent women. "You wanted to talk to her about it face-to-face."

"Woman to woman," Maggie added, playing along. "We're not press, by the way."

"Scott came in a separate car, one of the Lincolns, just after you arrived. Did Jase Norman arrive while you were there?" The timing had seemed to be close enough to make it plausible.

Laura's eyes narrowed. "I said no comment. I don't know what your agenda is, but the police are investigating Mr. Norman's death. You should ask them your questions."

Laura spun on her heel and started to walk away. Crys followed her. "Actually, I have. They're going to arrest Farrah, but I don't think she killed Jase Norman."

"My advice to her would be to get an attorney." She didn't slow down.

"Farrah and Jase knew each other years ago when they both served in Africa in the Peace Corps. She was surprised to see him after all these years. She invited him in, didn't she? To catch up with an old friend, someone she had once been very close to, not to murder him."

"That doesn't mean she didn't do it after I left."

They had almost reached the Danforth crowd. "You don't believe that, do you, Laura? How did Farrah react when she saw Jase? Shocked but pleasantly surprised maybe? The way any of us would look if an old lover showed up on our doorstep?"

Laura stopped and whirled around to face them. "What do you want from me?"

"Farrah can't defend herself. I'm just trying to understand what happened that day to try to help her and prevent an injustice from being done."

"Isn't that what you do in your work?" Maggie asked. "Fight injustice and help those who can't help themselves?"

Laura glanced again toward her husband, who was talking with Evan and another man. When she turned back to face them, her eyes were troubled. "She was shocked to see him. I didn't know who he was until later, but they greeted each other like old friends who hadn't seen each other in ages. Anyhow, our discussion was over when he rang the doorbell, so I left. She invited him in as I went out. That's it."

Crys was trying to picture the encounter, the four people in Farrah's entryway. "How did Scott react? Jase Norman had already met him at campaign headquarters, hadn't he?"

"Scott wasn't there. He'd already left. I'd forgotten my handbag, so I had come back in to fetch it."

Crys exchanged a look with Maggie. "You wanted to talk privately with Farrah about the rumors, didn't you?"

"What Farrah and I said is none of your business." She glanced again at her husband and then back, her lawyer's face impassive. "I have no more to say to you. There was no affair, and Jason Norman was alive when we left. Scott's a good man. Please—leave us alone."

She turned and headed to her husband. She took his arm possessively and smiled up at him.

Chapter Thirty-One

"WELL, THAT WENT well," Maggie said with a sigh. "She didn't deny that Scott had been there, or that they had a conversation about the rumors." Crys bit her lip. Laura Danforth was an attorney. She knew when to keep her mouth closed.

"What's next?"

Crys looked around the crowded room. There was no way she was going to be able to talk to Scott Danforth with so many people surrounding him and Laura on his arm. At least not now.

"How about dinner?"

Maggie wrinkled her nose. "I suppose we've paid for it, although I doubt that it matches the Riverview's quality."

They made their way to the buffet lines that had opened up.

"I can't believe Laura Danforth used the old *handbag left behind* ploy to return to the house to talk to Farrah," Maggie said. "Do you think she told her to keep her hands and other body parts to herself?"

"Could be. Or maybe she doesn't think there was an affair. I'd be telling Farrah to stay out of the spotlight and stop going to Scott's events where they could be photographed together."

"That's very civilized of you." They stepped forward in line. "She said Jase Norman showed up as she left. Do you think she was telling the truth about leaving, or did she stay around and kill him?"

Rick thought either of the Danforths could be the killer, but why would Laura murder Jase? "What's her motive, though? I can see her being angry at Farrah, but she said she didn't even know who Jase Norman was until later."

"What if she did know who he was and believed Farrah was being interviewed behind Scott's back? Maybe she tried to stop that from happening and just lost it."

Crys again pictured the three people at the door. "Assuming Scott had left, let's say just before the taxi arrived, and Laura is telling the truth about being on her way out—"

Maggie snorted.

"And if she didn't recognize Jase Norman... Remember, none of us had heard of him, and I doubt that Laura was present at campaign headquarters the previous day when he tried to interview Scott."

"Okay. And..." Maggie rolled her hand in a keep going motion.

"And she saw Farrah's shocked reaction. An old friend had shown up. They obviously had some catching up to do. She would just leave then."

"I still think she and Farrah had a cat fight worthy of Lifetime television or one of those housewives shows."

Crys laughed. "I can't see either one of them pulling hair or bitch slapping, if that's what you're imagining." They moved forward in the line again. "Back to your scenario, even if Laura was angry at Farrah and recognized Jase, I think she'd just go tell her husband. He would fire Farrah, and she would be rid of her rival."

"Damn! Where's the drama in that?" Maggie stepped back to allow a server carrying a full tray of cut submarine sandwiches through the line. "So, we're back to Jase alone with Farrah, which means she's the killer."

Something was bothering Crys about Laura's story. She pictured Laura watching Farrah greet Jase at the door. They probably only had eyes for each other. Laura turned and went down the sidewalk to her Kia...

A young man with a large SCOTT DANFORTH pin approached them. "Would you ladies like a bumper sticker or a pin?" He held out a fistful of campaign tokens.

"No, thanks," they both answered. He didn't seem surprised and continued on down the line.

"The Lincoln," Crys said aloud. She grabbed Maggie's arm. "Gary Zygman said the Kia arrived first and then the Lincoln. Both had two DANFORTH bumper stickers."

"Okay," Maggie said slowly. "You said they arrived separately. Laura arrives first and Scott parks behind her. He leaves first and she goes back to retrieve her purse."

"Gary saw the bumper stickers on *each* car. If Scott parked behind Laura, Gary wouldn't have seen the stickers on the Kia, unless he looked out his window before Scott arrived."

"Maybe he parked beside her. Didn't you say that Randy pulled up next to you in the driveway later? Is there room for two cars side by side?"

Crys's excitement fizzled. "Yes. Maybe that's it." She

tried to remember Gary Zygman's exact words. He'd said the Kia had been there first and then the Lincoln. Wouldn't he have said they had both been there at the same time, if that had been the case? Talking to Gary had been confusing at times. Maybe he had just been reporting on who arrived first, in which case, his observation of the Kia arriving first matched what Laura had told them.

"I'll be right back," she told Maggie.

She hurried back over to the Danforth camp, working her way through the crowd. With the buffet lines drawing people away, it didn't take her long to edge her way to the center. Laura had moved about six feet away from Scott. With several more "excuse me's," Crys came up behind her. She took advantage of a moment of laughter between Laura and two women with multiple piercings and spiky hair to ask, "How soon after you arrived did Scott pull up?"

Laura whipped around. "I told you, I have nothing more to say."

"It's just a simple question."

"He was right behind me. We went to the door together. There—now are you satisfied?"

"Did he park behind you or next to you?"

"Look, I don't see why that matters."

"Behind you?" she persevered. The two women were examining her as if they were wondering about calling security.

"I—yes, he parked right behind me. Now if you'll excuse me." She moved away, reaching for the arms of the two suspicious women to sweep them into her orbit.

"What was that about?" Maggie asked when Crys returned. The line hadn't advanced much. The man with the glassy stare behind them looked like he'd lost hope of ever being fed.

"Scott arrived right after Laura and parked behind her," she told Maggie. "They went to the door together." Gary Zygman had seen Laura's car arrive and then Scott's, just as he'd said.

"Then Scott left, Laura went back to knock on Farrah's door for her purse, and as she was leaving, Jase arrived."

The same sandwich server returned just then, carrying an emptied tray at his side. They stepped back to let him through.

"Wait a minute, what did you say?"

"I said Laura went back to knock on the door, and then—"

"That's it! She would have knocked, thinking that Farrah hadn't had time to go far from the door. That's what I'd do."

"She could have rung the bell. Does it matter?"

"It could. The Danforths told the police they arrived around eight thirty that morning, which was the first time Wes received an alert about someone at the door. Laura said they went to the door together, so only one of them needed to press the button. She said Jase rang the doorbell, so he would have been the second, which leaves the killer as number three."

"Or Laura rang the bell when she returned for her private chat and Jase was number three."

"No, she left them there together, as she said. It makes sense. Gary Zygman was telling the truth. He saw the Kia, probably after Scott had left, and then he saw a Lincoln parked in the driveway, in that order. Not just any Lincoln, but one registered to the campaign with two bumper stickers. Gary didn't see the Kia arrive or the taxi, so he probably didn't see Scott at all when he drove up to go to the door with Laura and then left."

"I'm confused. Are you saying Scott returned after Laura left?"

Austin had said there were two of them, same make and model, registered to the campaign. Evan had been driving one of the Lincolns when she'd run into him and Scott in the hospital parking lot last week and at the POW gala. Had Scott returned or had Evan shown up?

"He followed her," she said aloud.

"We know that. Scott followed Laura and then he left, but you're saying he came back after she left? Now we're talking some drama!"

Maggie took a step forward as the line moved up. They had finally reached the end of the buffet table. She handed Crys a plate.

"Maybe Scott. He could have waited for Laura to leave and then gone back to reassure Farrah, if she was his mistress." There was another possibility, though. "Evan Kruper drives a campaign Lincoln with two bumper stickers, too."

"You think he followed Laura? That makes sense. He followed her around the other night. Maybe he found out Laura and Scott were going to confront Farrah about the affair."

"That could explain what he was doing there," she said

slowly. "Following Laura and cleaning up after her. Making sure the campaign would continue to run smoothly."

"Damage control," Maggie said, reaching for silverware.

"Right. And inside, he finds Jase Norman, the prize-winning investigative reporter, enjoying a cozy chat with Farrah in her living room. He couldn't afford to lose another campaign to scandal."

"Another campaign?"

Crys craned her neck, looking for them. The Danforth table now only had a few people browsing through literature and tokens. "I don't see them."

"Excuse me," the man in line behind them said, looking like he'd emerged from his hunger daze. He had already grabbed a plate. "You're holding up the line."

Crys handed him her plate. "Go ahead. Have seconds."

"Have thirds," Maggie said behind her, shoving her plate toward him. "I won't tell."

They hurried to the DANFORTH sign. A young woman wearing a friendly smile and a large DANFORTH FOR CONGRESS button on her jean jacket was handing out campaign literature and the ubiquitous bumper stickers.

"Excuse me," Crys said. "Has Scott Danforth left?"

"Yes, you just missed him. Would you like to read about what he supports? And here's a sticker for your car."

Crys waved away the handouts. "What about Evan Kruper? Is he still here?"

The girl blinked. "The campaign manager?" She turned to the young man who had been handing out bumper stickers in the food line. "Jackson, have you seen Mr. Kruper?"

"Evan? No, he left about twenty minutes ago."

"Did he say where he was going?" Crys asked.

Jackson exchanged a look with the girl. "He wouldn't tell us that. We're just volunteers."

Maggie said, "I'm surprised Mr. Danforth didn't stay 'til the end of the event. Doesn't he normally do that?"

The girl looked at Jackson, who answered. "Yeah, normally. His wife told him something and they both rushed out. Family emergency, I think."

Crys ignored the girl's outstretched hand holding a pamphlet and led Maggie away from the table.

"We need to go to the hospital. I think Farrah may be in danger. I told Evan she was conscious and starting to remember what happened."

"We should call the police."

Crys shook her head. "If I'm wrong and we call them, I'll look like an idiot."

Maggie grabbed her arms and turned her so they were facing. "No, you won't. I trust your instincts. What you said about the cars and who arrived when makes sense. Come on—you can call Rick from the car."

She followed Maggie toward the entrance. The hospital had security. She had promised to share her plans with Rick before she took action, but what if she was overreacting? Besides, what could he do other than worry?

You promised not to protect him.

She pulled out her phone as they exited the building. It was only six forty-five, but the darkness made it seem later. She tapped in his cell number and listened to it ring. Had they finished eating? She hoped the kids were busy elsewhere.

"Hey, how's it going?" he answered.

"Maggie and I are leaving. We're heading to the hospital."

"The food was that bad?"

"No. I mean, probably. We haven't tried it. Rick, listen. The Danforths and Evan Kruper left early. I'm really worried about Farrah. We're going to go check on her."

There was a long pause. She had done what he asked and not protected him. Would he trust her? She stopped at Maggie's car and waited for her to click the doors open.

"You've figured something out."

God, she loved this man. "Yes." She slid into her seat and quickly updated him about what Laura Danforth had said and what she had realized about the three doorbell rings and the order of the cars arriving. "It had to be either Scott Danforth or Evan Kruper. They both drive the two campaign Lincolns."

"I'll call Mitch," Rick said. "If the killer shows up, you could be in danger, too."

She squeezed her eyes shut. "Could you come?"

It was a huge ask. Loading his chair into his car, driving, unloading the chair at the hospital... She was about to tell him to just call Mitch when he said, "I'll meet you there in the lobby."

"Okay. I love you."

"Love you, too, but don't try to be a hero."

Maggie glanced over at her after she disconnected. "I thought you still had a truce with Mitch. You don't trust him?"

The answer seemed clear to her now. "Actually I do, but Rick's the one I want to have my back."

Chapter Thirty-Two

THE HOSPITAL WAS lit up like a city at night. It probably housed as many people as Crys's small hometown. Visiting hours had lured enough vehicles to almost fill the expansive parking lot.

"It may take a while to find a parking spot," Maggie said, looking side to side.

"Drop me at the door." They had reached the end of the row, and Crys unclicked her seat belt.

"All right, but be careful. And wait for Rick or me. At least he can park in a handicapped space, if there are any vacant ones," she grumbled as Crys opened her door and hopped out.

Inside, Crys glanced around the lobby but didn't see Rick. She made a quick circuit as visitors came and left. The elevator doors opened and closed, loading and discharging passengers.

Wes was probably visiting. She should have thought of that. She could pop upstairs and see if he was with Farrah. Most likely, her fears tonight were groundless. She could be back downstairs by the time Maggie parked and Rick arrived, and then they could all go home and have a laugh.

She headed to the elevator, which opened before she

could press the button to summon it. A couple about her age stepped out, arguing about which pizza place they should choose for dinner. This was crazy. She should be home having pizza with her own family. Crys stepped inside and pressed the button before she could change her mind. She scanned the lobby for Rick or Maggie again before the doors closed.

The fourth floor was quiet. No guard, not even a chair for one. The deserted hallway gleamed under the florescent lighting.

She hurried to room 417. A dim light shone through the glass in the door. She peered inside.

A male in hospital scrubs bent over the figure on the bed, blocking her view of the patient. Wes wasn't there. Had Farrah been moved?

"Excuse me," she said, opening the door. "Is this—?"

The man jerked up and turned toward her. He pulled his hand away from Farrah's face and down to his side, but not quickly enough to hide the cloth he was holding.

"Ms. Ward," Evan Kruper said. "Just in time. I was checking to see if she was still breathing. Her color doesn't look good, does it?"

Against the white sheets, Farrah's pale skin had a blue tinge. Her partially opened eyes were unfocused, and her lips, dark in the dusky light, were parted. The sheet covering her chest hid any rise and fall that would indicate breathing.

"Maybe you should find a nurse?" he said, as if it were normal for him to be there in scrubs. "I'll stay with her."

Keeping her voice calm, she said, "Use the call button.

It's right there, at the side of the bed. That will be faster."

"Ah, I didn't think of that. Which button is it?"

She didn't move any closer. He had to realize that he couldn't go through with killing Farrah now. "It's the red one with the white cross."

"I guess that's obvious enough." He turned, holding the remote control device up for her to see. The red button was the largest one and hard to miss. Had he pressed it, though?

"I haven't been a patient," he continued, conversationally. "Guess I've been lucky. They should be here soon. I think she's looking a little better."

He bent over Farrah. Crys took an involuntary step toward the foot of the bed to watch what he was doing. He touched Farrah's neck, his fingers probing the skin below her ear. He bent his head close to her face.

Crys moved closer. She couldn't see his other hand or the cloth he'd been holding.

"Oh no," he said, softly.

She reached the foot of the bed. "Is she—?"

He snapped his hand back and lunged at her. Grabbing her wrist, he twisted it and bent her arm behind her back. Crys moaned as pain shot up to her shoulder. He jerked her against his chest. Before she could scream, he clamped the cloth over her mouth with his other hand and held it tightly over her nose and lips.

Crys struggled, trying to wriggle free from his grasp. Was there something on the cloth? If so, she should hold her breath, but panic was overwhelming her. She sucked in air, desperate to fill her lungs. His fingers were spread as they held the cloth, but the cotton fabric was a barrier to a full breath. She twisted again in a futile attempt to escape.

"Don't scream," he murmured, his breath hot on her ear. "If you're quiet, we'll leave here together and I'll let you go."

She didn't think she could scream. She was gasping now, straining to breathe.

She squirmed in his iron grip, but he only squeezed her tighter to his chest. His fingers closed, cutting off her air. The light in the room began to fade, dimming around the corners of her vision.

She stopped struggling. She wouldn't scream, not if he would uncover her mouth and nose. *Stay calm. Think.*

"That's more like it. Let's go."

The hand on her face loosened, and she breathed in precious air. He pushed her, forcing her forward with his chest still pressed against her back. He was steering her toward the door. There could be people in the hall, even though it had been deserted when she'd arrived. But the elevator wasn't far. He'd soon have her in there and then what?

Crys knew better than to leave with a killer. As he reached for the door handle, she stomped down hard on his foot. His soft leather dress shoes were no match for her chunky heel.

"Son of a—"

His grip loosened. She spun to face him, raising her knee toward his groin. He tightened his hold on her wrist and pulled. Her knee only grazed his thigh, but she fought him, lowering her head and twisting to escape from his grip. He shoved her hard toward the wall, headfirst. With a *crack*, her skull hit, and Crys saw stars. She slumped to the floor, blinking at the band of light that appeared as he opened the door. Evan's legs moved into the light of the hallway. The band of light narrowed to nothing as the door closed behind him.

She knew she had to do something, but her thoughts were scattering like a flock of frightened birds. She tried to focus on standing or even raising her head, but nothing happened. She couldn't move.

Oh god—was she paralyzed? What would her children do with two parents in wheelchairs? Tears stung her eyes, and the dim light became blurred.

A hand appeared in front of her face. She blinked, but the room was still a blur of gray fog swirling around her.

The hand waved again, followed by the sound of a familiar voice. "Crys! Are you okay? I'll get help. Don't move."

The hand disappeared, and her sluggish brain identified the voice as Maggie's. The hand had probably been hers, too. Don't move—that was rich. She didn't feel as if she had a body, at least not one she could command.

Her heart and lungs seized with panic. Had Rick felt this way when he'd been shot? She wanted to scream at her limbs to move but it was too much effort. She closed her eyes to stop the spinning of the room and steady her panicked thoughts. The sound of her ragged breath filled her awareness.

I can breathe. Evan hadn't suffocated her, but it had been close.

She sucked in a deeper, slower breath.

I'm alive.

Another deep breath calmed her. She could see and hear, too. She'd seen the hand, heard Maggie's voice. She began to use a breathing technique she'd learned in a yoga class to try to relax.

Healthy air in, fear out.

Within a few breaths, her panic receded. She opened her eyes. The spinning had stopped. The stars twinkled and then faded into the twilight of Farrah's room. She tried to raise her hand. Fingers, one wearing her wedding rings, appeared. She wiggled each digit, formed the okay sign with her thumb and forefinger. Afraid to try to move upright, she directed her brain to bend her foot and slide it along the floor.

For a moment, nothing seemed to happen. Then her knee appeared. She moved it left and right, right and left. She cautiously raised her other knee, lifted it an inch. There was no pain.

Her spine wasn't injured. There was no paralysis.

She closed her eyes and offered a prayer of thanksgiving.

Chapter Thirty-Three

THE DOOR OPENED, bringing back the bright light from the hallway and a team of reinforcements. Maggie had found a nurse and another male in scrubs. They glanced at her on the floor and then rushed to the bed.

"Call Dr. Park and fetch a gurney," the nurse said, pressing one of the call buttons. The nursing assistant left.

"Crys," Maggie said, "where are you hurt?"

She could smell her perfume and feel her warm hand stoking her hair. Somehow her friend had squatted at her side. Trust Mags to manage that move wearing a sheath dress.

"We'll check her out, ma'am," the nurse said, looking over her shoulder from Farrah's bedside. "Don't move her."

Crys smiled. The poor woman didn't know how much Maggie hated being called *ma'am*.

"Is Farrah okay?" she managed to ask.

"She's alive," the nurse said. "We'll have the doctor check her."

"He tried to suffocate her," Crys said. She shifted to a more upright position, and a few stars returned.

"Lie still," Maggie said. "You look like you're going to

pass out."

The door was shoved open as two men arrived with a gurney. They eased Crys down on a back board and raised her onto it. The sides were snapped into place. Soon she was on the elevator with Maggie still at her side.

"It took me forever to park," her friend said. "I saw one of those Lincolns with the Danforth stickers in the parking lot while I was cruising for a spot. I figured you'd already come up here. I had to wait in line to find out the room number, or I would have been up sooner."

"It's okay," she said as the elevator descended. "Thanks, Mags."

Had Rick decided not to come? She shouldn't have asked him. And what about the kids? She needed to go home.

The elevator doors opened, and they bumped into another brightly lit hall. The walls of the corridor flowed alongside her gurney like rivers of smooth cream. The stars again settled back in whatever universe they had come from.

"Doing okay?" the porter asked.

Crys wiggled her feet and gave him a thumbs-up.

THE ER DOCTOR was concerned that she might have a concussion and wanted to keep her overnight. Crys objected. She'd had a concussion in high school after being elbowed by an aggressive teammate in a volleyball game, and she had none of the nausea she'd experienced then.

Her skull ached where she'd hit the wall, but she'd had worse headaches. Her mind had cleared, and after thirty minutes or so of following the doctor's order to stay in bed until he returned, she'd managed to sit up with Maggie's help. The small wave of dizziness quickly passed. As soon as the doctor returned, she would insist on being discharged.

They both looked up as the curtain parted. Rick rolled in with Mitch following him.

"It's about time, guys," Maggie said.

Crys just smiled. Rick had come.

"We had a little business to attend to," her husband said, studying her with a slight frown. "You were supposed to wait in the lobby for me."

"I had a little business to attend to upstairs," she said tartly and then relented. "I thought Wes might be upstairs and I was overreacting. Instead, I found Evan Kruper in her room trying to kill her."

"We heard." Rick reached for her hand. "How are you feeling?"

"Not bad. Just a bump on the head."

He gave her a skeptical look and turned to Maggie.

"The doctor is worried about a concussion," her friend told him, "although she talked him out of keeping her overnight. She says she didn't lose consciousness."

"Traitor. I didn't pass out and I'm fine. What business did you have to attend to?"

Mitch snorted. "It seems Mr. Kruper had an unfortunate accident when he came down to the lobby. Some guy in a wheelchair knocked him over."

Crys's jaw dropped. She squeezed Rick's hand. "*You*

caught him?"

"Pinned him is more like it," Mitch said.

"It worked, didn't it?" Rick said. "Luckily he was already limping and couldn't run very far. You wouldn't happen to know anything about that, would you?"

"I might have stomped on his foot."

Rick nodded. A smile teased the corners of his mouth.

"Has anyone heard how Farrah's doing?" she asked.

Mitch jammed his hands in his jeans pockets. "Her doctor says she's okay. She even woke up and spoke. They've called her husband to let him know what happened."

"Lieutenant Ward?" A man and woman wearing badges appeared at the split in the curtain. Crys recognized the balding man, who had been on Rick's team when he was running the homicide unit. "Sorry to interrupt, Ms. Ward, but we need to borrow your husband for a few minutes," he said, smiling at her.

Rick released her hand. "Stay out of trouble until I come back," he told her.

"I will."

To her surprise, Mitch didn't follow him. Instead, he moved to the end of her bed. His hair was the usual bird's nest caught in a hurricane. In the harsh light of the emergency room, his face looked older with the furrows in his forehead and worry lines more pronounced.

"I think I'll find a ladies' room," Maggie said, glancing between them. On her way out, she made a flag-waving gesture and mouthed "truce" at Crys behind Mitch's back.

Muted conversations and sounds of machines filled the

dead air between them. Mitch gripped the foot of her bed. The scowling man staring at his hands as they clenched the foot of her bed was not the easy-going, cowboy character she was used to seeing.

"Mitch? Are you okay?"

He moved then, coming to her side. Coming alive.

"Hell no, I'm not okay. When Rick called me, he said you were going to the hospital to confront Jase Norman's killer. I was clear across town. I tried to talk him out of coming. What the hell, Crys? You couldn't call me? You didn't have to call Rick out. He has no business—"

"Rick wanted to come. He doesn't want us to protect him, Mitch. Not anymore. It might be a hard habit to break, though—for both of us."

He rubbed a hand impatiently on his neck. "You still should have called me."

"Would you have believed me? You were positive that Farrah was the killer."

"I'd have listened."

She gave him a skeptical look.

He sighed and dropped his hand. "The other day when you asked me if I would accept the alibis of the Lincoln and Kia drivers if they weren't considered sensitive, I realized that the answer was no. I talked again to the guy across the street, Zygman, the next morning. He hadn't seen either driver, but he said the Kia wasn't there long. Just after he saw it pull in, he had to answer a phone call and make a few more, which lasted about twenty minutes. The Kia was gone by then, and the Lincoln was in the driveway."

"That was Evan Kruper."

"Yeah, well, he noticed the bumper stickers on the back and figured it was one of Ms. Compton's campaign buddies, or maybe the candidate himself. He also copied down the license plate numbers, something he hadn't told us when we first interviewed him."

"There were two Lincolns. Scott Danforth had arrived behind Laura and left. Evan must have followed one or both Danforths that morning, probably to make sure Farrah toed the party line and didn't speak to the press about the alleged affair. He walked in to find Farrah talking to Jase Norman, the hot-shot reporter, without his permission."

"I could tell when I interviewed him he didn't like the guy."

"And he didn't know that Jase and Farrah were former lovers."

Mitch's eyebrows went up. "Lovers?"

"When they were in the Peace Corps together. Farrah's best friend told me that." She continued before Mitch could yell at her about not sharing that information. "Evan probably didn't intend to kill anyone. Jase Norman either said something that upset him or tried to defend his former lover. Evan grabbed the statue and killed him. Then he made sure Farrah Compton's fingerprints were on it so she would be framed. It was his word against hers, and all of the evidence pointed to her."

"Yeah, and she didn't remember what happened."

Crys pulled the light blanket over her lap. Why do they keep hospitals so cold? "Exactly. Evan thought he was in the clear. At first, the victim was identified as her husband

and then the Kia and Lincoln drivers, the Danforths, were cleared by the police."

"Crys, about that—"

"I'm not blaming you, Mitch. There was nothing really pointing to him as the killer, unless Farrah regained her memory."

"That's not exactly true. I did a little digging on Mr. Kruper when I learned Ms. Compton worked for the campaign. Nothing criminal, although he picked the wrong horse to back in the last mayoral election."

"Rick told me about that. He said they couldn't prove Kruper knew what was going on with the embezzling." She felt the back of her head where a knot was forming. It was tender to her touch. Thank god they had rushed to the hospital, especially after she had set Farrah up for elimination by Evan. A minute later and Farrah could have been dead. She shivered and pulled the blanket higher.

"You should be lying down," Mitch said. "You could be concussed, even though I know how hardheaded you are."

Before she could respond, he tossed the blanket aside and lifted her legs. He placed them back on the bed, forcing her to lower her head onto the pillow. "You might as well enjoy a rest while you wait for the doctor to release you," he said, spreading the blanket over her.

"Don't go yet." She reached for his wrist. "There's something else. I think Randy may have been trying to extort money from Evan. He may have killed Randy, too."

"Nothing like tidying up loose ends. Anything else?"

"Thank you for coming," Crys said. "And for caring

about Rick. I'm sorry I've been…"

"A pain in the butt?"

She smiled. "Someone who should have forgiven you a long time ago."

Patches of red appeared on Mitch's cheeks. He rubbed a hand through his impossible hair. "I hate hospitals. Next time call me before you end up in one."

"I will." She hated hospitals, too.

WHEN RICK RETURNED to her bedside, she sent Maggie home. Mitch had already left to check on his team and the on-site investigation. The doctor finally discharged her around ten.

She sat in Rick's passenger seat and watched as he transferred and stowed his ultralight traveling chair in the backseat. He settled behind the wheel and turned to her.

"Come here," he said, opening his arms.

She rested her head on his strong shoulder and breathed in the smell of him.

"I'm glad you came."

He chuckled. "You should have seen Kruper's face when he noticed me barreling toward him. He looked like a deer in headlights."

"And then you ran him down." She looked up at him. His eyes were bright. "Back in the action, Lieutenant?"

He traced her cheek with his finger. "Next time, let me handle it."

She smiled at him and then sobered. "Next time call

Connie. What were you thinking leaving Kurt and Dana alone?"

"I told you. Legally, they're old enough to be left alone for a few hours. Kurt has a phone if he needs it. Maybe you should trust my judgment."

"That's a two-way street, buddy."

"Huh," Rick said, starting the car. "As long as you don't pull any more stunts like you did tonight."

"Stunts? I'm not the one who used his wheelchair to run down a murderer."

Rick's eyes were shining. "Dugan and his partner were impressed."

"I bet. I'm sorry I missed it, Rambo. Let's go home before I have to have a doctor look at your swollen head."

"Damn, the look on his face…"

Crys smiled. She was impressed, too.

Chapter Thirty-Four

TWO WEEKS LATER, Crys turned into the Compton-O'Malley driveway. The freshly mown and raked yard looked immaculate, marred only by the two SCOTT DANFORTH FOR U.S. HOUSE OF REPRESENTATIVES signs back in place, side by side, facing the street. The signs, like the campaign, looked a little battered and slightly bent, but they seemed solidly stuck in place and not going anywhere.

Crys parked and grabbed her notebook before heading to the front door. The doorbell still had a trace of sticky residue around the camera, a faint but easily removed reminder of what had happened here. This time she pressed the bell and was relieved to hear footsteps approaching from inside.

Farrah greeted her with a bright smile. She wore dark blue jeans that appeared new and a cream-and-tan striped jersey top. She still looked pale, even with makeup, but her eyes were clear and sparkling. Her hair was loosely waved, making her appear younger.

"Wes told me I couldn't even peek at the office until you were here. For once I had to agree with him. You deserve to be here for the big reveal. Thank you again for saving my life, Crystal." Farrah's hug was strong, like her life force.

Tears stung Crys's eyes. "I hope you like it."

Farrah's smile widened as her gaze traveled around the organized office. "The new desk is even better than what I remember ordering." She laughed. "That seems like a lifetime ago." She touched the surface. "It looks so much more modern than that heavy wooden monstrosity I used to have."

"It takes up less space, too, and the glass top makes it seem almost weightless." Crys liked the style so much that she planned to order one for her new office upstairs as soon as she could afford it. It had been Rick's suggestion to convert their former master bedroom/spare closet/sewing room/storage dump into the headquarters of Organizing Chicago. The kids could work on their computer in the basement. He seemed to be more supportive now that she was including him as a partner in the business. She hadn't had the conversation about creating a website or using social media to advertise, but she would soon.

Farrah sat in her new chair and ran a finger along the edge of the desk's thick glass surface as she gazed at the few items around her open laptop.

"What a perfect place for sticky notes and pens," she said, touching the acrylic container that held the items. She reached for the framed photo of her and Wes at the beach.

"I thought you might want that picture closer to your workspace instead of on a shelf."

Farrah smiled. "I do," she said simply.

They both glanced up as they heard the garage door open.

"He's moved back in, you know."

"I'm glad."

"Wes has been wonderful," Farrah said, still gazing at the picture, "about everything. He had become frustrated with Randy, but despite that, he's been a great comfort."

"I think he loves you very much." She had already told Farrah how sorry she was about her brother's death.

"Yes. I think we needed to remember what's really important in life." Farrah placed the picture back on the desk facing her. "I told him about Jase Norman. We fell in love years before I met Wes, but then it ended. It's been over for a long time."

Crys hesitated. Should they talk about the reporter, or was Farrah still fragile from the emotional trauma of witnessing his death?

Her client seemed to read her thoughts. "It's okay—you can talk about him. I know Alana filled you in. I wasn't sure how I felt about seeing him again. It was a surprise. We'd only just started to talk about what happened in Africa when Evan showed up."

"He thought you were talking to Jase about the campaign."

"He was furious. He accused me of all kinds of betrayal. I told him I wouldn't do that to Scott." She moistened her lips. "He grabbed my arms. He must have pushed me or hit me. I fell. I saw Jase come toward me…and that's the last I remember."

The theory Crys had shared with Mitch that night in the hospital had been more or less accurate. Farrah's mind must have shut down to protect her from the shock. At least she was no longer in danger. Evan was in jail and bail had been denied.

Farrah's face relaxed. "Anyhow, I'm going back to work next week and plan to spend plenty of quality work time right here in my beautiful new office space. When I'm not with my husband, that is." She glanced behind Crys.

Wes stood in the doorway, a broad grin on his face.

THAT EVENING RAFE volunteered to help her fix dinner. He'd already settled in as if he'd lived with them all of his life. Even Connie had decided he might need some banana bread, seeing as how he was a growing boy with a good left hook on the basketball court.

"Dora has a friend who's helping her move her stuff to a storage unit this weekend," he told Crys as she pricked the potatoes with a fork to see if they were done. She had made roast beef, a rare treat. Farrah and Wes had given her a generous check today.

"I need butter and milk from the fridge," she told him. "Dana, please set the table. We have six eating here tonight with Mitch coming."

Her daughter, seated at the kitchen table, had her nose in a Laura Ingalls Wilder book. Ever since her grandmother had told her that her great-great-grandparents had traveled to Wisconsin in a covered wagon, she had been obsessed with pioneer families. She sighed, inserted her bookmark, and left the frontier to lay out place settings.

"Mrs. Ward, will you come help set up my room after the furniture's gone?"

"Absolutely." She handed Rafe the potato masher. "Go for it. I'll add a pat of butter and a little milk."

"Don't forget salt," Dana said, pulling silverware from the drawer. "Maybe some cheese, Mom?"

"Not tonight. We have gravy to go with the roast." She reached for the dish towel to dry her hands. "Cheese would be a little over the top."

"Way over the top," Mitch said, coming in with Kurt. "Even for a cheese head from Wisconsin."

Crys flicked the dish towel at him. He easily dodged it and grinned at her.

"You two go wash up," she told them. "Kurt, tell your dad that dinner is almost ready."

She reached for a bowl for the potatoes, smiling at Mitch's teasing. He seemed like the old Mitch. Or maybe she was the old Crys. No, she would never be that woman again, but there was something to be said for letting go of things that no longer served you, like her anger toward Mitch. Wasn't that what she told her clients?

She folded the dish towel over the oven door handle and smoothed it. It had a few faint stains, but it was still mostly white.

Just like a truce flag.

The End

Don't miss Crystal's next adventure in book 2, *Deadlier Than Fiction*!

Join Tule Publishing's newsletter for more great reads and weekly deals!

Acknowledgments

My thanks to my sister Judy and niece Katy for their feedback, sharp-eyed copyediting, and technical medical advice. They are always willing beta readers, no matter what I write.

A shout-out to Nan Reinhardt, whose career I have followed since she helped me set up my Kindle and make my first e-book purchase (her book, of course). Nan is a role model of persistence and commitment to the craft and a brilliant romance writer. Thanks, Nan, for suggesting that I submit my manuscript to Tule Publishing and for your generosity in continuing to answer my questions about this business. Also, thank you for your careful copy editing. I'm so grateful that you caught my outdated words and references and nudged me to replace them. I'm a better writer because of your editorial guidance.

At Tule, Jane Porter, Meghan Farrell, Nikki Babri, Cyndi Parent, and the rest of the editorial and acquisition team have my sincere appreciation for taking a chance on a new writer and being so supportive. Thanks too, to everyone else at Tule who made publishing this book possible. I'm proud to be a Tuligan!

And last but not least, many thanks to my editor, Julie Sturgeon, for her insightful comments and suggestions that raised this novel to a much higher standard. Her belief in this book has been unfailing and inspired me at every step to "knock her socks off."

If you enjoyed *Room for Suspicion,*
you'll love the next book in the…

Cluttered Crime Mysteries series

Book 1: *Room for Suspicion*

Book 2: *Deadlier Than Fiction*
Coming in September 2023

Available now at your favorite online retailer!

About the Author

Carol Light is an avid reader and writer of mysteries. She loves creating amateur sleuths and complicating their normal lives with a crime that they must use their talents and wits to solve. She's traveled worldwide and lived in Australia for eight years, teaching high school English and learning to speak "Strine." Florida is now her home. If she's not at the beach or writing, you can find her tackling quilting in much the same way that she figures out her mysteries—piece by piece, clue by clue.

Thank you for reading

Room for Suspicion

If you enjoyed this book, you can find more from all our great authors at TulePublishing.com, or from your favorite online retailer.

Made in United States
Orlando, FL
11 February 2024

43546066R00195